FOR A MOMENT, PICARD DID NOT REALIZE WHAT HE WAS SEEING.

Then he knew that it was the narrow edge of the wormhole, so thin that it could not be seen, fine enough to cut blood vessels in half. If anyone was standing in its path, the boundary would slice, cleanly in two, every cell it encountered, right down to the smallest platelet. The action was swift, reminding him of the old trick of pulling a tablecloth out from under plates, glasses, and silverware.

"No!" Riker shouted as the small section of Epictetus III separated from the rest of the planet and began to pass above the wormhole, continuing in the planet's orbit.

"Distress call coming in," another officer called out.

Riker sat down at his station and leaned forward. "It's Deanna," he said, "calling for help. She's on that fragment."

Picard's stomach twisted inside him. "Deanna!" he shouted as the wormhole swallowed Epictetus III. "Deanna!" But there was no answer.

Look for STAR TREK Fiction from Pocket Books

Star Trek: The Original Series

Star Trek: The Next Generation

Star Trek: Deep Space Nine

Star Trek: Voyager

A FURY SCORNED

PAMELA SARGENT AND GEORGE ZEBROWSKI

POCKET BOOKS

New York   London   Toronto   Sydney   Tokyo   Singapore

An *Original* Publication of POCKET BOOKS

POCKET BOOKS, a division of Simon & Schuster Inc.
1230 Avenue of the Americas, New York, NY 10020

A VIACOM COMPANY

This book is published by Pocket Books, a division of Simon & Schuster Inc., under exclusive license from Paramount Pictures.

ISBN: 978-1-4516-4169-1

First Pocket Books printing November 1996

10 9 8 7 6 5 4

POCKET and colophon are registered trademarks of Simon & Schuster Inc.

Printed in the U.S.A.

This shore leave is dedicated to James Gunn, who introduced us to John Ordover, Master of All Print Trek; to Gregory Benford, who suggested we take a slice out of Epictetus III; and to Charles Pellegrino, who has a genius for the wonder of details.

A FURY SCORNED

Chapter One

As HE WAITED in his ready room, Captain Jean-Luc Picard wondered exactly what Starfleet wanted from him. The Federation Council had given no orders to Starfleet Command and seemed uncertain of what to do; he suspected that the Council was waiting for its advisors to come up with a plan of action. In the meantime, he was faced with a dilemma that was probably unsolvable and very likely to end in tragedy.

No, he told himself. Tragedy was not an outcome to dwell on; he would do whatever it took to prevent it. But what could mere mortals, even a highly trained starship crew, do about a nova that threatened a world of twenty million people? How could the *Enterprise* help when only days remained before Epictetus III was swallowed by its sun?

The Federation Council clearly wanted to do something helpful and compassionate, if possible, during the short time remaining to the people of Epictetus III. If indeed nothing could be done, the Federation could not leave the planet below to its doom without at least a show of concern and an effort to help. There had to be a presence, so that these Federation citizens would know that they were not to be simply abandoned and forgotten. He wondered how much comfort that would be to this proud and thriving colony world, and concluded that he was not seeing the entire problem. There had to be much more to it, and it would take all the skill and ingenuity present in his crew to find a solution—or, at least, to make certain that there was none.

Picard touched the panel in front of him. "Captain's Log, Stardate 46300.6." He leaned forward, resting his arms on the table. "We have reached Epictetus Three and are awaiting Starfleet's further instructions. Our on-arrival conference with Admiral Barbieri will begin in five minutes." He had an impulse to add a few words about his hoped-for meeting with Samas Rychi, whose work he had long admired, but such a personal comment seemed inappropriate now.

Samas Rychi, one of Epictetus III's most eminent archaeologists, had been the first to uncover a site revealing the existence of a highly advanced ancient humanoid civilization on his world. His subsequent excavations, which had revealed a large number of sites containing hundreds of monumental and majestic structures, had shown that this early culture had abruptly disappeared. Had it collapsed suddenly, as had the Mayan civilization of Earth? Or had those people made contact with a far more advanced civilization and abandoned their home planet in the wake of a geological disaster, as some recently discovered etched metallic plates seemed to suggest? Rychi would never know, Picard thought. The sun that illuminated his world would destroy any evidence that these ancient people had ever existed.

Rychi, ironically, was also the archaeologist who had so recently found evidence of exactly how powerful the previous inhabitants of his world had been before their culture had vanished so abruptly. Their humanoid civilization might well have found a way out of this dilemma. Now Samas Rychi would be facing the death of his work, the death of his world, and very likely his own death as well.

There was one course of action for Picard to take, although it presented painful and perhaps even unethical choices. The *Enterprise* could save perhaps a few thousand people and a few of Epictetus III's most precious cultural artifacts. Had Starfleet Command and the Federation Council already concluded as much, that the situation was hopeless, and ordered him into a predicament in which he would be forced to do the absolute minimum because it was the only choice?

No, Picard told himself. It was not like the Council or Starfleet to be so vague, so—*uncertain.* They expected more from the *Enterprise* than a token act.

Somewhere, in all the information that was now being examined by the Council, his own science officers, and his crew, there might be the pieces of a solution, just waiting to be assembled. Solutions were often like that, needing no new discoveries, only existing knowledge put together in a new way. under the stimulus of an overwhelming danger.

But as he rose to go out on the bridge, determined to do everything he could, a feeling deep within him told him that he might have to face the conclusion that there was no good solution to the problem of saving the people of Epictetus III because there was not enough time left to help them. The *Enterprise* had used up much of that time in getting here, and now the planet's expected lifetime could be measured in days. He hoped that the scheduled conference with Admiral Barbieri would not be an exercise in futility, and that the presence of the *Enterprise* in this system would not raise false hopes that might only be dashed in the end.

As the crew on the bridge listened again to Admiral Barbieri's recitation of the grim facts about the coming nova, Lieutenant Commander Data considered the problem presented by the unstable star. This was not a star of the classic eruptive novas. It was certainly not a candidate for a supernova. It was simply not massive enough for either of these states. This was a sun like that of Earth, except that it had been affected in some way to bring on this sudden instability. The star presented an extremely perplexing problem, but his mind was already searching for explanations, and a solution.

The Federation Council was tacitly treating the rescue of Epictetus III's population as an impossible task. Data admitted to himself that there might be no way to solve this particular problem, that twenty million people might suffer a scorching death. It was only a matter of days, perhaps a week, before the great death took place. And, as he considered the facts that Admiral Barbieri was repeating, it became even more clear that no earlier warning had been possible.

He reminded himself that the *Enterprise* was also at risk. The unstable sun might bloom into a nova with almost no warning, and any malfunction delaying the *Enterprise*'s departure could conceivably doom the starship. It was not likely to happen, but the risk could not be ignored.

". . . and it now appears," Admiral Barbieri was saying, "that the attractions of this system were too good to be true. Thanks to Samas Rychi, we now know that the star of Epictetus was stable because of a previously undetected device left within its subspace core by the ancient humanoid civilization that once lived on the planet. Professor Rychi recently discovered a site that is apparently a station linked to the sun's stabilizing device, along with some visual depictions that seem to give a picture of the device and how it was placed. Now we're convinced that this highly advanced technology must be failing, because the sun's emissions suggest all the classic signs of instability."

The admiral paused, reached toward a panel in front of him, then turned his great weight in the zero-g environment that had been his home for the last thirty years, and from which he routinely communicated with the Federation Council. It was unusual for a human being to be so massive in size, but the admiral reportedly had both a rare chaotic metabolic disorder and a great love of food. He was a remarkable man, Data thought, recalling what he had read about Pietro Barbieri in the records: the admiral had earned a degree in astrophysics at fifteen, had been one of Starfleet Academy's most brilliant students after that, and had spent twenty years as a starship captain, when his incurable metabolic ailment and increasing corpulence had made a life aboard ship as an active officer impossible. From what Data knew about Admiral Barbieri, he spent almost all of his time thinking, but clearly the admiral had not had much time to think about this nova.

"The *Enterprise,*" Barbieri continued, "was the only vessel close enough to get to Epic Three within a week. There's no chance of routing additional Starfleet vessels to you in time to help out." An uneasy look passed across his round face, as if he were feeling the emotion called shame. Perhaps he was ashamed, given that he had so little advice to offer. Starfleet and the Council depended upon the admiral as they would a natural resource. If a problem seemed intractable, it was said, ask Pietro Barbieri. He was capable of vast intuitive leaps— many of them illogical, of course, but always interesting as hypothetical proposals that were often justified much later. It was said that Barbieri prided himself on being able to help guide Federation Council decisions with his intuition and intellect alone, although Data suspected that this widespread assumption was inaccurate. The admiral was, after all, only one individual. Many others also advised the Council, and perhaps the admiral had simply accumulated credit for the results of larger brain-storming efforts.

"But now that we're here," Picard asked from behind Data, "exactly what can we do?" Data glanced back for a moment to see the captain lean forward slightly in his station chair. "It's impossible to move twenty million people in so short a period. We couldn't even begin to set up our transporters to beam up and temporarily store that many people in a week's time. Even if we had the time, no one has ever tried such a procedure on that large a scale. The error rate would be enormous."

Data knew that this was so, and that only lip service would be devoted to this illusory possibility. Glancing aft, he could see Lieutenant Commander Geordi La Forge, who was sitting at his engineering station, nodding in agreement with Miles O'Brien, the transporter chief, who was at mission operations. Interesting as it was to speculate about such a transporter feat, it was far beyond what could be done reliably within a week. To place that many people safely in the transporter's pattern buffer, assuming that the extensive modifications to make that possible could be made quickly, would require that a beam operate day and night for months. Quantum errors would make a substantial loss of the human data inevitable. Even if those losses were accepted, the power and a sufficiently detailed pro-gram were just not there, leaving aside the problem of exactly where such a vast block of human information could be rematerialized in time to prevent deterioration.

"You're quite right, Captain." Barbieri's jowls trembled as he shook his head. "There's no way out of it. When the time comes, you may have to settle for taking the few people you can, along with one or two cultural treasures. You'll just have to assess the situation personally and decide what is to be done. That's all I can tell you. We cannot leave this world to its fate without some demonstration of concern and an effort to help, however futile." The admiral grimaced. "There has to be a presence, so that other Federation worlds will know that we tried, that the people of Epictetus Three were not completely abandoned."

Admiral Barbieri was correct, Data concluded, given what they knew so far; the situation seemed intractable, perhaps even truly hopeless. But Data also concluded that no one yet had all the facts about the threat to Epictetus III. And where there seemed to be a poverty of both facts and assumptions, there might also be alternatives.

Lieutenant Commander Deanna Troi glanced to her right at Captain Picard, then turned back toward the viewscreen. The captain's concern was obvious. Jean-Luc Picard would do whatever he could even while knowing that his efforts were useless, but she sensed the strain inside him and the anger he felt at his helplessness. Admiral Barbieri's heavy-lidded brown eyes hinted at his own suppressed rage. He would have to suppress it, having nowhere to direct it.

It was the *Kobayashi Maru*—the no-win scenario. To save some two or three thousand lives out of all the millions was to do almost nothing, however precious those individual lives were. Save a few, abandon the many, and call that success.

This mission was impossible, its criterion of success too narrowly defined; it would certainly lead to severe strains on the personalities of the officers and all the members of the crew. Too many lives were at stake, too many would vanish as though they and their world had never existed. Troi had never faced such an overwhelming eventuality, even in her worst nightmares. She could almost feel the insides of the doomed millions beginning to press in on her, as if somehow she might be a refuge into which they could escape.

Everything in her suddenly rebelled against her training, her duty, this mission. No one, not even the organized intelligence of a starship crew, should have been put into such a position of responsibility, forced to make such horrifying and impossible choices. Yet she did not know what else could have been done. For the Federation to have made no effort at all would have been even worse. Even among the wild animals on her world of Betazed, and among some species on Earth, mates or siblings would stay close to a dying member of their species, to keep company with the life that was slipping away. Rational beings could do no less.

Captain Picard seemed steadier now, and she felt

more confident that he would hold himself together. But another crew member on the bridge was containing emotions tied into knots of agony. Troi turned her attention to Ensign Ganesa Mehta, the officer sitting at the controller station next to Data. The young woman's back was stiff, betraying the ensign's tension. Ganesa Mehta had remained at her station, asking not to be relieved, and Commander Riker had honored that request. Now Troi was beginning to think that he should have insisted on replacing her with another officer.

Ganesa Mehta, Troi thought sadly, had come home to Epictetus III only to see her homeworld die.

Ensign Mehta seemed to be holding up—so far. Commander William Riker had worried about leaving her at her post, but she was an extremely promising young officer, and he had trusted her when she had told him that she was able to stay on duty. "I must do what I can," she had told him. "To sit around waiting—that would be worse."

Admiral Barbieri was now speaking of the slight risk the mission posed to the *Enterprise*. Riker did not like the idea of putting the starship so close to a nova, despite the fact that there would be plenty of warning to allow the ship to get clear. Plenty of time, he reminded himself, as long as nothing went wrong, as long as no unforeseen malfunction developed. He had played poker enough times to know that a player could lose even when holding a good hand, and the stakes this time would be the lives of the entire *Enterprise* crew. Unfortunately, this was a hand he could not fold or refuse to play; but his poker player's heart was warning him that it was not wise to play poker with a sun about to go nova, that some unanticipated circumstance might somehow fatally delay the *Enterprise.*

As he listened to Admiral Barbieri, Riker tried to banish his irrational fear. If it persisted, he would have to talk to Deanna Troi about it. He shifted in his seat, then glanced past Captain Picard at Counselor Troi. She was sitting perfectly still, and he could almost see the doubt within her that she would never allow to be seen in her lovely face. And he also knew that he would do his duty, even if it cost him his life.

As Admiral Barbieri signed off, the crew members on the bridge were silent. Then the viewscreen showed the sun that promised to release an impersonal violence vastly greater than a star's usual seething cauldron. Outwardly, the sun did not betray the presence of the fury, so long imprisoned, that was readying to wipe all life from this system's third planet. Riker knew that the *Enterprise*'s instruments had already recorded enough information to predict with certainty the coming hellfire.

Then he noticed something else, and leaned forward to study the panel in front of his station. The *Enterprise*'s sensors had detected twenty sublight spacecraft accelerating toward the edges of this solar system. They had to have been boosting for some time to have gone so far, and they could only have come from Epictetus III.

"Twenty sublight ships are leaving this system," the deep voice of Lieutenant Worf said from his station behind Troi.

"Computer," Picard said, "view aft." The viewscreen revealed the tiny dots of the sublight craft. He turned toward Riker. "Where can they be going?"

The question was rhetorical. Picard was obviously well aware that with a standard sublight boost, the best those ships could achieve would be to reach interstellar space. Out there, they had a chance to survive the shock of the nova, but there would be nowhere for them to go, no port for them to reach in any reasonable time.

"Clearly, Captain," Riker replied, "they expect to be picked up."

Chapter Two

As THE BLUE-GREEN GLOBE of Epictetus III appeared on the bridge's main viewscreen, a wave of anxiety washed over Deanna Troi. She sat back at her station, shaken by the sensation, then regained her self-control.

Epictetus III, she knew, had a reputation for beauty, and its inhabitants were noted for their artistic accomplishments and their appreciation of all the arts. Images of the planet's cities had shown her graceful buildings set among flowering gardens. Most of the Epictetans lived along the east, south, and west coasts of Themis, a continent about the size of Earth's Australia that lay on Epictetus III's equator, but some two hundred thousand people lived in the city of Boreas on the much smaller northern continent of Metis.

The two continents were the only landmasses on a planet whose surface was over ninety percent ocean. These continents had presented some obstacles to settlement. The coastline of Metis was barren and covered with rocks, while the middle of that continent was thickly forested land. The interior of Themis was a sand-covered expanse known as the Korybantes Desert, bordered by the high peaks of the Kuretes Mountains in the east and the Kabeiroi Mountains in the west.

Federation colonists had come to this watery world of so little land, and had fallen in love with its beauty. To an Epictetan, Troi had heard, no other planet could be as beautiful. The stark contrasts among the flowering hills overlooking the ocean, the magnificent mountains, the wide grassy plains, the orange sands of the desert, the rock-strewn shoreline in the north, and a forest of trees that were many times larger than Earth's sequoias had only heightened the colonists' appreciation of their world's beauty.

Now that world would be forever lost.

The torment of twenty million people again threatened to fill her; she felt their growing terror and despair pressing in around her. And then, below the inner storm of fear and anxiety, she heard a deeper song: the love of this world's people for their planet. The roots of the song reached back to a time before this world was settled, and seemed linked to the long-dead alien civilization that had once flourished here, and whose absence had never been adequately explained. This songful bond with the long-gone inhabitants had been forged by a century and a half of growing familiarity with the landscape and through various archaeological clues, much as the owner of an old house develops a sense about the previous dwellers and comes to feel that he knows so much more than he can say, much less prove.

The story of that long-ago culture had also been one of love for a beautiful world surviving in the hostile glare of an unstable sun. Recently uncovered evidence suggested that the earlier people of Epictetus III had sought to protect their world from danger by stabilizing its sun, because they could not bear to see their world perish. And it had not perished, even though those past inhabitants were gone; now their song continued in the minds and hearts of new settlers, opposing the sun's renewed enmity.

So much of life's meaning, Troi thought, lay only at the edge of extinction. . . .

Picard straightened at his station and said, "This is Captain Jean-Luc Picard of the *U.S.S. Enterprise. . . .*"

The face of a handsome gray-haired woman appeared on the viewscreen, stopping Picard in midsentence. Troi sensed that the captain had not been sure of exactly what to say after the routine hailing phrases, and was now content to remain mostly silent.

"Captain Picard," the woman said, "I am Minister Mariamna Fabre of our world's governing council, and I have been chosen to speak for the council." She paused as the view pulled back to show eight other figures sitting with her at a long table covered with a lacy white cloth and set with flowers in enameled vases, delicate glass pitchers, and elegant silver goblets. The faces of the nine ministers were grim, and one man with a thick mane of white hair was whispering to a younger woman. Another man, with black hair, fine features, and intense dark eyes, scowled at Mariamna Fabre. Their expressions told Troi that, even though the council was deferring to Minister Fabre for the time being, some of its members were wishing that her authority were not so great, especially during this deadly crisis.

The young woman sitting with the white-haired man suddenly struck the table with her fist, knocking over a goblet. "This is no time for the niceties of diplomacy!" she cried out. The white-haired man nodded in agreement. "We have nothing to lose now by speaking honestly, even harshly."

"Captain Picard, that was Minister Dorcas Dydion," Minister Fabre said. "She's quite understandably distraught—please pardon her for failing to introduce herself." Fabre sat back in her seat. "Go on, Dorcas," she murmured. "Say what you have to say." Troi sensed the iron will underlying Fabre's conciliatory tone; the minister was tougher than she seemed, but always willing to bend rather than break.

The young woman looked away for a moment. "I'll yield to Samas," she murmured, and Troi saw that Fabre had intimidated her more than a little.

"Very well." Minister Fabre gestured at the black-haired man. "Samas, you may speak. Captain Picard should know how it is with us."

The man lifted his head; his dark eyes gazed out from the viewscreen. "I am Minister Samas Rychi."

Troi saw Picard tense with recognition. "Professor Rychi," Picard said, leaning forward, "I'm an admirer of your work. Archaeology is a keen interest of mine—I've read all your books, including your recent account of your excavations on Epictetus Three. You make the past live in your words. I hadn't realized that you were a member of your world's council."

"An election was held only a few months ago. I haven't been on the council of ministers long. It seems I was destined to help govern our world only at the hour of its demise." Samas Rychi rested his arms against the table, and Troi realized that the captain's sincerely meant compliments had not moved the archaeologist at all. "Captain Picard, exactly what can you do for us in a week's time?"

"All that is possible," Picard replied in a flat, unemotional voice, but his eyes betrayed his concern and dismay.

Rychi's mouth twisted. "And exactly what is possible?"

"They should go after the ships," the white-haired man shouted. "That much should be possible."

"I assume," Picard said, "that you mean the sublight craft fleeing from your system."

"Yes."

"Well, of course!" Rychi burst out. "We all know why that's your first priority, Czeslaw."

Minister Fabre's face sagged with fatigue, and Troi glimpsed despair in her eyes for an instant; but then the minister straightened and gazed directly at the

17

white-haired man. "Samas has the floor," she said in a quiet but hard voice, reasserting her control of the meeting.

"Naturally Czeslaw wants the *Enterprise* to go after those ships," Samas Rychi said. "His son's on one of them."

"I see no reason—" the white-haired man began.

"Silence." Minister Fabre had pitched her voice low, but both men immediately turned toward her. "I was chosen to speak for the council, so you will allow me to speak." She paused. "Some of us are ashamed of what those craft represent, Captain Picard. Three ministers in this chamber have family and friends aboard those ships." Her face revealed her shame at having to make such an admission, and Troi felt sympathy for the woman's pain and courage. "Minister Czeslaw Peladon's son is among the passengers."

"I make no apology for that," Czeslaw Peladon said, drawing his bushy white eyebrows together. "I took the chance to save my only child and his wife. Ministers Lise Turano and Lev Robert were my partners in this enterprise, and used their influence to save those close to them—I can only commend them for agreeing to act quickly when it was necessary to act without hesitation."

He waved his arm at a fine-featured blond woman and a mustached gray-haired man; the two shrank back in their seats, looking embarrassed. "But we did not try to save ourselves," Peladon continued. "Keep that in mind before you rush to condemn us."

"You want the *Enterprise* to save the people

18

aboard those ships," Minister Fabre said. "I must disagree. Who would we put in a lifeboat if only a few could be saved? The children, of course. A starship is limited in the number of people it can rescue, so as many of this world's children as possible should be saved."

"How many people are aboard the sublight ships?" Picard asked.

Fabre glanced at Czeslaw Peladon. "Three thousand and sixty, Captain," the white-haired man replied.

"We could accommodate that number," Captain Picard said, "but to chase down each of those ships would take time away from whatever we might be able to do here."

"Wait!" Minister Dorcas Dydion, the young woman who had spoken before, was leaning over the table; a lock of her long reddish hair fell across her face. "Do you mean you're the only ship? Didn't Starfleet send any others?"

Picard shook his head. "We were the closest. There was no time for anyone else to get here before the nova. Several ships are on the way, but they won't be here in time unless by some chance the nova's delayed. And even then, for them to orbit your world and transport people aboard would put those starships in jeopardy if anything went wrong."

Troi imagined a horrifying picture. Starships standing off in low planetary orbit, beaming people aboard—a very small number—and then being forced to shut down the transporters at the last moment and race to outrun the nova. It might be done if the ships could get here before the end, but fifty or even a hundred ships could do little for most of the twenty million people. Mobs would be fighting one another below to get a chance at rescue, perhaps storming the places where transporter beams were to touch down, making it impossible to do anything more than to beam up jostling bodies in bits and pieces.

"So your ship is all there is?" Dorcas Dydion was saying, her eyes wide with disbelief.

"Yes," Picard said, and Troi caught the undercurrent of rebellion in his emotions.

"Then there is only one rational course to take," Samas Rychi said, but his voice broke and he paused. Minister Fabre was waiting for him. He nodded at her, then went on, "You can't save our world or most of its people, but it might be possible to save our culture. Some of us on this council are its custodians, people who have done what we can to uncover and preserve this world's past. Others, such as my colleague Mariamna Fabre, have enriched our culture with their contributions to its science and art—she is, as you may know, one of our most gifted composers."

Fabre grimaced, as though resenting his mention of her accomplishments in so grave a context.

"And all of us here," Rychi continued eloquently, "were elected to our positions because others trusted us to serve and to guide our world. We and a few of those like us must survive. Take some children, of course, but take other people as well—our best and most accomplished people, along with some of our most treasured artifacts. What will those children have if there is no one left to remember, and no one left to teach them what we had here?"

"I see your point," Picard said, but Troi sensed the captain's dismay. He had admired Samas Rychi's work and thought something of the man, and now disillusionment was clearly setting in. Rychi's argument might be sound—she could grant him that much—but she also sensed what seemed to be fear and self-interest behind his statements.

"I'm partly in agreement with Samas," Dorcas Dydion said, "but Czeslaw has a point, too. Take what people and artifacts you can from our planet, then go after the sublight ships." She looked around at the other council members, who seemed to be agreeing with her.

"What would we be saving?" Minister Fabre asked. "Our world's life will die, and will not live again in the few who survive. It's not the few who need to be saved. It's our world that needs saving." She spoke with despair in her voice, and there was no hope in her eyes.

"That is not possible, Minister," Picard said softly. "I wish it were otherwise. If only we had known earlier what had kept this sun stable—the Federation wouldn't have risked settlements here until more was known."

Fabre bowed her head. "We were so in love with this world," she said, "these few generations that have lived here, that perhaps we didn't wish to look too closely at the great gift left us."

Troi knew what was coming now. The presence of the *Enterprise,* rather than giving comfort and safety to some, would drive many to desperate and violent acts. The starship could easily repel boarding parties, but the agony of having to do so would place cruel emotional strains on the crew. Below, on the planet, the suicide rate was likely to rise quickly; many would prefer a peaceful end in place of a conflagration.

She caught a wave of distress and agony, at close range this time. At her station, Ensign Ganesa Mehta was as still as stone as she watched the viewscreen. How would the young woman react if she had to refuse desperate friends and relatives passage on the *Enterprise?* Would she be able to bear up if people she cared about chose to take their own lives before the nova flared? What would the ensign do when the last messages came, when her world began to die? She shouldn't be on bridge duty, Troi thought; she's close to falling apart now.

"May I ask another question, Minister Fabre?" Picard said. "Our records show that you have at least two cargo-carrier-class starships."

Fabre nodded. "Yes, we do—the *Olympia* and the *Carpathia.*"

"Where are they?"

"On their way here with cargo from several ports of call," Fabre replied. "They're scheduled to arrive three weeks from today. Their captains have said that they won't turn away from a course for home until all hope is gone." She folded her hands; her knuckles were white. "We were building a third cargo carrier, as well as a cruiser-class starship, but they can't be completed before the end. The twenty others we had, all nonwarp intrasystem craft, were, as I said before, commandeered by three of my fellow council members before anyone else could get to them." The minister averted her eyes.

Troi almost heard Picard try to say, "Perhaps a way can be found to save your people," but he held back, obviously knowing that hollow words, even from a starship captain, would be useless to set a brave example in a hopeless situation. Minister Fabre's people would show their best and worst, and mere words would not bring dignity to the coming disaster; nothing could.

Minister Fabre ended the meeting quickly. There was nothing more to say, and she and her colleagues would have their hands full struggling to keep some order among their people before the end.

Picard found himself gazing at the screen, which was again showing the planet below. He felt the eyes of his officers on him, but for a moment he did not look back.

At last he turned toward Riker and said, "There is only one course of action to take, as unfair as it is. We have to start beaming up as many people as we can take, together with any essential or especially precious artifacts and documents, immediately. And we don't have the time to start any kind of fairness lottery for which deserving three thousand or so people can come aboard. Three of the council members have already sent away those nearest and dearest to them, so the six remaining ministers might as well pick the rest, themselves included. Chance would be just as unfair as what's already happening. A technical fairness would be cold comfort."

Riker frowned. "As you say," he began, "there's no fair way to handle this, except perhaps to reach down into populated areas and simply beam up people at random, which would be dangerous."

"Permission to speak, sir," said the young officer sitting at the control and navigation station, and Picard recalled that the young pilot, Ganesa Mehta, was from Epictetus III. It was unfortunate but unavoidable, since Starfleet made a point of recruiting from as many Federation colonies as possible.

"Go ahead, Ensign Mehta," Riker said.

"You can trust Mariamna Fabre to be fair," the dark-haired ensign said. "She's been a member of the council for nearly twenty years. There's never been a hint of scandal involving her, and she's scrupulously honest. That's why she keeps getting reelected and why she's almost always asked to speak for the council as a whole. If anyone must make difficult decisions, she's the one to do it." Ganesa Mehta lowered her eyes. "You can't say the same for some of the other ministers."

"La Forge and O'Brien," Picard said, standing up and turning aft, "how long to beam up three thousand? And how crowded would we be?"

"If we use all six personnel transporters," Geordi La Forge replied, "we could beam up seven hundred persons per hour at most."

"If we reset the cargo transporters to handle life-forms," Miles O'Brien added, "we could manage an additional three hundred per hour."

Data turned his chair around and said, "Therefore, the shortest amount of time it would take for three thousand is three hours, but it would be safer to allow a bit more time than that. Our life-support systems can handle that many additional people, and there is enough space to hold them, despite the crowding. It is deciding which persons to bring aboard that is likely to take most of our remaining time."

And then, Picard thought to himself, we simply leave this planet to its fate.

Riker stood up and went over to Ganesa Mehta's station. "Ensign," he said softly, "I'm relieving you of duty."

"Sir," she replied, "I can handle my duties at conn."

"Perhaps," Riker said, "but the next few days will be hard on all of us. I don't want any of us strained beyond our limits. I'm putting you on the inactive list for the time being."

Ensign Mehta nodded, and for a moment her eyes met Picard's. He felt an instant of sympathy, then got up and started toward the forward turbolift, intending to keep his appointment in sickbay. He had been scheduled for his physical just before the order to head to Epictetus III had come in from Starfleet Command. Dr. Crusher would be even more eager to examine him now, to make certain that he was up to the demands of this tragic mission.

Data caught up to him and said, "Captain, may I speak with you in private?"

Picard gazed into Data's expressionless yellow eyes, but there was no way to tell what the android had in mind. "Of course."

He led the way to the ready room. When the door had slid shut behind them, Data said, "Captain, I would like permission to beam down with Lieutenant Commander La Forge to the site of Professor Rychi's recent excavation, the one that houses the station that may be linked to the alien sun stabilizer technology."

"Do you think that can help us?" Picard asked.

"Probably not, Captain, but perhaps we might find some way to slow up the nova for a month, perhaps longer. What we need is more time for evacuation. It is worth the effort to see what this surviving technology might suggest to me and to Lieutenant Commander La Forge that would gain us that time."

"I'm sure Samas Rychi won't have any objection to your visiting the site under the circumstances." Picard sat down, suddenly feeling very tired. "Don't be long—a few hours at most. We'll have you pinpointed for beam-up on a moment's notice."

"The nova is not likely to pose a danger to us in that length of time," Data said.

"It isn't just the nova I'm thinking about. I don't want you and La Forge falling hostage to anyone who might demand refuge on the *Enterprise.*"

"I believe the site is in the middle of the Korybantes Desert, at a great distance from any populated areas," Data said.

"Whatever do you think you'll find?" Picard asked, feeling a surge of curiosity touched with hope.

"I do not expect to find anything, Captain. If the engineers Professor Rychi brought in have not learned anything in the months they have had to examine his discovery, I do not expect to learn much in only a few hours."

"Still," Picard murmured, "at least we will have explored every possibility."

"Indeed. That is all that we can do, Captain." Data turned toward the door. "I will speak to Lieutenant Commander La Forge at once."

Finally, Captain Picard was on his way to sickbay for his physical. Beverly Crusher smoothed back her hair as she prepared to leave her private quarters. She had managed to squeeze in a nap, knowing that there would not be much chance to rest over the next few days. She would have to be at her best now.

Jean-Luc Picard was physically fit; she had no doubt of that. But fatigue and the emotional stress of this mission would take a toll on the captain and the crew. At the moment, her sickbay had as patients only two crew members rapidly recovering from minor accidents. She did not expect it to remain that unpopulated for long.

Beverly stepped toward the door, then remembered that she had not yet viewed her son's latest subspace message. Wesley's message had been waiting for her earlier, but she had decided to look at it after getting some sleep. She had better look at it now, while she had some time. She went to the panel over her desk and activated the small screen.

Wesley's face appeared, and she saw the worry in his eyes. "Mother," he said, "I hope you're all right. We've heard about the mission. I—" His throat moved as he swallowed. "I've got a favor to ask of you. Krystyna's been trying to get a message through to her parents, but hasn't had much luck."

The young woman's name had come up often and warmly in Wesley's recent messages. Krystyna was a promising young cadet at Starfleet Academy who had already earned a reputation as one of the school's most brilliant students. Her mathematical skills had first attracted Wesley's notice, but Beverly suspected that the two had grown much closer in recent months. Now she saw tension and worry in her son's face, and guessed the reason. Krystyna had grown up on Epictetus III.

"Anyway, I told her I'd contact you and ask if you could find out about them. She just wants to know if they're all right, and then—" Wesley's face grew even more serious. "They haven't answered her calls. There are a lot of things she wants to say to them before—" He looked down and murmured, "They were angry with her for coming here. Krystyna hadn't told me that before. They had a big argument about it. Her father insisted that the universities on her own world were the equal of any in the Federation and that she belonged there, doing mathematics. Not that any of that matters now." Wesley shook his head, obviously struck by the tragic irony that Krystyna would survive because she had defied her parents' wishes, and that they might even be glad now that she had done so. "If you can find out anything, let me know. I have to go—I'm already late for a class, and Krystyna's supposed to meet me after that."

Wesley's face winked out. Beverly went toward her

door, thinking about her son and the young cadet who would never see her home planet again.

Beverly found Jean-Luc Picard in the sickbay, talking to one of her two recovering patients. "Well, Ensign Chang," the captain was saying, "I hope you'll be ready for active duty soon."

Ensign Chang Jun-shing sat up in his biobed. "I'm fit now, sir, but Dr. Crusher refuses to discharge me."

Beverly glanced at the display on the screen over the ensign's bed and saw that Chang's fractured ulna had not quite mended. "Tomorrow, Ensign Chang," she said. "I'll release you then."

Beverly motioned for the captain to follow her into her office. "Ensign Chang's been extremely impatient to get out," she said as the door closed, "especially since this mission began. I suppose I can't blame him."

"He's a fine young officer," Picard said, sounding almost like a proud father. "He'll make an excellent starship captain someday."

"You *do* think a lot of him," she said.

"Yes, I do." As Beverly took out her tricorder, Picard said, "I've conferred with the council of Epictetus Three. I don't know if you happened to view that discussion."

"I was sleeping. I expect I'll have my work cut out for me for the next few days, and decided I'd better rest up while I could. But I'll play it back."

"You won't find it pleasant," Picard said as he sat down on the examination table.

Beverly peered at the tricorder readings as she

scanned the captain. "There was a message from Wesley," she murmured. "He's awfully worried about another cadet, a young woman he's been seeing. She's from here, and she's been trying to get a message through to her parents."

She looked up from her tricorder to find Picard gazing at her with sorrow in his eyes. "Wesley told me not long ago," Beverly continued, "that his friend's grandfather is a member of the council, so you might have spoken to him already. Her name is Krystyna Peladon."

Picard's eyes widened slightly. "Then her grandfather has to be Czeslaw Peladon." He shook his head. "Minister Peladon and two other members of the council used their influence to get those close to them aboard their world's twenty sublight craft. Those ships are now attempting to reach the outskirts of this system, where they hope to survive the nova. So I can tell you where the parents of Wesley's friend are—on one of those ships."

Chapter Three

Geordi La Forge was not on the bridge when Data came out from the ready room. The ship's computer informed him that the chief engineer was in Ten-Forward, where he often relaxed after going off duty.

Data found his friend sitting at the bar with Ensign Ganesa Mehta. A glass of synthehol, obviously untouched, sat in front of the young woman. The ensign looked extremely unhappy, which was understandable under the circumstances. Geordi's customary amiable mien had deserted him as well; he was slumped forward, his mouth set in a frown, his arms resting on the bar.

Guinan finished serving two people several stools away, then approached Data. She wore her usual gentle smile, but her eyes were solemn. "What'll it be?" she asked.

"I do not think I require anything at the moment," Data replied.

"Thanks for coming here with me," Ganesa Mehta said to Geordi. She turned to Guinan. "And thank you for listening. I think I've wallowed in my fears enough—right now, I'd better get some rest so I'll be fit for duty later on, if I'm needed. And I'll have to think of what to say to my parents and brother—" Her voice caught on the words.

"If you need to talk some more, I'll be here," Guinan said.

The ensign slid off her stool and left. "Poor Ganesa," Geordi said. "I don't know what would have been worse for her—being at the other end of the galaxy and not having a chance to say good-bye to anyone, or being here, knowing her whole world's going to die, and not being able to do anything about it."

"Not much of a choice," Guinan murmured.

Geordi sipped his drink. "There's no way to save this world. That offends me a lot." He glanced at Data. "And I'm sure it offends your encyclopedic intelligence greatly."

"I take no offense," Data responded, "but my curiosity has been greatly affected. There is no politically humane solution to the problem as it now stands, only an exercise in lifeboat logic of the most extreme sort. There may, however, be other solutions."

Geordi smiled ruefully. "We'll have to get out of

this system long before we can find an answer. There's just no time to find any other solutions."

As Data reviewed all his stored knowledge about novas and the course of stellar evolution, his attention was caught by a peculiar artifact shaped like a bird that stood on the bar next to a glass of water. The bird dipped its beak into the water, straightened, then dipped its beak into the water again.

"I see you've noticed my new toy," Guinan said. "It was a present from Lieutenant Griffin. He told me it was a popular bar decoration on Earth during the mid–twentieth century." She left them to serve another crew member a few seats away.

Data studied the bobbing bird for a while, then turned toward Geordi. "May I request," he said, "that you beam down to the surface with me as soon as possible?"

"For what reason?" Geordi asked.

"There is a particular site I wish to have you examine with me. The captain has already given us his permission, and was about to contact the person in charge of this site, Professor Samas Rychi, when I left the ready room."

"What do you have in mind?"

"I would rather not tell you just now," Data replied. "I prefer that your mind not be prejudiced by anything I might say before we examine this site together."

"You do have something in mind!"

"Indeed," Data said. "I ask you to, as you might say, humor me. You are not only an extremely competent engineer, but also possess a strong and imaginative grasp of technology. I would very much like your opinion after we have viewed this particular site."

"And I can guess what site this is." Geordi leaned toward Data. "You want to take a look at that station, the one that seems to be linked to the so-called stabilizer inside this sun."

"Yes."

"What do you think we can do—find some way to repair the stabilizer? From what I've heard, Samas Rychi has had engineers puzzling over the station ever since his team discovered it, and they haven't been able to figure anything out except that it's linked to the sun stabilizer somehow."

"Perhaps they are too close to the problem," Data said. "Perhaps their fears have clouded their judgment, and they are incapable of seeing what they might have otherwise. If we could find a way to delay the nova even a few months longer, there would be time to save more people—maybe everyone."

"It's worth a try," Geordi said. "Let's go take a look."

They would be examining an alien technology, Geordi La Forge thought as he stepped onto the transporter platform. The odds of understanding any part of it, let alone finding a way to use it to delay the nova, were not simply long, they were obscure. But in the little time they had left in this system, he was curious to see what the people of Epictetus III had unknowingly depended on for the last century.

"Energize," he said, and the transporter room and

the lanky form of Lieutenant Jake Dane, the officer on duty, vanished.

He and Data were abruptly standing in front of a domed silver structure with a high ridge of excavated sand behind it. A desert of orange sand stretched around them on all sides. The heat was dry but intense; through his VISOR, La Forge could see the pale rippling infrared waves reflected by the sand.

Two small vehicles were parked in front of the silvery building. Two men were standing at what appeared to be the entrance to the installation; Samas Rychi was one of them. The archaeologist lifted a hand in greeting.

"Professor Rychi," La Forge said, "or perhaps you'd prefer being called Minister Rychi."

Samas Rychi shrugged. "It makes no difference to me. I haven't been on the council long enough to get used to being addressed as Minister."

"I am Lieutenant Commander Geordi La Forge, chief engineer of the *Enterprise.*"

Rychi nodded. "Captain Picard told me to expect you, but I don't know what you expect to accomplish here. A number of engineers have looked at this installation already without finding out a thing."

"I'm aware of that," La Forge said.

Rychi gestured at the tall, wiry gray-bearded man on his left. "This is Hakim Ponselle, one of my associates. He was a member of my team when we discovered this place, and he's practically been living here."

Hakim Ponselle squinted at La Forge's VISOR. "Got a problem with your eyes, young man?" he asked.

"I was born blind," La Forge explained, "but this VISOR allows me to see selectively almost all of the electromagnetic spectrum."

Ponselle grinned. "Then you can see a lot better than the rest of us."

"Better still, I can see out but you can't see in." Ponselle chuckled as La Forge motioned to his friend. "And this is Lieutenant Commander Data, our operations officer."

"I am a fully sentient android," Data added.

"Meaning," Ponselle said, "that you're probably smarter than I am, have a much better memory, and don't have all my emotional distractions."

"I should say, however," Data responded, "that I have made a great study of human emotions, and must admit that they are not as irrational as they are often made out to be."

Ponselle laughed again. La Forge smiled, impressed that the gray-bearded man was still able to retain his sense of humor. Samas Rychi, however, appeared distinctly uneasy with them; his stance was rigid, and he did not smile.

"What can you tell us about this installation?" La Forge asked.

"Tell you while we show you." Ponselle turned and extended his arm to the wall. A doorway suddenly appeared in the wall, but retracted so quickly that the opening seemed to have appeared almost instantaneously.

Ponselle led the others into a wide hallway. The

walls were covered with etchings. One was clearly a detailed depiction of a sun and its corona. Another was of two humanoid figures sitting in front of a cylindrical object adorned with what appeared to be the image of a star, and still another showed a vessel with sails. The craft might have been a sailboat of some kind, but to La Forge it looked more like a sunjammer, a spacegoing vessel that used its giant sails to catch the solar wind.

"We've found etchings and artwork at almost all the ancient sites," Rychi said. "Even in an installation like this, the old ones tried to create some beauty."

They crossed the hallway and went down a steep ramp, walked along a wide walkway, then descended another ramp. "Many of the ancient structures here have levels kilometers below ground," Rychi explained. "This one isn't quite as deep. There are no signs of any lifts or other means of descending to the lower levels, so we're assuming, based on old etchings and other artwork that depict people inside these buildings, that they used small antigravitational devices attached to belts to move up and down. We've been making do with the ramps."

La Forge could hear nothing except the soft sound of footsteps against the ramp. "Awfully quiet in here," he said, and the air seemed to swallow his words.

"We had some of our archaeologists and a few engineers working here up until a few days ago," Ponselle said, "but they've all gone home now." He spoke casually, as if telling them that the others were simply taking some routine time off and would return. "Our sun here had been unusually quiet before it began to show the signs of instability common to eruptive variables. That quiet was noticed by the first colonists, who concluded that it was unusual even for a star of roughly Sol's mass. When it began to show instabilities that were also uncharacteristic for a sunlike star, our astrophysicists were completely baffled. The puzzle teased us for nearly a decade. Then when Samas and I and our team found this building, we finally learned that something had been put into our sun to keep it stable."

"Put into the sun?" Data asked.

"Yes, you'll see," Rychi said.

The second ramp finally ended at a large open arch; La Forge and Data followed Ponselle and Rychi into a long chamber. At the far end, shadows played on what seemed to be a gray wall. One image was that of a white, pulsating sphere. At its center sat a jet black sphere. As La Forge looked at the image, it seemed to rotate slowly and acquire a three-dimensional reality.

"That," Ponselle said, "is a view right into our sun, into what you'd have to describe as a subspace pocket inside the star. That pocket holds what we call the stabilizer. All solar emissions confirm that it's failing now, and there doesn't seem to be a damn thing we can do about it."

"Are there any controls here?" Data asked.

"If there are," Rychi said, "we haven't been able to understand them or even find them. It may be that the pocket itself is failing for some reason, and that the integrity of the stabilizing device will soon be destroyed. We don't know how to remedy that." He sighed. "I had the best engineers we've got exploring this site, hoping they might see something my team and I couldn't see. None of them could gain any insight into how this stabilizer works."

As La Forge looked down the long chamber at the ghostly image of the star, he realized that he was looking into a limited visualization of subspace. A small pocket of it had been opened inside the star, to make a place where the stabilization device could survive and presumably control the star's use of hydrogen fuel, thus preventing its arrival at the eruptive variable or nova stage.

"You'd almost think," Ponselle said, "that a link station like this one couldn't have been made just to display this control of the sun. That's what I keep thinking anyway. I mean, it doesn't seem likely that the ancients would have put this whole thing up just so people could come out to the middle of nowhere and gawk. This installation might have been used to control the sun in other ways. But in all the time we've been here, we've never found anything else to do in here except watch. It's maddening!"

"Perhaps that was this station's purpose," Data said, "to warn anyone watching of when the sun could no longer be delayed from becoming unstable. That could be why the alien civilization that built it is no longer here. They might have left at the very first indication of instabilities to come, of which a nova is the most extreme. This display may be nothing more than an alarm, which you have come upon very late in the day, so to speak. There may in fact be nothing here or inside the suncore that can be repaired."

"That's the same conclusion I finally reached," Rychi said, "but I keep suspecting there's more to it, that we're missing something." He folded his arms. "The civilization that built this station erected a great many other structures. Most of their sites remind me of certain ancient Egyptian monuments on Earth—they're all filled with statues and etchings I can only describe as monuments to glory, to a people who accepted their power and delighted in it." He stared at the metallic floor. "We don't have their power, we've been recklessly unobservant in settling this world, and now we'll pay the highest price for our century and a half of happiness."

"I would not go that far in any criticism," Data said. "Until you saw the obvious fluctuations in your sun's output, it would have been difficult to conclude that anything could go wrong in such a short time as a century or two, or even in a millennium. Human beings do not often look ahead more than a few generations, and are not likely to do so until they have lives that extend over millennia."

"You're being kind and generous to the doomed," Ponselle muttered, "but what it comes down to is that the people who settled here made a big mistake, and it's going to cost us dearly. We were just plain stupid."

"No more so," Data replied, "than any form of life that has to survive on a planetary surface. Planetary ecologies have always been dangerous to the life-forms of their worlds. Technologically advanced civilizations may lower the numbers of their yearly dead, but they cannot eliminate the loss entirely."

Rychi's eyes narrowed as he looked at Data; he was clearly growing annoyed. The archaeologist, La Forge thought, was losing patience with Data, not understanding that the android's literal-minded and long-winded manner of speaking was often his way of thinking aloud or prompting his thoughts, and that Data liked to share the process.

"It seems you've come here," Rychi said, "just to arrive at the same assumption I had. Our sun can't be stopped from going nova. Hakim wants to believe it might be otherwise, that this place can control the device inside the sun, but that's probably only hope and desperation talking. This station or monitoring system is here simply to signal when all hope is gone, to give a warning when the stabilizer can no longer extend the star's life. It did that a long time ago, and this world's people left—very early. For some reason, we haven't been so lucky."

"We may still be wrong about this being a warning system," Data replied. "What I am thinking of doing now is beaming down some of our probes and monitoring equipment and linking this system to that of the *Enterprise*. There are a few diagnostics I would like to try."

"And what'll that do?" Ponselle asked. "Find us a way to restabilize our sun?"

"Even a small delay would be helpful. It would give us more time to evacuate people from this planet and system."

Ponselle turned to La Forge. "Can we hope for that?"

"Let's find out," La Forge said. "I don't want to raise false hopes, but—"

"Raise them all you like, young fellow. Any hope's better than none."

"Do whatever you like here," Rychi said softly. "You have my permission. Scan the installation, analyze it, blast it apart if you like. Can't do any harm. It doesn't matter now."

La Forge pondered what Data had said as they followed the two archaeologists out of the chamber. Data's words had triggered something in his imagination. He knew that his friend's mind was already listing the various possibilities, and that they all assumed that a starship could be an extremely versatile instrument in the right hands. But he also knew that Data would not guess blindly, imagine gratuitously, or mistake wishful thinking for reality. Data would propose a course of action only when he was sure it had a chance of working.

The two *Enterprise* officers were gone. Samas Rychi gazed at the spot on the sand where they had been standing. La Forge and the android called Data could always escape, he thought. They would return to poke around this site, to pretend that they might actually be able to grant his world a reprieve, and then they would beam aboard their ship just before the end came. They would convince themselves that they had done all they could, that they had honored their oaths as Starfleet officers.

"Samas," Hakim Ponselle said, "I'm thinking of heading back to Nicopolis. I want to be with Asela before—" His voice trailed off.

"Of course," Rychi said. "I'll probably be in Nicopolis myself before long. Mariamna Fabre is bound to call at least one more useless council meeting during the time we have left." He glanced at the older man. "I thought you might want your wife to come out here so you could both watch those two Starfleet officers at work. As an engineer herself, Asela might be curious about exactly what they hope to find."

"I don't think they're going to find anything. And you don't, either."

Rychi turned toward his colleague. "Then you don't really believe your own hypothesis about this place."

"That this station might have a way to control the device inside the sun? I still think that's possible, Samas. I just don't think we'll have time to find out how to use it."

"Go," Rychi said. He was about to say "give Asela my best," then realized how empty that would sound. "Thank you for working with me all these years, for being my friend." It occurred to him that this might be their last moment together.

Hakim Ponselle shook his hand, then clasped his shoulder. "If you need me for anything during the next few days, let me know. I'll come right out here—Asela, too."

"I will."

Hakim walked toward his flitter. Rychi would be alone until the two officers from the *Enterprise* returned with their equipment. When they learned nothing, they would leave, and he would be by himself once more. There would be one last meeting of the council, which he would attend out of duty, and more useless chatter about which small portion of the population and cultural heritage of his world most deserved to be saved. Then he would come back here, to be alone again before the destruction. It seemed appropriate for him to meet his end in the solitude of this place.

He had always been alone. Hakim Ponselle and the people who had worked with him over the years—his students, colleagues, and mentors—had been his only friends, yet he had known little of them apart from the work they had shared with him. His mother and father had become parents late in life, and had died by the time he entered the University of Nicopolis. There, and at the Sorbonne and Cambridge, the universities on Earth where he had done his graduate work, he had acquired a large circle of acquaintances but few friends. There had been infatuations for him but no abiding love and no wife, protégés but no children, and he had preferred it that way.

His work had been his life, the past inhabitants of Epictetus III more real to him than the people among whom he had lived. He had uncovered their metallic walls of etchings and their monumental statuary and had imagined himself among them, walking the wide and open streets of one of their cities, resting in one of their vast rooms or indoor courtyards, watching the competitive displays of physical strength in one of their huge arenas. Their art and their buildings had told him that even their personal lives had been conducted on the grand scale, with great passion and an indulgence of all their senses and emotions. Their ancient structures, the monumental towers with their underground levels, had withstood all the geological and meteorological forces hurled against them over the ages, and seemed designed to stand forever.

In much of their art, great ships were depicted, great oceangoing vessels that looked as though they could hold the population of a small city. The old ones had apparently not feared to leave their continents far behind and sail the vast ocean of their world.

Rychi had pored over their documents, their recorded images and the alien symbols etched into pages of metal foil, in his attempts to decipher their language. He had dreamed of finding the key to that linguistic code, of opening up the inner minds and thoughts of that past race, of truly entering their world at last.

But their language had remained a tantalizing mystery, just out of reach, and now there would be no time left for him to solve it. The solid walls of their monuments could not survive a nova. Because their remains would be completely destroyed, the ancient race of Epictetus III would vanish from the universe without a trace, forever lost to any future intelligence that might have treasured their legacy.

Rychi had seen the look in the eyes of Mariamna Fabre when he had said that their duty now was to save the custodians of their world's culture. He was certain that he had glimpsed a flicker of contempt for him in the eyes of Captain Jean-Luc Picard.

Why couldn't they understand? He had not been thinking of saving himself, but of preserving the memory of the race that had once dwelled here. It had taken him nearly thirty years to gain even a superficial understanding of what that culture might have been. Without the monuments and artifacts, the shards of old tools and the remnants of an ancient technology—without this planet itself— even his most accomplished students and colleagues would never advance beyond his own limited comprehension. But if he could preserve enough data, take enough images of Epictetus III's artifacts and records with him, he might eventually manage to decipher the language that would open the minds of those ancient people to him at last.

They should have understood. That man Picard, who clearly fancied himself a student of archaeology, certainly should have grasped his motive in suggesting that his own life be saved. Instead, the captain was probably thinking that Samas Rychi was a coward, pleading for himself from purely selfish reasons.

They did not understand. He would have accepted death if he had accomplished his aim, if he had been able to translate just one ancient document and know that his interpretation of it was accurate. Then he would have been able to leave a Rosetta Stone for others, a key to this world's past that others might have used. Eventually another archaeologist might have been able to build on his legacy even if there was nothing left of that ancient civilization except what survived in databases.

But he would leave no legacy now. That was what pained him most, far beyond the prospect of his own death. His world would become a vapor in the heavens, and everything he had given his life to would be forgotten. This world's past inhabitants, with their power to control a star, had unwittingly lured Rychi's grandparents and others to settle this world. He would wait in this station, in this place built to warn those ancient humanoids of approaching doom, knowing that his life had been wasted and would vanish without a trace, and that their world and culture would be erased with him.

Chapter Four

Samas Rychi was alone at the alien site when Data returned with Geordi. The archaeologist waited inside with them as the probes and consoles of monitoring equipment beamed down from the *Enterprise,* rematerializing inside the alien station's long chamber. Data could clearly see that Rychi expected nothing from these instrumentalities, that the man had reached the state human beings called resignation, or perhaps despair. It was often difficult for Data to tell the difference between the two emotions; resignation, when not mistaken, was a rational state of mind, a recognition of the inevitable, but rarely free of emotional despair in a human being.

"You had no problem requisitioning all this equipment?" Rychi said.

"Not at all," Data replied. "Your people are in a most perilous situation. Captain Picard feels that, under the circumstances, every hand must be played, so to speak."

"Including weak hands and long shots," Geordi added, bending over to move a sensor closer to the wall of dancing subspace shadows. He straightened, then removed his tricorder from his belt. "I'm going to scan this room for concealed controls."

"It's been scanned," Rychi said, "many times. You won't pick up anything new. This isn't a long shot—it's wasted effort."

"To quote an extremely old adage," Data said, "whaddya got to lose?"

Rychi folded his arms and frowned. "Exactly what do you hope to accomplish here?"

"If I knew that," Data said, "I would not have to gather more information first."

"Perhaps you could be more enlightening, Lieutenant Commander La Forge."

"Don't ask me," Geordi said as he put away his tricorder, then moved another probe console closer to the gray wall of shadows. "This is Data's show at the moment, but you can trust he wouldn't be going to all this trouble on a lark—especially under these circumstances."

"I'll be leaving here when Minister Fabre calls another meeting of the council," Rychi said. "She'll probably summon us at almost any moment, but feel free to stay as long as necessary while I'm away—not that you're likely to accomplish much."

"Do you have an associate who might be willing to come out and stay here in your absence?" Data asked. "I would like to have someone at this site to call on after we leave."

"Yes, I do. You met him before—Hakim Ponselle."

"Perhaps you could contact him now."

Rychi sighed. "I'll do it from my office—just go up the ramps to the ground-floor hallway and turn left. Head for that ugly plasteen dome at the end of the corridor. We set it up a couple of months ago."

As the archaeologist trudged up the ramp, Geordi shoved a console against the wall on Data's left, then turned around. "Data, my friend," he said, "I wish you'd tell me what you're up to. Professor Rychi's colleagues are going to want to spend what little time they have left with their loved ones, not out here staring at our equipment on the slim chance that we might need their help. You might have considered that."

"But perhaps," Data replied, "this will gain them some more time." He turned away, ignoring Geordi's quizzical look.

Data and Geordi beamed back to the *Enterprise* after Rychi told them that Hakim Ponselle would return to the ancient installation with his wife, Asela Ibanez, an engineer who was familiar with the site. Geordi had restrained himself from asking more questions, but Data could see that his friend was growing ever more impatient.

"There is no point in wasting time explaining my ideas to you," Data said as they left the transporter room and hurried toward a turbolift. "Our limited time is best spent by my showing you."

"Okay, okay, Data," Geordi said.

The turbolift whisked them to deck 36, where they went directly to the main engineering control station. Data moved quickly to the display console and set the controls, opening up a direct link to the probes and sensors on the surface and making certain that the ship's other essential operations would not be affected by what he was about to try. By then, the personnel on duty in engineering were gathering around the console.

Data turned on the console's small viewscreen. The chamber inside the alien installation appeared; the shadows flickering on the station's gray wall were clearly visible, unchanged.

"Working from here," Data said, "I have all of the *Enterprise*'s sensor systems available to explore not only the stabilizer, but also the suncore."

"But we know nothing about how the alien system works," Geordi said. "All that we *think* we know is that the device inside the suncore kept this star from going nova some time ago."

"Ah, but our field resonance detectors . . ." Data paused. "Let us see what happens on the first scan."

Lieutenant Anita Obrion, one of the engineering officers, shook her head, then glanced at Geordi. "Do you have any idea of what Lieutenant Commander Data's up to?" she asked.

"No," Geordi replied in a whisper, "but he seems determined to follow his hunch."

"Determination and hunches have nothing to do with my motivation," Data said.

"Yes, Data," Geordi said.

Slowly, Data reached out with a narrow sunspace

resonance probe, nudged the alien device, and watched the console's instruments for a reaction.

"Nothing," Geordi said. "Nothing at all."

"That is what I expected," Data said. "We have to see how stable the suncore implant is, whether anything we do will affect it in any way."

"Maybe it's stopped functioning completely."

"I do not think so," Data said. "If that were true, the subspace bubble would have collapsed, destroying the device and erasing all traces of its existence. In that case, the link station on Epictetus Three would have seemed most mysterious indeed, since it would have been difficult even to guess at its physical connection with anything in the sun. But the device is still maintaining itself and the subspace bubble, which is what I expected to see."

"And that's good?" Geordi asked.

"Indeed it is."

"So maybe now you can tell us what you're up to," Geordi said.

"Not yet. I prefer that you arrive at the idea independently."

"But why, Data?" Geordi shook his head. "I know it's not because you're insecure."

"Not at all. I have completed a long chain of reasoning to arrive at what I will propose to the captain. You will not have enough time to repeat that same line of deductions. I want to see if you will leap to the same conclusion I have reached, as a check on my reasoning."

"You're pretty sure I'll get it right, then."

"Watch this." Data slowly opened a tight subspace link into the suncore device, and waited. All of the instruments indicated that the alien subspace implant was still stable. The ship's sensors monitoring the sun still showed the same rate of deterioration toward a nova state.

"Now I've got it!" Geordi cried. "You're thinking of drawing power out of the star along that tight beam."

"Precisely."

"But why?"

"Think."

"Is it that obvious?" Geordi asked.

"Apparently it is not yet obvious to you, but ask yourself this question. What could we do with the power of a star?"

Geordi rubbed at his forehead above his VISOR. "But to collect all that power from the star will only hasten the nova!"

"Unfortunately, that is so. But the risk might be worth it to save an entire world. What I propose to do is open a wormhole in front of Epictetus Three and permit the planet to pass through it into an orbit around a nearby star. There is one about fourteen light-years away that would do nicely."

"Data," Geordi said, "there are theoretical formulas for opening a wormhole. And if you're right, the sun would provide enough power. But the chance of success is so small . . ."

"Any chance," Data replied, "is better than none."

Geordi looked thoughtful. The others around the console were murmuring excitedly to one another. "And using the star's power would mean that it'll pay for the havoc it's about to cause."

"A nice piece of irony," a technician said.

Data leaned forward. "We will test to confirm that power is actually drawn, and then attempt to convince the captain of what we might be able to do with it."

"It could work," Anita Obrion muttered.

Perhaps, Data told himself, well aware that he would not only be putting the ship in grave danger, but also risking even the small number of lives it could certainly save from the coming holocaust.

His opponent lay dead at his feet. Worf leaned against a tree, still panting. No weapons this time, only bare hands, and yet he had vanquished his foe too easily, too quickly.

The image of the dead Klingon warrior vanished as the program came to an end. Worf decided that he would program in more difficulties next time, give himself a more demanding opponent. Taking his exercise in this peaceful setting had also made the battle a somewhat less satisfying experience, but the other crew members on the holodeck, knowing that hard days and extra turns on duty awaited them, had insisted on a more serene holographic environment.

Worf strode through the woods toward the river up ahead. He had slept for a couple of hours, had his recreation, and soon he would have to go back on duty. There would be no more time for anything except this mission and its demands.

It was a most disturbing mission. The star shining on Epictetus III was a deadly enemy, one impossible to fight. The predicament of the planet's inhabitants was unfortunate, and he felt a bit of pity for them, but some of them might have shown more courage in the face of disaster and death.

Cowards, he thought. Had they possessed more sublight vessels, probably even more of the wretches would have been fleeing to the system's outer reaches, hoping to survive, if living without honor could be called survival. No Klingon would have behaved so dishonorably. Had Epictetus III been a Klingon world, its council would have asked the *Enterprise* to save the best and strongest three thousand, then chosen others to be given passage on the sublight craft, and the rest would have prepared for death bravely, even joyfully. Klingons would not have disgraced their ancestral lineages by giving in to fear; none would have behaved so dishonorably as had many of these Epictetans.

Worf came to the edge of the woods. Ganesa Mehta was sitting on the riverbank. He made his way down to her. A smile flickered across her face as she saw him and then faded as he sat down.

"Greetings, Worf," the dark-haired young woman murmured.

"Greetings."

The ensign looked frail, her bones almost as light as a bird's, so unlike the powerful frame of a Klingon female. Her soft brown eyes were those of a gentle soul; so Worf had thought when Ganesa Mehta was first assigned to the *Enterprise* almost a year ago. But her record had revealed a citation for exceptional valor received during her first mission, when the starship on which she was stationed had encountered and was forced to fight and repel an intruding Romulan ship threatening a Federation outpost near the Neutral Zone. Her physical strength was no match for the Klingon warriors of his favorite holodeck program, but she had used guile and tactics to wrest a few victories from her holographic opponents. She had never shown any fear of him, or nervousness around him, and that had also won his respect. They had become friends over the past months, and his son, Alexander, had taken an instant liking to her. Worf felt it was unfortunate that others of her people did not share her fortitude.

"I spoke to my parents," Ganesa said, "and to my brother. Dalal is twelve—he was hoping to follow me to Starfleet Academy someday. I had to tell him and my parents that there was nothing I could do for them—not that they would have asked. They're being very brave about it all. They know I have to follow the orders of Starfleet and Captain Picard."

"That is so," Worf said.

"But my place is with them, not here. I keep wanting to leave the *Enterprise* and go to them. I don't know if I will survive the death of my world."

"To give in to such feelings shows weakness," he said. "I didn't expect that of you, Ganesa."

"If I could do something for them—" She drew up her legs and wrapped her arms around them. "But I can't. And I won't be losing only them. My family, my relatives, my first love, all my old friends—" Ganesa paused. "How will I bear it? I often see myself taking my own life."

"Such thoughts are unworthy of you," Worf said. "Your parents would want you to remember them, to honor their courage. The best thing you can do for your people now is to follow the orders of your commanding officer. You won't help those you love by becoming yet another defeat for Captain Picard."

"I know." Ganesa gazed out at the river. "I've told myself the same thing, but I'm completely useless here. Commander Riker has temporarily relieved me of duty. I think he's afraid I'm not up to performing well, and maybe he even thinks he's being kind, but waiting without being able to do anything to help is even worse."

"The commander would not have taken his action," Worf said, "if he had complete confidence in you. Therefore, you must restore his trust by convincing him that you can and will carry out his orders, no matter what happens on your world. You were to be reassigned to operations—inform Lieutenant Commander Data that you are prepared to resume your duties. Let him go to the commander and ask that you be put back on active duty. Commander Riker will go along with what he recommends if Counselor Troi says you're fit to return to your post."

"She must have sensed what I was feeling on the bridge." Ganesa lifted her head. "But I'm past that now."

"Then harden yourself, Ganesa. Forbid your fears to overwhelm you. Throw them aside."

"I shall," Ganesa said, looking determined. "Thank you, Worf. I knew what I had to do, but hearing it from you helps."

He allowed himself a brief smile. Ganesa never took his sternness the wrong way, as some of the other human crew members occasionally did. She bore his reproaches as a comrade might, one who needed only a few firm words to remind her of her duty. It was another quality he respected in her.

"I'll do everything I can to get Krystyna's message through," Czeslaw Peladon said, "but it may be difficult. The crews on the sublight vessels aren't responding to any messages. They may have closed their channels. I think they fear—" His throat moved as he swallowed.

"Go on," Beverly Crusher said to the image on the small viewscreen.

"You must realize that the people aboard have already said their farewells," Minister Peladon continued, running a hand through his unruly white hair. "If they now start receiving messages from those they left behind, some of them might have a change of heart. The last things the crews need now are mutinies among their passengers, or battles between those who might want to turn back and those who want to press on."

"I understand," Beverly murmured. The fleeing Epictetans also might react badly if they learned of the steadily increasing number of suicides on their world; some passengers, out of guilt, might take their own lives as well, or threaten others aboard.

"At least you can tell my granddaughter that her parents have a chance to survive," the minister said.

If the sublight craft could reach a safe distance from the nova, Beverly told herself, then Epictetus III's two cargo-carrier starships or other Starfleet vessels would be able to reach those craft. Captain Picard had already decided that the *Enterprise* was needed here, and would not go after the fleeing ships, which were in fact slightly better off than the people of the planet.

"I'll tell Krystyna about her parents in my next message to my son," Beverly said, "and relay any message from her to you. I can say that you'll try to get her message through to them."

"I'm grateful, Dr. Crusher." Czeslaw Peladon's image winked out.

Beverly rested her elbows on her desk. Her next message to Wesley and Krystyna would have to be carefully worded. She was not sure how the young woman would react to the news that her parents were safe for the time being only because her grandfather had used his influence to help them flee. Would Krystyna be thankful that her mother and father had a chance to survive? Or would she feel shame at what they had done to save their own lives?

As it happened, Beverly felt more sympathy for Czeslaw Peladon than she had expected to feel. He had explained the reasons for his actions to her. He had known that, after the shock of learning about the nova had worn off, people would be storming Epictetus III's spaceports trying to get a place aboard the shuttles that would take them to the sublight ships. There were likely to be riots—too many people struggling to get aboard, perhaps damaging the shuttlecraft in their desperation. Better to commandeer those ships immediately and make sure that some people had a chance, Minister Peladon had told two of his fellow ministers, Lise Turano and Lev Robert. Better for the three of them to act on their own, while Minister Fabre and the other council members were dithering, than to waste precious time seeking their assent to the plan. Czeslaw Peladon had shown some ruthlessness, and had chosen to save his own son, but Beverly was finding it difficult to condemn him outright. She wondered what she would have done if Wesley's life had been at stake on Epictetus III.

The door behind her slid open. Beverly turned in her chair and saw Deanna Troi standing in the entrance to her office.

"Come in," Beverly said, noting the shadows under Troi's dark eyes. The counselor was already showing signs of fatigue and the effects of sensing too many intense emotions. "I have a prescription for you, Counselor. Sleep, a minimum of five hours, to be taken immediately."

Troi sat down. "I was on my way back to my quarters," she said, "when one of your assistants summoned me here."

Beverly had forgotten. "Oh, yes," she said. "We're having a problem with Ensign Chang Jun-shing. He's been insisting that I return him to active duty, and I keep telling him that he needs another day of rest. Now he's after my staff all the time to—"

"You won't have any more problems with Ensign Chang. I sensed that he had some sort of attachment to Epictetus Three, something that was markedly increasing his anxiety, and he finally admitted that a young woman he was once deeply involved with is studying at the university in Nicopolis."

Beverly sighed.

"He's very conflicted about what happened between them," Troi continued. "He feels that she
wouldn't have come to Epictetus Three at all if she
hadn't been so bitter about their breakup. She felt
that his obligations to Starfleet made any kind of
bond between them impossible, and wanted to go to
a place where nothing would remind her of him."

"So he's feeling guilty," Beverly said.

"His guilt would be greatly relieved if there were
something he could do to help his former love and
the others on this world. Unfortunately, there won't
be much he can do even on active duty."

"There isn't much any of us can do." Beverly
leaned back in her chair. "I've got to send a message
to Wesley. He's been seeing a lot of a cadet named
Krystyna Peladon. Maybe you can advise me on
what I should say. Krystyna's grandfather is Minister Czeslaw Peladon, and I have to inform her
that—"

"Counselor Troi and Dr. Crusher," the computer
interrupted, "please report to the conference
lounge."

The message to her son would have to wait.
Beverly rose as Troi got to her feet, and followed her
out.

Picard studied the officers he had summoned to
the bridge. They were sitting around the table in the
conference lounge, listening as Data outlined his
proposal for saving Epictetus III. Data and Geordi
had sketched out the plan for Picard earlier, in
enough detail for him to know that it would have to

be seriously considered and discussed among his most trusted officers before he presented it to the Federation Council, but he still felt wary and apprehensive.

Picard could see the skepticism in the faces of the others as Data spoke. Riker was rubbing at his beard, never taking his eyes from Data. Counselor Troi would be thinking of the effect this proposal might have on the people of the planet, and whether offering this possibly false hope might only increase their suffering. Worf looked ready to attack any flaw in the plan, however much he respected the intelligence of Data and Geordi La Forge. Beverly Crusher would probably have little to say about the proposal's technical aspects, but as chief medical officer she might have insights into any ethical considerations the plan raised.

"There are of course certain facts that we must consider," Data continued. "To use the sun's power to open the wormhole, we must tie in via a subspace link into our warp drive, since opening wormholes is based on the same physical principle as the warp drive."

Picard saw Riker's eyes narrow; the commander was gazing even more doubtfully at Data.

"During the period of time in which we are opening the wormhole," Data went on, "the *Enterprise* will be unable to leave this system, since at least eight hours or more would be needed to put our warp drive back into service. The ship will be helpless during that time, unable to outrun the nova if it occurs. Once we have opened the wormhole, the *Enterprise* must continue to channel the star's energy, to keep the wormhole open long enough for the planet to pass into it. Once that passage begins, the wormhole should stay open without our support, but then begin to collapse behind Epictetus Three some thirty minutes after the planet enters. The orbital motion of the planet will be what sends it through. I can vector the course of Epictetus Three so that it should emerge around a G-type star about fourteen light-years away, at a distance of anywhere from point eighty to one point two astronomical units from the star."

"Can you be sure of those figures, Data?" Riker asked. "If the planet emerges too close or too far away from its new sun, what then?"

"I cannot be absolutely certain about the exact distance of the world's new orbit," Data replied, "but at the very least the planet should escape the nova and emerge from the wormhole into a relatively safe orbit. If that orbit then proves to be inadequate, we will have time to evacuate the planet. At best, Epictetus Three will have a new sun and a livable orbit."

Riker still looked dubious.

"What are the chances," Picard asked, "of the nova beginning while the wormhole is open? You've admitted that we'll be bringing the nova on sooner by draining the sun of power. Will we have enough time to get our warp-drive engines back on-line?"

"As I mentioned before," Geordi said, "I think I can rig our plasma injectors to get our drive back within eight hours."

Riker shook his head. "But what if the nova doesn't give us even a half hour? What do we do then? Both of you must have considered that possibility."

"We'll be cutting it awfully close," Geordi said. "I won't minimize the risk to us. But we should still have enough impulse power to enter the wormhole behind Epic Three and escape that way if necessary."

"The risk seems very great to me," Picard said. "The lives of everyone on board will be at stake. Twenty million Epictetan lives against our thousand makes a compelling argument for trying this, but it's still possible we could lose both the planet and the *Enterprise.*"

"That is possible, Captain." Data sat up even straighter in his chair. "But we could also lose the *Enterprise,* yet save the planet. Or we could lose the planet but not the *Enterprise.* Or we could lose both through some unforeseen circumstance."

Troi said, "In other words, we could lose everything."

"I do not consider that the most likely possibility," Data responded.

"Not the most likely!" Troi leaned forward. "Is that all the assurance you can give us?"

"Please do not underestimate my caution," Data said. "It is possible to accomplish this if we plot each step carefully."

"I don't know," Beverly Crusher murmured. "We can be certain of saving at least three thousand Epictetans if we beam them aboard and leave. There's a chance the people on those sublight ships could be picked up later by other Starfleet vessels. That isn't saving very many, but if this plan fails, we would lose everything—there would be nothing at all left of Epictetus Three and its people."

"And possibly nothing left of ourselves and the *Enterprise*," Riker added.

And I, Picard said to himself, may have to give the orders putting the *Enterprise* at such great risk. What would his officers and crew decide if they were given the power of decision? He knew the answer to that question. If there were any chance at all of saving everyone on Epictetus III, they would all willingly take it—after suitable discussion, of course.

"Data, how sure can you be?" Picard asked.

"Nothing like this can be one hundred percent certain, Captain. But there are a finite number of steps to be taken in this procedure, and they can be analyzed exhaustively. Our success should be nearly as certain as the fact that the nova will happen—except of course for unforeseen accidents or mistakes on our part."

Worf scowled. "Mistakes and accidents," he said, "are always possible. To attempt a dangerous action previously untried makes them even more likely. Our chances of success with this plan of yours are not good, since it may require perfect execution."

"If we had known earlier that we might be able to do what Data suggests," Troi said, "we might have left our saucer module at a safe distance and come in with a volunteer crew. I still have my doubts about this proposal. Sending the saucer module away right now, on impulse power, wouldn't get it far enough away, would it?"

"No," Geordi replied.

Troi bowed her head. "And your plan may also deprive the Epictetans of some of the little time they have left."

"Here are my orders," Picard said. "You'll all remain on the bridge until we hear from the Federation Council, as I expect we shall momentarily." The Council should be responding to his subspace request for an emergency meeting almost any minute now. "In the meantime, I'll ask Minister Fabre to call another meeting of the council of Epictetus Three, so that we can decide which three thousand of their people should be beamed aboard. We can hope to save that many at the very least."

The officers around the table were silent.

"Data," Picard continued, "please summarize for the others how far along you are with your preparations."

"Lieutenant Commander La Forge has already started modifications in our warp-drive inputs," Data said, "to allow for and set up a subspace output channel from the sun's core."

"How soon could it be ready?" Picard asked.

"Two days," Geordi replied, "give or take an hour or two. I'll admit that's an optimistic estimate."

Riker nodded. "Maybe wildly optimistic," the commander said.

"What about the fleeing sublight ships?" Beverly Crusher asked. "If we proceed with this plan, the nova may come on sooner. There may not be enough time for them to escape. We'll be destroying whatever chance they now have."

Picard sighed. "They'll have to take shelter behind

any large planetary body available and ride out the nova. Data tells me there are several on their present course—a gas giant with six moons, for one. We could come back later and search for survivors, or Epic Three's own incoming ships, the *Carpathia* and the *Olympia,* can rescue them."

"Will that be enough to give them a chance?"

"I assume they also have deflection shields. Shields and a body large enough to eclipse a ship should be enough at the distance they've already attained. They simply have to be told what to do as soon as possible and warned that the nova may come sooner than they expect."

"Then we may have a problem." The chief physician folded her hands. "I spoke to Minister Peladon not long ago. He says that the sublight craft aren't responding to any messages, and may not even be receiving them."

Worf drew his brows together. "The deserters should have remained on their world. Cowardice doesn't deserve any consideration."

Troi glanced at the Klingon. "If we can save their world," she said, "their shame may be enough punishment. Think of how difficult it would be for them to return home afterward."

"Quite right, Counselor Troi," Picard said. "We'll have to do what we can. Minister Fabre may find a way to get through to the sublight craft." He paused. "Number One, we'll need—"

"Captain," the computer said, "subspace communication coming in from Vida Ntumbe of the Federation Council."

67

"I'll speak with her on the bridge." Picard got up and hurried to the door as the other officers followed him.

Picard had finished outlining the procedure for moving Epictetus III. He gazed at the viewscreen, unable to read the expression on Vida Ntumbe's face. He had been relieved to know that she had been the first Council member in San Francisco to respond to his request, that she would be one of the people advising him.

Picard did not know the three Council members who were sitting in her office with her. The man from Galen IV, Jeremy Curtis, had posed his questions about Data's proposal in an especially belligerent manner. Picard, fortunately, had been able to field them easily without calling on Data or La Forge for a more detailed explanation. It was important, he felt, to show that he both understood the intricacies of Data's proposal and had some faith in the plan himself. But he did not know if he had convinced Curtis; and Lxiti Lons, the Betazoid delegate sitting at Ntumbe's left, still looked skeptical.

Only Raul Zender of Pellegrini IV seemed moved by Picard's words. "It might work," he said, glancing at the other Council members.

Vida Ntumbe was staring at a console in front of her. Other Federation Council members and advisors, including the president of the Council in Paris, would be listening to the discussion, perhaps offering their opinions.

Picard suddenly longed for the Council to tell him what to do. He would have to follow their orders. It would be easier to have the decision taken out of his hands.

The round face of Pietro Barbieri suddenly appeared at the bottom of the viewscreen. "It's a clever plan," the admiral said. "It even has a kind of brilliance. Extremely risky, of course, long odds, but perhaps—" Barbieri's image faded out.

"With so much at stake," Ntumbe said, "maybe boldness is called for in this situation. I don't much care for the idea of saving only three thousand Epictetans and condemning the others to death."

"Are you saying that we should proceed with this plan?" Picard asked.

"We're not saying you should or you shouldn't." Ntumbe propped her elbows on the table, resting her chin in her hands, and Picard saw the fatigue in her dark brown face. "We can't really advise you. You're the closest to this situation, you'll have to make the final decision about what to do. There won't be time for us to review the calculations and preliminary tests of your officers and issue orders to you. You're in the best position to assess the risks, to see if the plan has any chance of working. What do you intend to do now?"

He knew what his answer would have to be. "Lieutenant Commanders Data and La Forge will continue with their preparations," Picard said. "I'll postpone any decision until we see the results of their tests. In the meantime, I'll inform the Epictetan ministers to prepare their people for their world's possible passage through a wormhole by instructing them to shelter themselves in structures that can withstand severe quakes, tidal waves, severe storms, and other possible seismic and atmospheric disturbances. That's what their world will face if we go ahead with this plan, so they have to be told."

Vida Ntumbe said, "No," and a look of pain passed across her face.

"But they must have some warning of what to expect," Picard said, "or many of them will die even if their planet is saved. People are dying right now, killing themselves because they have no hope. They have to be told there's a chance for them, Vida."

"You can't tell them anything about what you hope to do," Ntumbe said softly. "I'm sorry, Jean-Luc, but you still don't really know if it will actually be possible to save Epictetus Three. What if you announce to the people there that you're going to save their world, and then you fail to do so?" She lowered her eyes. "Other planets in the Federation will be quick to believe that you lied to the Epictetans, that your warning was only a cynical move designed to keep them calm and distracted until their inevitable deaths. Trust in Starfleet and the Federation would be destroyed, especially on worlds that were once antagonistic to us."

"If we stay silent," Picard said, "more of the Epictetans will choose suicide."

"I know that." Ntumbe sat up and folded her hands. "But we must weigh that against the possible damage to the Federation if you offer false hope and then fail to save the planet. You can't tell the Epictetans a thing about your plan until you've made your decision."

The painful ethical dilemmas in which he was trapped were multiplying. He also knew what Vida

Ntumbe was not saying: if he took the great risk of proceeding with Data's plan, and then failed, the Federation would have a convenient scapegoat. All the planets could be told that Starfleet had done everything in its power to save Epictetus III. If his starship survived, Picard could shoulder the blame for the plan's failure. It might mean a court-martial, disgrace, and the end of his career, but the needs of the many—the United Federation of Planets— easily outweighed the needs of one man. Trust in the Federation would be preserved.

"I understand," Picard said at last.

"I knew you would." Ntumbe looked around at her colleagues. "Does anyone else have anything to say?" No one spoke. "Then this meeting is concluded." She lifted her head. *"Bonne chance,* Jean-Luc."

The viewscreen went blank. The officers on the bridge were silent.

Picard turned toward Riker. "Number One," he said, "I want an away team ready to beam down to Epic Three for the next meeting of the council of ministers. Some of our people should be there when they decide which three thousand should be beamed aboard the *Enterprise."* Riker nodded. "But you are not to beam down yourself unless the situation demands it—I need you here."

Commander Riker leaned back in his seat, still looking doubtful.

"Data and La Forge," Picard continued, "you'll return to main engineering and continue with your tests. I'll contact Minister Fabre from the ready room."

He stood up. Somehow, he would have to find a way of convincing her and the other ministers to move their people to shelter without telling them of Data's plan, without violating Vida Ntumbe's directive. To accomplish even that small task seemed almost as impossible as saving the planet.

Chapter Five

"I NEED TO CONSULT with you about the away-team personnel," Riker said to Deanna Troi after Data and Geordi were gone. He and Troi had remained on the bridge, just below Worf and his tactical station. Troi sank wearily into her station chair. "And after that, I order you to get some sleep."

The counselor nodded. Riker felt edgy and apprehensive about sending people to the surface of Epictetus III without being able to lead the team himself. But he had to be here to take over when Captain Picard was resting; even Jean-Luc Picard could not go without sleep indefinitely. The captain would also need his first officer aboard to help him assess Data's plan. The burden of that decision would be weighing heavily on Picard; he would want his executive officer near him.

"You heard the word from the Federation Council," Riker went on. "This particular away team is going to have rough duty. They won't be able even to hint at what the captain's hoping to do. They'll have to be reassuring without giving anything away. And there's always the chance they might get stranded there, that we may not be able to get them back aboard if we run into unexpected problems."

"I understand," Troi murmured.

"You'll have to go, of course." It was difficult to tell her that, to send her into such danger. "We'll need an experienced counselor there to handle our direct dealings with the Epictetan council. I've also decided that Lieutenant Worf should go. You'll command the team, Counselor, but you may turn command over to Worf if you find it advisable." If, he thought, Data's brilliant plan didn't pan out and they were suddenly forced to fold this hand, Worf might be the only one who could get the away team back to the ship safely.

Worf was gazing at him from his control panel. "Is that wise?" Troi said. "Part of our mission, as you say, will be to offer some reassurance, and Worf—" She glanced up apologetically at the Klingon. "Lieutenant Worf might not seem so reassuring to the Epictetans."

"That's true," Riker admitted, "but there's always the chance that people who believe they have nothing to lose might try to use the away team as hostages in order to board the *Enterprise*. Worf's presence should make that possibility more unlikely. Yeoman

Parviz Bodonchar should be part of the team, too, for some of the same reasons." The strapping yeoman was the only member of the crew who was nearly as physically imposing as Worf, but his kindly demeanor would also make him seem less threatening than the Klingon. "Do you feel sure of him?"

"Very much so," Troi replied.

"Yeoman Bodonchar is an excellent choice," Worf said, "and I would also recommend Ensign Ganesa Mehta."

Riker shook his head without hesitation. "She has family on Epic Three. That might interfere with her willingness to carry out certain orders."

"I'm inclined to agree," Troi said. "The pressure may be too much for her. She won't even be able to tell her own family what the captain is hoping to do."

Worf glanced from Troi to Riker, then said, "But you know that I would not make such a recommendation if I had any doubts."

That was true, Riker admitted to himself. The Klingon would not be swayed by sentimentality, pity, or any other emotion he considered a sign of softness or frailty. He was saying that he trusted the ensign to carry out her duties, and face the prospect of death as a Klingon might.

"I'll leave it at this," Riker said. "If Counselor Troi thinks she's emotionally fit, she'll go. If not, Ensign Hughes Holman will take her place." He sighed. "I'd add Ensign Chang Jun-shing to the team, but I believe he's still in sickbay. Captain Picard thinks he's starship commander material, and that's recommendation enough for me." Also,

Ensign Chang, as Riker had learned to his cost, was one hell of a poker player. The away team might need someone who could play out a very weak hand, and Chang wasn't someone who would fold too soon.

"Ensign Chang will be discharged by the time we're ready to beam down," Troi said. "I spoke to him in sickbay just before the captain called us to the bridge. You should probably know that a woman he was once involved with is now on Epictetus Three. I would trust him in spite of that—maybe trust him even more because of it. He'll see this mission through both out of duty and for personal reasons."

Possibly, Riker thought. Chang and Mehta had more incentive than anyone else on board to do everything they could to help Epictetus III. They would have less reason than others to fear death while on the surface; they might even welcome death if the mission failed. But they also had a lot more reason to cut and run if things started going wrong, to give up on their mission too soon and try to get to the people they cared about. Nothing in either of their records indicated that they were capable of desertion, but neither young officer had ever faced this kind of situation.

"Very well," Riker said. He would trust the counselor's judgment, but still felt uneasy. "Get some rest, both of you."

"I have already had sufficient rest," Worf objected.

"Get some more—you'll need it. Meet me back on the bridge at oh seven hundred for your briefing.

By then we should know when the council meeting will take place."

Troi got up from her chair and went to the aft turbolift, followed by Worf. Riker went to his station in the command area and sat down. He needed some rest himself. He rubbed his temples, wishing that he could shake off his lingering doubts.

"Minister Fabre has informed me that the council will meet in five hours," Picard said as Riker entered the ready room.

"The away team will beam down by then," Riker said, sitting down at the table. "You should grab some sleep before the meeting."

"I'll try." Picard leaned back in his chair. "Minister Fabre also told me that the sublight ships still aren't responding to messages."

"There's still some time left to get through to them. At this point, I think they have a much better chance, slim as it is, for escaping this catastrophe than anyone else does, including the personnel aboard this starship."

Picard sat up slowly, his eyes on Riker.

"I don't care what Data says," Riker went on, "or how many arguments he makes to support his plan. I have a very bad feeling about this whole business."

"Do you have any specific objections, Number One?" Picard asked. "Or is it just your poker-playing heart telling you not to bluff the cosmos?"

"Maybe it's partly that, but I do have some specific worries. Staying in this system to run tests is putting us at more risk—if anything goes wrong, we might not have time to outrun the nova. And even if

Data actually manages to do what he hopes to do, even natural wormholes are sometimes misshapen. You can go through some of them in seconds, while others stretch subjective time. To open an artificial one, and with the energies we'll be using, is just asking for unreliability. Even Data and Geordi aren't completely certain they can pull this stunt off. I'm surprised they didn't bring up a long list of possible complications."

"But we have no choice but to explore this possibility," Picard said. "Should we simply pack in three thousand randomly selected people and leave? You know we can't do that when there's any chance that Data's plan might work. If we can save this planet and its people, then almost any complications and risks will be preferable to the alternative."

"You mean you're willing to die trying," Riker said.

"And so are you, Number One."

The captain, of course, was right. For twenty million lives, it was worth the risk. The Federation Council had not ordered the *Enterprise*'s crew to risk everything, but the starship's company would never hold up their heads again if they did not. They had their pride, and the traditions of Starfleet, but this was much more than a matter of pride.

"Would you give up one finger, agree to have it chopped off your hand, in order to save a thousand lives?" It was an old question, one Riker had first heard as a boy at school in Valdez, and it had provoked a lively discussion among his classmates. He had known then that there was only one way to answer that question. To abandon the Epictetans before everything possible had been tried was to say, in effect, that one finger did indeed mean more than a thousand lives.

"I suggest," Picard said, "that you discuss your objections with Data."

"Data damn well already knows each and every one of them." Riker got to his feet. He would do what he could; they would try everything. He would conduct himself as a Starfleet officer, yet still wished he could rid himself of the growing conviction that this might be the *Enterprise*'s last mission, that his true duty here might turn out to be seeing that the people under his command died with honor.

Twenty million lives for one starship? It was a bargain. No doubt about it.

Geordi looked up from the console, sighed, then turned toward Data. "I've just finished my third simulation run," he said, "and everything came out differently than in the first and second runs."

"My results are similar," Data said.

Geordi glanced at the other crew members in main engineering; all of them looked as discouraged as he felt. Anita Obrion was staring fixedly at the panel in front of her, with an uncharacteristic expression of passivity on her face.

"We do not know enough," Data continued, "to predict exactly how the operation will run, from the initial drawing of power and the problems that presents, to the opening of the wormhole and keeping it both large and stable, and then to the passage of the planet through the wormhole, with all the inertial stresses that will cause." He did not sound at all discouraged. "But keep in mind that the variants emerging in our models may belong mostly to those models, not to the reality in which we will be working."

"You think reality will be more forgiving?" Geordi asked.

"Perhaps not. But reality may give us more time to react and adjust, to improvise if we must, as we proceed. The models are inevitably more limited, because they cannot be identical to the richness of reality. They are merely mathematical sketches, to which we must add as much detail as possible, until the simulations begin to run more successfully."

"Somehow, I don't feel comforted by your words," Geordi said.

"Our aim is to make our plan work, not to feel comforted, although I well understand—"

"No, I don't think you do." Geordi spoke more sharply than he had intended. "Sorry, Data—didn't mean that. I'm not really offended, just jumpy and nervous."

"I did not mean to give offense," Data said, "but I understand that you will not be able to avoid unease. You must ignore the feeling. Keep in mind that this plan will reveal its difficulties only in the doing, even though I am convinced that its general sequence will work exactly as predicted."

Geordi turned back to the console. "Here we go

again." He nodded in Anita Obrion's direction. "Ready on mine."

"Ready," Data said.

After Riker was gone, Picard realized that he felt more disturbed by the commander's doubts than he had wanted to admit. He was stretched out on a couch, trying to sleep, but sleep would not come. Too much adrenaline, he thought; his body was preparing itself for what lay ahead.

What Riker had been getting at was quite clear: the *Enterprise* could be considered expendable in this operation. In fact, it had to be considered expendable, given the stakes. Of course that did not mean that the ship and all its lives would definitely be lost, only that they might be lost. That possibility had to be faced without illusions, eyes wide open, with an unflinching will. And he was the only one who could make the final decision—or, in effect, ratify it, since he was sure that all the crew would back him up on whatever he decided to do.

The Federation Council could live with losing this starship and crew. Indeed, if efforts to save Epictetus III failed, it might be better, in a political sense, if his ship were lost. The United Federation of Planets would have an example of how much Starfleet would risk to save a member world, and the Federation Council could console themselves by remembering that they had not ordered the *Enterprise* crew to sacrifice themselves. It was a cynical thought.

Still, there had to be a reasonable expectation of success for him to proceed with Data's plan. If the risk was too great, and he took the chance anyway but lost the planet, a court-martial was almost inevitable if the *Enterprise* somehow managed to survive the disaster. The Starfleet prosecutor could argue that Picard had recklessly endangered his ship and crew in a misguided effort at glory; that would be how his actions would appear to many. But if he took the certain course of saving only a few thousand Epictetans, knowing that he had turned away from the chance to save more, he would never be able to live with himself.

And, as he tossed uneasily on the couch, Picard reminded himself that more people on Epictetus III were probably committing suicide even as he lay here pondering his personal dilemma, and that he was forbidden to offer them even a scrap of hope.

At last he sat up and touched his communicator. "Picard to main engineering—Data, La Forge."

"Yes, Captain?" Data's voice said.

"How are you proceeding with your tests?"

"Nearly two dozen simulations now," La Forge replied.

"And?"

A few seconds passed. "They differ wildly," La Forge finally said, "but they all seem to work for the most part."

Picard did not like the hesitancy and uncertainty he heard in the chief engineer's voice. "Data, is this going to work?" he demanded, knowing suddenly that he wanted to be convinced by Data, not by La Forge, that in fact he wanted to ignore Geordi's obvious uneasiness.

"Is it going to work?" Data repeated. "I would reply that even with difficulties—yes."

"What kinds of difficulties?" Picard asked.

"Difficulties such as power-flow handling, which we can adjust for. There is also the size and stability of the wormhole, which I think we can control. Then there is the planet's passage through the wormhole, during which there will be inertial stresses that we cannot prepare for. And there is also the problem of the time element—our own departure from this system, once the planet has gone through, cannot be predicted to the hour. Those are some of the difficulties, Captain."

"Have you had any scenarios in which the *Enterprise* is lost?"

"We sure do," La Forge said, still sounding nervous. "We can get caught in the nova. It's unlikely—someone would probably have to take a phaser to our warp and impulse engines to prevent our leaving, but if anything else happened—"

"What else?"

As Geordi began to detail the other possibilities for catastrophe, Picard realized again that a possible outcome of this mission might be the destruction of the *Enterprise*. He would not be around then to answer for his decision to open a wormhole. The planet might survive, and he would never know. . . .

The possible disasters seemed to proliferate as Geordi continued outlining them. Picard suddenly did not want to listen to the engineer anymore. Enumerating all the ways in which things could go wrong wasn't getting him any closer to understanding if this plan had a chance of working.

"I get the idea," Picard said when Geordi finally

fell silent. "Data, is it possible that Epictetus Three could be destroyed inside the wormhole, even if the opening is wide enough for the planet to enter?"

"Yes, it is possible, if the wormhole is not of sufficient size all the way through."

"Then it can vary in size."

"Yes, it can."

For an instant, Picard thought that it might be best after all to pick up as many people as possible from Epictetus III and leave. That would be the safest choice, but it would also be the choice with the least possible reward. The saving of a whole world beckoned to him, but it might be only a tempting illusion that would lead both his ship and the planet into oblivion. He was not entirely immune to the temptations of glory.

"My last question for now," Picard said. "How soon will you two be ready to move beyond planning and simulation?"

"My best estimate now," Data replied, "is within forty to forty-eight hours."

Not much time, Picard thought, but in that forty to forty-eight hours, more Epictetans might take their own lives, might seek that final escape from their impending doom. Forty to forty-eight hours was enough time for people to give in to despair, to consider desperate measures, to curse the Starfleet officers who could do so little for them.

Chapter Six

Samas Rychi had not slept at all. He was up early, staring at copies of ancient documents, when Mariamna Fabre's message came.

She was calling the ministers to a meeting in the council chamber in Nicopolis at the eighth hour. Captain Picard would address the council by viewscreen, but an away team from his starship would also attend.

"I know what we're facing," Minister Fabre's message continued. "I know that all of you would rather pass this time with those closest to you, but—" Her face contorted and she looked, for a moment, as if she might lose her usual composure. "We must decide which people from our world should be taken aboard the *Enterprise,* and how to choose them. We must do what we can right up to the end. I won't give up hope, even now. I'll struggle against the inevitable until I am no longer capable of fighting."

The message ended there. Mariamna Fabre, Rychi thought, had always searched for the fairest solution to any problem. Her desire for fairness and justice was one of her defining characteristics. Now she was deluding herself into believing that her hope could be transformed into a saving reality, that even a nova might be forced to grant her doomed people and world some measure of justice.

Alien, indecipherable letters swam before his eyes. Rychi turned off his reading screen and got to his feet. For a moment, he had imagined that he might see something in these old records that he had missed before, a symbol or a mark whose meaning would suddenly become clear. He had thought of the silvery foil documents of this world's ancient culture as nearly indestructible; now they would prove to be only too ephemeral.

He left the plasteen dome, walked down the wide shadowed hallway with its etchings, and went outside, breathing deeply the dry, clean air. The sun was above the horizon in the east, looking much as it did every morning; the dark pink sand of the desert was deepening into orange. He turned west. A small black speck was dropping from the sky in the distance, then swelled as it shot toward him, becoming a bullet-shaped vehicle with a transparent domed top. Rychi watched the flitter land, then went to meet it.

Hakim Ponselle slid one of the side doors open, climbed out, then held out a hand to his wife. Asela Ibanez waved as Rychi came closer. "We heard," she called out, "just before we left, about the council meeting."

Rychi frowned. "What's Mariamna Fabre doing—making it a public meeting? Is she going to put it on the net?"

Hakim shook his head. "There wasn't any announcement, but word gets around, and people know there's going to be a meeting."

"A crowd was already starting to gather in Kerulo Square when we left Nicopolis," Asela said. The silver-haired, brown-skinned woman was as short and round as her husband was tall and lanky. "Rumor has it that a group from the ship is going to beam down to the meeting."

"That much is true," Rychi admitted. Somebody on the council must have leaked the news of Mariamna's summons. What good would it do to have everyone find out that a meeting was to take place, and that its purpose was only to decide which tiny fraction of the population would be given a chance to live? There might be riots. He would have to land his flitter behind Michio Hall, away from Kerulo Square, and hope more people had not collected there as well.

He almost smiled. What did it matter if the crowds inconvenienced him, kept him from this meeting, even if they rioted? If they turned their rage and despair upon the ministers, he would die only a little sooner.

"I'm curious to see what those two Starfleet officers left here," Asela said. "Why would they have bothered to leave so much equipment behind?"

Rychi shrugged. "They didn't exactly go out of their way to explain what they were doing." He glanced at the timepiece on his wrist. "I'd better get going, or I'll be late. I'll contact you as soon as the meeting is over, and get back here as soon as I can."

"Safe journey, Samas," Hakim said.

Rychi hurried toward his flitter, then looked back. Hakim was gazing after him, his arm draped over Asela's shoulders. The two might be hoping for a miracle to happen, but at least they had each other, they had lived their lives, and neither would have to face death alone.

Rychi turned away, his mind filling with regrets. He suddenly wanted to live, to complete his work, to be a true friend to those who had offered him friendship in the past. He ached for the impossible, for what countless other doomed people must be longing to have—another chance to lead his life as he might have been leading it all along.

From the garden tiers on the roof of Michio Hall, Deanna Troi gazed down at the sandy orange beach and the blue-green expanse of the Geryon Ocean. Nicopolis had been built overlooking a bay, and the two horns of the crescent-shaped city curved to the north and southwest. Nearly every white-walled dwelling and massive stone structure bordered a grassy green park or flower garden; rows of slender saaphan trees, with their fernlike green branches, lined the wide city streets and walkways. In the mountain foothills to the east of Nicopolis, ancient silvery towers built by this world's original inhabitants gleamed in the distance.

Parviz Bodonchar moved closer to the balustrade, propping his muscular arms against the carved metal railing. A smile slowly spread across the yeoman's face as he took in the view.

"Pleasant place," Worf said. "I see why humans wanted to settle this planet." Coming from him, Troi knew, such words were high praise.

"They say that there's a view of the ocean from almost every house," Ganesa Mehta said, "and that one can walk from anywhere in Nicopolis to the beach in only a few minutes."

"This city wasn't your home, then?" Ensign Chang Jun-shing asked.

"I've visited Nicopolis several times," Ganesa said, "but I grew up in the city of Hierapolis, in the plains east of the Korybantes Desert." Troi sensed Ensign Mehta's distress, her sudden urge to run from this place and find some way to reach her family, but she was keeping her troubled feelings under control.

The away team had been instructed to beam down to this roof garden. It would have been just as easy to rematerialize inside the council chamber, but Minister Fabre, Ganesa had explained, was apparently observing the formalities; the ministers were always seated before others attending the meetings were led to the council chamber by aides. Fabre might also need extra time to deal with any dissension among her colleagues before the away team was admitted.

Several flitters sat in the spaces between the garden tiers. Troi knew why the ministers had parked their vehicles there; crowds surrounded Michio Hall on all sides. Below, in Kerulo Square, people stood shoulder to shoulder, silent, waiting.

She touched the Starfleet insignia on her chest. "Troi to Captain Picard," she murmured into her communicator. Ganesa moved to her side as Troi reported that this building was surrounded, that she assumed it was closed off from the crowd, but that she did not know what other arrangements for securing it had been made.

"May I say something to you and the captain?" Ganesa asked. Troi nodded. "I'm surprised that Minister Fabre didn't make this an open meeting. All of those people could have been in their homes watching the meeting with their families instead of gathering here. As it is, they may be thinking we're here only to help the council and those closest to the ministers get away."

"Perhaps we'll find out why this meeting was closed." Troi touched her insignia again, signing off. "Are there any special courtesies we should observe, Ensign Mehta?"

"The council has chosen Minister Fabre to speak for them," Ganesa said, "so address any questions to her, even if another minister has the floor at the time. But if another minister asks you a question, direct your answer to that particular minister. We sit in the chairs to the right of the council, where invited guests are seated—others sit on the left. I don't know if any university professors will be at this meeting or not, but if so, they'll be in the seats to the left."

"Do professors usually attend council meetings?" Troi said.

"Of course, if the meetings are open, and they usually are. Otherwise, only people who were past members of the council are allowed in. Two of the current ministers, Samas Rychi and James Mobutu, are professors at the University of Nicopolis, and others who used to be on the council make a habit of attending meetings in person whenever they can, since Michio Hall is so close to the campus."

"It is?" Ensign Chang said, moving closer to the two women.

Ganesa nodded, then waved an arm at the slender towers on the other side of Kerulo Square. "Those are two of the office and classroom buildings. Most of the apartments and houses from Kerulo Square down to the beach are faculty and student housing."

Ensign Chang tensed. Troi was certain that he was thinking of the woman he had once loved. She might be there now, inside one of those buildings, or down below in the square, waiting.

"Greetings," said a voice to Troi's left. She turned to see a slender olive-skinned man with graying dark hair walking toward them.

"I've been sent to usher you into our meeting room," the man continued. "I am Minister Rohin Nowles." As the man spoke his name, Troi sensed wariness and distrust inside Ganesa Mehta. The ensign did not fear this man, but did not entirely trust him, either.

"Greetings," Troi replied.

"My greetings as well," Ganesa said, then turned

toward Troi. "Minister Nowles was elected to the council from Hierapolis just before I left for Starfleet Academy." She turned back to the minister. "We'll do everything we can to help. You must know how sincerely I mean that, how hard we're trying—after all, this is my homeworld, too."

That was, Troi thought, as much as the ensign dared to say, but Minister Nowles was clearly unmoved by the young woman's sentiment. "Normally, an aide would have come to get you," he said coldly, "but there aren't any aides here now. Minister Fabre didn't see any reason for them to waste precious time coming here until we've heard what your captain has to tell us."

Troi sensed his animosity then, entwined with bitter anger. "Come with me," Minister Nowles said, leading them away from the balustrade.

Troi felt the hostility emanating from Rohin Nowles increase. He did not want them here; that much was clear. He had not spoken to them in the lift, and said nothing as he left her side to take his place at the long table with the other ministers.

There were no flowers on the table this time, only glass pitchers and silver goblets. Only seven of the nine council members were present. Lise Turano, one of the two ministers who had conspired with Czeslaw Peladon to commandeer the sublight ships, was not here; Troi wondered why. Minister Lev Robert, Peladon's other accomplice in that deed, was slouched in his chair, his face looking sallow, his eyes blank.

Except for the ministers and the away team, the chamber was empty. High-backed chairs with arms lined the walls to the left and right of the table where the ministers were seated. A viewscreen on the wall behind them showed a landscape of green hills dotted with flower beds.

The atmosphere in this room was disturbing, even disorienting. Troi sensed the underlying conflicts among the Epictetans, and also a wild hot rage struggling with dank, cold despair inside one minister. Now she knew why Fabre had kept the meeting closed. The nerves of these people were frayed, their emotions barely under control.

Troi introduced the members of the away team, then led them to the row of chairs at the right of the table. A viewscreen much larger than the one behind the ministers covered most of the wall above the entrance to the chamber. Captain Picard's image gazed into the room from that screen; Commander Riker sat at his side. Troi was sure that Data and Geordi were monitoring this meeting from main engineering as they ran their tests.

Minister Fabre looked tired. Her gray hair hung loosely down her back, as though she had not had time to pin it up. She seemed about to speak when Rohin Nowles leaned forward. "Exactly what are these people doing here?" he said loudly, gesturing at Troi.

"I explained that," Fabre replied. "To help us decide who should be rescued—"

"They didn't have to come here for that. We could decide all of that by ourselves. What's their real purpose—offering us Starfleet's heartfelt condolences in person before they beam back to their ship and leave us to burn?"

Minister Samas Rychi laid a hand on Nowles's arm. "Steady, Rohin. Let's at least hear what Captain Picard and his people have to say." He lifted one brow, as if expecting to hear little of importance in spite of his diplomatic words.

Troi sensed another wave of anger and hopelessness, then found the source. One of the ministers was sitting with her elbows propped on the table, her face in her hands; she straightened and shook back her long reddish hair. Troi recognized Dorcas Dydion, the young minister who had been so distraught when Captain Picard had first spoken to the council. The woman's eyes were rimmed with red, her face ravaged by grief.

Fabre turned toward the younger woman, as if also sensing her anguish. "Dorcas," she said, "you didn't have to come. If you want to leave now—"

"Oh, I'll stay," Dorcas Dydion said hoarsely. "I should have gone with Edmond, I should have taken his way out. I don't know why I'm here, but I'll stay."

"Please understand," Fabre said, looking back at the viewscreen. "Minister Dydion has suffered a painful loss, and—"

"Say it!" Minister Dorcas Dydion shouted. "Edmond is dead! My husband took his own life! He didn't want to wait until our world was dying, and I was too much of a coward to go with him!" She covered her face again, her shoulders shaking as she wept. Czeslaw Peladon reached for her hand, trying to calm her.

"I'm very sorry," Captain Picard said from the viewscreen, and Troi knew how deeply he meant the words.

"You may as well know," Minister Fabre said softly, "that two of our council members, Andrew Kolodny and Lise Turano, have also died by their own hands. Minister Kolodny was a man of integrity, and he'll be greatly missed." She glanced at Czeslaw Peladon. "Minister Turano, as you already know, was one of the three among us who commandeered our sublight craft and made sure their own relatives and cronies got aboard." Fabre folded her hands. "We still haven't been able to get through to those ships to tell them that the nova may come sooner than they expect." Troi had sensed the disdain in Captain Picard for those fleeing in the sublight ships, but he had insisted on doing everything possible to warn them nonetheless. They could not be told anything about the possibility of opening a wormhole, only that their sun was approaching a nova state more rapidly and that they should immediately seek shelter behind planetary bodies.

Minister Robert sank even farther into his chair; he did not look well. Troi felt shaken. Two ministers were suicides, a third was mourning her dead husband, and Lev Robert seemed about to lapse into a catatonic state. More might choose to die; people might be dying now, even as Data and Geordi and the *Enterprise*'s engineers worked to avert this world's doom, and she could say nothing about their plan. She glanced at Ganesa, sensing that the young woman was thinking the same thing. It would be even worse for Ganesa; she would be worrying that people she knew might become suicides.

No wonder, Troi thought, that Minister Fabre had wanted this meeting closed. She would not have wanted her people to see how conflicted their council was, to hear that two of their ministers had so lacked faith in Starfleet's ability to do anything for them that they had taken their own lives. Such news might only encourage others to follow their example.

Minister Fabre said, "We must discuss what we can accomplish, little as it is. We're ready to hear from you, Captain." Troi sensed the small bit of hope that still burned inside the gray-haired woman.

Picard gazed at the images on the bridge viewscreen. He was finding it acutely painful to speak to the Epictetan ministers, knowing that he would have to conceal his plan from them. Preserving the Federation outweighed his offering a premature and perhaps false hope to the Epictetans in an effort to prevent more suicides. The demands of politics could be as inexorable in their way as a sun's inevitable progression toward the nova state.

But he had been given some room to maneuver, limited as it was. He had received a subspace communication from Vida Ntumbe two hours ago, telling him that the Federation Council had discussed his dilemma in more detail. He could not tell the Epictetans about a risky plan that might not work, but he could urge them to take whatever measures they could to save themselves, even if the chances of doing so were infinitesimally small. A hastily called conference with the science officers on duty had given him the opening he needed. He now had a way to tell the ministers that the Epictetan cities should be evacuated, without giving away Data's plan.

Such an evacuation would be necessary, given that most of the planet's population lived in cities on seacoasts. If Data and Geordi succeeded in opening a wormhole and sending Epictetus III through it, the resulting quakes and tidal waves would kill millions if the people remained in their coastal cities. They had to move to places away from the threatened areas which could also withstand quakes. But he could not tell them the true reason for going there.

His problem, Picard thought, would be to convince the ministers to follow his advice and evacuate their cities. They weren't idiots; they would see how slight their chances were. They might refuse to subject their people to such disruption on top of all they already had endured.

"You already know that we can take three thousand of your people aboard the *Enterprise*," Picard began. "You must decide who should go as soon as possible. Lieutenant Commander Troi and her away team will do everything possible to get them beamed aboard quickly."

"Three thousand," Minister James Mobutu said bitterly, "out of twenty million."

"What's the point of saving so few?" Minister Rohin Nowles asked. "Is it only so that Starfleet and the Federation can salve their consciences by making some small gesture?"

"Being able to do so little is as distasteful and

morally demeaning to me as it is to you," Picard replied, "but it's still preferable to saving no one at all."

"I agree," Samas Rychi said. Picard focused on the archaeologist, surprised at the strength he heard in the man's voice. "Let's decide how we're going to proceed—we don't have much time. How shall we choose the three thousand to be beamed aboard the *Enterprise?*"

Picard leaned back slightly in his station chair. Samas Rychi had clearly found some inner strength. "Random selection," Fabre said, her voice sounding steadier. "The census bureau's computer will generate a program to select people at random from its list. Only children fifteen years of age or younger should be eligible. The older ones must be old enough to look after the younger ones, and be able to remember something of our world."

"Mariamna is right," Minister Dorcas Dydion said. The young woman's voice was still hoarse, but her face seemed more composed than it had been earlier. "It's some of the children who most deserve a chance now." The other ministers apparently agreed, since no one seemed about to object.

Fabre folded her hands. "That's it, I suppose," she said. "Perhaps we can send a few of our cultural artifacts with the children."

"There's one more thing I wanted to discuss," Picard said, "the possibility that more of your people might be saved than those three thousand."

Czeslaw Peladon frowned. "Exactly how do you propose to do that, Captain Picard?"

Picard took a breath. "I've consulted with some of

my science officers. There's a very small chance that if the side of your planet on which your continents lie is facing away from your sun when the nova blooms, then people who are in underground shelters might have a chance to survive. I won't deceive you—their chances of surviving would be vanishingly small."

Nowles grimaced. "Almost nonexistent, I'd say."

Picard nodded in agreement. "We have few enough options," he said. "I'd rather keep as many of them open as possible, however slight they are. People would have to go to underground sites with enclosed ventilation systems and some life support to have any chance at all. We could beam down devices for producing air to any sites where they're needed, along with food, water, and medical supplies. Later, when it's possible, any survivors could be rescued."

"You want us to wait out the nova underground?" Peladon shook his head. "You'd just be sending us to our graves."

Picard gazed at the white-haired man steadily. "That's very likely. I can't deny it."

Mobutu leaned forward. "You're asking us to spend what little time we have left on this hopeless effort? I see no reason—"

"James, please." Fabre held up a hand. "Captain Picard has admitted that being underground in enclosed shelters probably won't save anyone. But isn't a tiny chance better than none at all? I'd rather spend my last days clinging to whatever hope there is than giving up completely." She sighed. "But exactly where could our people go?"

Rychi said, "I have an idea." He stood up quickly, turned to the viewscreen behind him, and pressed a panel; a map of the two Epictetan continents appeared. "Look here. We have three important archaeological sites in western Themis with underground levels that could probably house most of the people in Nicopolis and its suburbs." He pointed at the three silver dots marking those sites. "There's another site north of Austra, and four near the eastern coast that could shelter most of the people from Hierapolis and Epira, and probably everyone in the outlying communities as well." He indicated those sites, then gestured at the northern continent of Metis. "In the north, I'd suggest that everyone in the city of Boreas be evacuated inland, to the site bordering the Dryon Forest. Even though we found another site near Boreas a couple of years ago, most of it hasn't been uncovered."

That might work, Picard thought. From what he had read about the sites in Rychi's writings, the structures seemed quite sturdy. They might very well survive a passage through a wormhole.

"Those ancient structures have survived for eons," Rychi continued. "Many survived being buried under landslides until we excavated them. They've been undamaged by even the most powerful of quakes. Our scans show that the material used to build them can withstand extremes of heat and cold and even assaults by weapons of mass destruction. If anything can give us a chance—"

"Do you really believe they can outlast a nova?" Peladon shouted. "You've always had something of a proprietary interest in those sites, Samas. Now you're ready to delude yourself into thinking they can save us. I think I'd rather spend my remaining time at my house in Epira instead of huddling inside some ancient alien artifact that even you, after years of study, don't fully understand."

Rychi's face flushed with anger. Picard saw that Peladon's words had cut deep. "I understand enough," Rychi said evenly, "to see that those sites offer us a sliver of hope. As Mariamna said, that's better than no hope at all."

Peladon stood up. "Samas, you're a fool."

"And you're a selfish old man who made sure your own son got aboard one of our sublights. I only hope he has enough of a conscience to feel some remorse—if he lives."

"Enough," Fabre said. "I want to hear a constructive proposal, not pointless bickering."

"I propose that we encourage as many people as possible to go to the archaeological sites," Dorcas Dydion said, "and make the evacuation as orderly as possible. Of course we can't force anyone to go, and I think we have to admit openly that their chances of survival there will hardly be any better than if they stay where they are. Anyone with any sense is going to know that anyway. But it's better to die trying."

Minister Peladon sat down, looking defeated. His heart, Picard thought, wasn't in this meeting; Peladon would be thinking of his son and all the others aboard the sublight ships.

"I think we'd better start drawing up evacuation plans," Fabre said. "I'm in agreement with Dorcas and Samas, but I must hear from the rest of you."

"We might as well follow Samas's suggestion,"

Mobutu said, "useless as it'll probably turn out to be. I can't think of a better idea anyway."

Nowles sighed. "I'll go along, too."

Peladon bowed his head. "So will I." Lev Robert nodded passively.

"The away team will help with any evacuations and with beaming children aboard," Picard said, a bit heartened that the ministers had been able to reach a consensus. "We'll beam down replication equipment and supplies to all of the evacuation sites to supplement whatever your people take there with them. We'll have to make sure that transceivers and other communications devices are at all those sites as well. That way, we can warn you when the nova is imminent." If Data's plan actually came to fruition, he would need a way to announce that the planet would be passing through a wormhole, in the hope that people who had chosen not to go to the sites might still have time to get to safety.

He tried not to think of another possibility: that Data and La Forge would fail to open their wormhole, and that the archaeological sites would indeed become graveyards. No, he told himself. If only a few could be rescued later from those sites, if only a few beat the odds, the evacuation would be justified.

Troi was exhausted. The Epictetan ministers were drawing up their evacuation plans, contacting aides, parceling out responsibilities. The strong emotions she had sensed in the council chamber had nearly overwhelmed her, but the ministers had finally pulled themselves together.

Despite their feelings and fears, their efforts to save some of their people, however futile such efforts might be, were all that mattered now. Troi had found it a bit easier than she had expected to prompt the ministers with suggestions, to deflect outbursts that might have led to recriminations or unproductive expressions of remorse. She had come to respect most of the members of the council. They had been pushed to the breaking point by a crisis that would have tested the strongest. Whatever their weaknesses and failings, they had rallied and now seemed ready for whatever lay ahead. Troi had been able to report to Captain Picard that the council would do whatever was necessary, however useless it might seem to them.

But she had also sensed something else inside Minister Fabre, and in Minister Rychi—a suspicion that they had not been told everything, that Captain Picard and the away team were hiding something from them. She had sensed some doubt in the other ministers as well. These people had to have sound political instincts, or they would not have been elected to their council. They were all very clearly aware of how vanishingly small the chances were of surviving the nova at the archaeological sites, however insistent Picard was that people take shelter there. They had felt, however unconsciously, that something important had been left unsaid.

Delicate lamps shaped like flowers cast a soft glow over Michio Hall's roof garden. Troi moved to the balustrade and looked down. Evening had come, and Nicopolis was now an arc of bright lights.

Instructions on how to prepare for evacuation had been put on the net. The crowds in Kerulo Square had finally dispersed; Minister Fabre had addressed them from the terrace outside the council chamber, eloquently rising to the occasion. The theme of her speech had been that it was more noble to resist even a death that seemed inevitable, to stand against it and seize whatever shred of hope one was given right up to the end. They would probably all die anyway; they could choose to do so with courage, grasping at even the slimmest of chances.

If Epictetus III survived, Troi thought, that speech was likely to become legendary.

She took a deep breath. Sometime that night, a list of the three thousand children to be evacuated to the *Enterprise* would be posted. By morning, the children would be on their way to various locations, where members of the away team would join them to make sure that they were beamed aboard safely and efficiently, by providing lock-on coordinates for the transporter, and to calm the fears of the young people.

Worf was still in the chamber with Czeslaw Peladon, helping the minister in his efforts to get a message through to the fleeing sublight ships; the Klingon, to Troi's relief, had restrained himself from revealing his distaste for the people aboard those craft. Ensign Mehta was probably still talking to her parents and brother, who were under the impression that this would probably be their final conversation. Ensign Chang and Yeoman Bodonchar were waiting with Troi on the roof until Minister Fabre came to take them to the census bureau offices. Fabre wanted Starfleet personnel with her to certify that the list of children to board the *Enterprise* had been randomly generated.

Troi heard footsteps behind her and turned. Mariamna Fabre was walking toward her, accompanied by Samas Rychi. She could still sense the fear inside the archaeologist, the dread and terror of losing his life and world, but he was now keeping that fear at bay.

"Greetings, Lieutenant Commander Troi," Minister Rychi murmured. "Have you finished your report to Captain Picard?"

"Yes." She had given that as one excuse for coming up here with Chang and Bodonchar, not wanting to admit that she had also needed a short respite after the intense emotions of the meeting and the saddening strain of concealing what she knew about Data's plan.

Fabre greeted Bodonchar and Chang, then said, "The census bureau is ready for us. I'll take us there in my flitter."

"Before you leave—" Rychi held up a hand. "Ensign Chang, I had just enough time to check on that young woman you wanted to find out about."

Troi sensed the sudden tension in Chang. She had seen him take Rychi aside earlier, and had heard him ask the archaeologist if a woman named Teodora Tibawi was still a student at the university. Chang had referred to her as an old friend, but Troi knew that she had to be the woman he had once loved.

"Is she here," Chang asked, "in Nicopolis?"

"I'm afraid not," Rychi replied. "She graduated and left Nicopolis nearly a year ago."

Chang tensed. "Is she still on this planet?"

"Yes." Troi caught the hesitancy in Rychi's voice and sensed disdain inside him. "She's at the Tireos Oceanographic Institute."

Fabre's eyes widened slightly; Troi sensed her surprise. "Is that an institute connected with the university?" Chang asked.

"No," Fabre replied. "They're—shall we say—a somewhat eccentric group."

"Eccentric?" Rychi grimaced. " 'Demented' would be a more accurate description. The Tireos Oceanographic Institute is some thirty-five or so misfits in an underwater base on the ocean floor near the northern polar icecap, who believe that there's intelligent life in our oceans."

"That's not such an odd hypothesis," Bodonchar said. "Many worlds have intelligent ocean-dwelling species."

"But there's one difference here," Rychi responded. "There's absolutely no evidence that any of the life-forms in our oceans possesses intelligence. The Tireos people persist in thinking that our nereids are intelligent because they so closely resemble Earth's dolphins, but not one marine biologist here agrees. There's actually more evidence that they're nearly as mindless as plants, but that doesn't stop the fools at Tireos from assuming otherwise."

"You seem to have almost a personal dislike of these people," Troi said, glancing uneasily at Chang.

"Some of them actually claim that the nereids are what's left of the ancient race that once lived here." Rychi scowled. "As an archaeologist, I can assure you that not one Epictetan scholar in my profession thinks that's even possible. Those Tireos idiots see that great ships, oceangoing vessels, and long sea voyages are often depicted in the ancient artwork we've found, almost obsessively depicted, and they leap to the conclusion that the ancients loved the sea so much that they decided to return to it. Anyone who studies our ancient documents and artifacts knows that's impossible. It's offensive even to think that such a great race would devolve into something as stupid as a nereid."

"Teodora was always suggestible," Chang murmured. "That was one of the reasons for our—disagreements. Will she have time to get to one of the ancient sites?"

"Dorcas Dydion will inform the Tireos people that they may go to the site near the Dryon Forest," Rychi said. "If they don't, that's their choice. Given their disorderly thought processes, I have no idea what they'll decide to do."

If this world was sent through a wormhole, Troi thought, then an underwater installation, one probably designed to withstand quakes, might be one of the safer places to be. Chang would be aware of that, too.

Rychi sighed. "I'd better be on my way to the university archives," he continued. Troi sensed the sadness inside him. Captain Picard had asked Rychi to select the cultural data to be transmitted to the *Enterprise*'s computer for preservation, and the other ministers had agreed to put him in charge of that. "Then I have to go to the Bharati Museum to decide on which ancient artifacts and works of art get beamed aboard. The children can carry some of the smaller pieces."

Troi nodded. The children to be transported to the *Enterprise* from this city were to be brought to that museum, which had the additional advantage of being surrounded by wide canals. The bridges over the canals could be blocked off, making it harder for any despairing, angry mobs that might gather to storm the museum. It was, as Worf had put it, necessary to consider such possibilities.

"We're betting against the house," Rychi went on. "That's what your captain's asking us to do, and the house always wins in the end. Or maybe a more apt comparison is buying a ticket in a lottery where the odds are millions to one. If even twenty people out of twenty million emerge from those ancient sites alive, they will have beaten the odds." His eyes narrowed, and she felt his doubts again. "Unless of course the house is rigging the game in some way we don't know about."

Troi kept her face still, searching for something to say as she sensed the struggle that was still going on inside him, but Rychi had already moved away from the balustrade and was walking toward his flitter, taking his turmoil with him.

Chapter Seven

THE SUN CREPT UP over the horizon and seemed to boil the edges of the atmosphere. It was, of course, an unconscious enemy, animated but without any kind of life, a machine powered by gravitational collapse, incapable of animosity.

None of which mattered, Czeslaw Peladon thought; the sun was still an enemy greater than anything purposeful and self-aware. Only intelligent life could match the destructive power of this god of the dark, this frenzied clumping of geometry and mass in the metric of space-time. It did not help him now to know that the intelligent life of this world had once restrained this fury for a time, and had then abandoned the effort.

The expanse of ocean to the east was greener

today, the breezes blowing in his direction hotter and drier. A molten white light blazed where the sun met the water. He had often come out on this terrace early in the morning, to sit with his wife Emilie until the sun rose and the city of Epira began to come to life around them. During the past days, he had found himself feeling grateful that Emilie had not survived to face the death of her world and to see their son leave it forever.

He had acted quickly, contacting the crews of the sublight vessels and allowing them to think that he, Minister Lise Turano, and Minister Lev Robert were speaking for the entire council. His son Casimir had been easily persuaded to leave on one of the craft with his wife Oliva, because it was the only way to save her, and because Casimir had usually given in to his father's demands.

Now Lise Turano had committed suicide, and Lev Robert had become a silent shell of a man at the latest council meeting, but Peladon still felt justified in his actions. Better for Casimir to be within reach of safety than to have to take shelter in one of Samas Rychi's questionable sites. His son still had a chance, even if the nova came on sooner than expected.

Suspicion stirred in him once more. Evacuating people from the cities, in the hope that they might survive the nova? Rescuing a few more people might be preferable to doing nothing at all, but Captain Picard had seemed too intent on pursuing such a minuscule chance of saving lives. Peladon had been skeptical of the notion immediately, but had seen which way the other ministers were leaning.

There had been no point in opposing them, no more time for arguing; he had always been a practical man.

Now he was wondering if Picard was plotting some course of action that wasn't so obvious. Something was wrong, something else was going on—his instincts told him that.

Flitters were rising from the houses nearest the beach. Those who had homes along the shoreline were to be evacuated first, to be followed by those living near the center of Epira. They were to bring food, water, bedding, and extra clothing, and were to proceed to the archaeological site to the west of the city. The rest of Epira's inhabitants had been directed to head north, to another site of monumental alien structures. Some people, of course, would choose to stay in their homes.

His neighbors were getting ready to leave. Peladon watched from his terrace as two boys carried hampers of provisions to their flitter, followed by their parents. Apparently neither of the boys had won a chance to be transported to the *Enterprise.*

Peladon turned and went inside. Emilie had decorated the sitting room and hung her own paintings on the walls. She had most loved painting the landscapes of their world. There was the Korybantes Desert at dawn, pink sand tinged with orange under a violet sky. Another painting was of a mountain gorge through which the Arion River flowed from the Kuretes Mountains on its way to the eastern plain. His wife had been a gifted artist, but even her genius had not quite captured all of the beauty of Epictetus III.

111

Peladon peered at the timepiece on his finger. The children to be beamed aboard the starship would already be on their way to the Warren Institute, located on one of the high hills to the west of the city. The *Enterprise* away team had been transported to their ship from Nicopolis, for a brief meeting with Captain Picard, but they were to beam down to the Warren Institute soon, to help with the children. Peladon had promised to join them there; as the minister for this district, his presence would be expected by the children's parents. After that, he was to join the other evacuees. If any of his people survived, they would remember that he had been there with them, clinging to life right up to the end; if they did not survive, as was likely, nothing he did would matter anyway. He had already packed what he needed in his flitter for when he left Epira.

I can't, he thought. He could not leave his home, not yet, not until he was certain that a warning had gotten through to the fleeing sublight ships.

Beverly Crusher sat back as the face of Czeslaw Peladon appeared on her desk's small viewscreen. "Minister Peladon," she said, "there's a message from Krystyna for you. I'll relay it to you now."

"Thank you, Doctor."

"By the way, have you heard from Captain Picard?"

Peladon shook his head.

"His subspace radio message has been received and acknowledged by the captains of your two incoming carrier-class starships, the *Olympia* and the *Carpathia*. They were told that the nova might come sooner, and now they're trying to contact your sublights to warn them about what to do. A message went out to all the ministers informing them of this—you should have had yours by now."

"I noticed that a message was waiting for me," Peladon said. "I was just about to retrieve it when you called." He paused. "The crews on the sublight ships have no reason to refuse messages from our own ships. They'll surely be warned in time. At least I hope—" His voice trailed off.

Beverly felt uneasy. She had contacted Czeslaw Peladon only because she had promised Krystyna that she would; but she had been hoping that he might not be there, that she could leave a message without having to speak to him. She did not like having to deceive him about what Captain Picard hoped to do.

What would Peladon think when he learned that his world might survive, that his son might have stayed there instead of running away? She reminded herself that Data and Geordi were still running tests, that there was still little hard evidence that their plan would actually work.

"Evacuating people to those sites," Peladon said then. "It's a ridiculous idea, you know."

"It's a chance," Beverly said carefully.

"It isn't any chance at all, and you know it. Even Captain Picard admitted how slight a chance it is."

"It's better than—"

"I know the argument, Dr. Crusher. My colleague Mariamna Fabre put it quite eloquently. Better to cling to any chance, however slight. Better to die bravely, fighting for one's life." He said the words mockingly. "A futile effort—unless your captain's actually up to something else. Is he?"

He had almost caught her off guard, with his jabbing, reproach-filled question. Beverly composed herself. "I wish he were up to something else," she said carefully.

"Samas Rychi was so quick to recommend those sites," Peladon said. "Grasping at a chance for glory, however slight it may be. He almost considers the sites his personal property, you know. He's the kind of person who falls in love with the past, who romanticizes it, who lives vicariously in antiquity. I've always wondered how someone so impractical and removed from the present, someone who likes nothing better than to pore over old documents and sift through ancient artifacts while telling himself stories about the past, ever got himself elected to our council. Now he's fooling himself, thinking his discoveries can save lives and vindicate his own life."

"Perhaps they will," Beverly said.

"Don't patronize me, Doctor. I know you don't believe that."

"I can hope for it." She wished even more fervently that Data and Geordi could bring off their miracle. "Minister Peladon, I have to leave my office now and go to a transporter station to help with the children when they arrive. Any other messages for you will be relayed automatically to the transceivers at your evacuation site. Where will you be?"

"Site A, to the west of Epira."

"I know how hollow and empty this must sound,"

she said, "but please don't give up hope." She could give him that much. *Enterprise* out."

Beverly Crusher's face faded. The pretty, rounded face of Peladon's granddaughter appeared.

"Grandfather," Krystyna said, "Dr. Crusher's told me about Mother and Father." Her bright blue eyes were rimmed with red; he saw her hand tremble as she pressed it against her lips. "I just want you to know—" Tears trickled from her eyes. "I love you, Grandfather. I wish Mother and Father could hear that, too. I'm not angry anymore, Grandfather—I wanted to say that to you."

"I thought you'd be proud of me," Krystyna had said, "that you'd be happy for me. This is what I want." Peladon remembered hearing her shout those words at her father. "All you've ever wanted was what Grandfather wanted for you."

Casimir's response to his daughter had been harsh. "Go, then. Waste your gifts on Starfleet instead of developing them here. Throw your life away taking unnecessary risks for strangers and aliens and worlds that mean nothing to you. Do what you like, Krystyna—I can't stop you. But I have no daughter now. Do you hear me?" There had been the sound of a fist striking a solid surface. "Your mother and I will not receive your messages. We will not communicate with any of your teachers or fellow cadets about your welfare, and will not travel to Earth to see you receive your commission. Come back here, and our door will be closed to you. Do you understand? I have no daughter! My daughter is dead!"

Peladon remembered his son's words only too well. They had been his own words. He had told Casimir to say them, thinking that they might frighten Krystyna into a last-minute change of heart. Instead, they had driven her away. She had left for Earth and Starfleet Academy the next day, on schedule.

"You weren't trying to be deliberately cruel," Krystyna went on from the viewscreen. "I know that now. All of you just wanted to protect me, to keep me safe, to do what you believed was best for me."

"You were right to go, dear Krystyna," Peladon murmured, forgetting that she could not hear him. "You'll live because you did go. And I'm glad now that you went."

"Please—send a message if you get a chance. Dr. Crusher will relay it to me. I forgive you, Grandfather—Father and Mother, too." The image of his merciful granddaughter vanished.

He got up from his transceiver and went to the nearest wall, straightening Emilie's paintings, wondering irrationally if he should take some of them with him. At last he left the room and descended the stairs that led to his garden. His flitter waited on the pale, flat flagstones bordering the bright red blooms of his melathe flowers. He walked outside into the bright white light of the sun.

The transporter room disappeared, and Worf was standing with Ganesa Mehta on one of the hills of Hierapolis. Rows of stone steps wound down from the hills to the footpaths that bordered the long, wide, twisting expanse of the Arion River. The diamondlike structure of Riverside Arena, where the away team was to meet the next group of children to be transported to the *Enterprise,* was within a short walking distance; light glinted from the arena's facets as they caught the early-morning sun. Ganesa had told Worf about her city, its hanging gardens, and the vast plain surrounding Hierapolis, where the high blades of tarendra grass moved in the wind like the waves of a vast green sea.

Two black-haired boys stood below them on the steps. One was stocky and sturdily built, with a broad bronze-skinned face. The other was small and slender, with dark eyes that resembled Ganesa's; he was clutching a flat rectangular case. The boys gaped at the two Starfleet officers, and then the smaller boy ran up the steps to them.

"Ganesa!" he shouted. He threw his arms around her, and then a man and a woman were running toward them from a nearby house, calling out Ganesa's name. The stocky boy was still staring at Worf, his mouth hanging open.

"I can't stay," Ganesa said as the man and woman clutched at her, patting her face and smoothing back her dark hair. "My commanding officer ordered us to go directly to Riverside Arena. The only reason I was able to come here first is that it's so close by."

"I'm glad you came," the slender boy said. "Zamir's going to go with you to the *Enterprise.* He came here to say good-bye to me."

Ganesa quickly freed herself from the embraces of the older man and woman, then introduced them to Worf. As he had already guessed, the couple were her parents. The slightly built boy was Dalal, her twelve-year-old brother, and the stocky boy was Zamir Yesed, Dalal's best friend.

Zamir Yesed continued to gape at Worf. "This is Lieutenant Worf," Ganesa said, "chief security officer of the *Enterprise* and my friend."

"Pleased to meet you," Dalal Mehta said, obviously impressed that his sister had a Klingon as a friend. Worf bowed slightly toward the boys. Zamir nodded back at him, then managed a smile.

Ganesa's mother embraced her again. "I wish I could stay here with you," Ganesa said.

"No, you don't," her father replied. "We wouldn't want you to stay. You'll have to remember us." He rested a hand on his daughter's arm. "I hate to tell you this, Ganesa, but better to hear it from me than from someone else. The Velensos have already said their farewells to this world. At least their suffering is at an end, if that's any comfort."

Worf saw the pain in his comrade's eyes before she bowed her head. Said their farewells—the meaning of that euphemism was clear.

"You'll have to remember them, too," Mr. Mehta continued. "They were our closest friends."

"I can't even tell my own family." Ganesa had said those words to Worf on the way to the transporter room, and he had heard the torment in her voice. "I'm forbidden to give them any hope." He knew that she would abide by that order, but could see how much her obedience to duty was costing her. Now she would be thinking that she might have prevented the deaths of her parents' dear friends.

"I loved the Velensos, too," Ganesa's mother said,

"but they were wrong to take that way out." She was heavier than Ganesa, but had the same soft brown eyes. "I won't go looking for death." Her eyes hardened. "It's going to have to come looking for me, and even then I'll give it a fight." Worf found himself liking the woman, but then, she was Ganesa's mother.

"We'd better go," Dalal said. "They'll be waiting for you at the arena."

"Your brother is right, Ganesa," Worf said. "We must beam the children aboard as quickly as possible."

"I guess that's one good thing," Zamir muttered. "If you have to beam us up fast, we won't have to listen to Minister Nowles give one of those long, boring speeches of his."

Dalal laughed. They were fine boys, Worf thought; with their refusal to show the fear they must be feeling, they reminded him of his own son.

"Your parents should have come to see you off," Ganesa's mother said to Zamir.

"Mama was afraid she'd start crying again if she came," Zamir said, "and that wouldn't have done much good. Anyway, she and Papa still have to get ready to evacuate. They gave me some holos and stuff to remember them by." He sounded as though he might choke on the words; his black eyes glistened.

"We'll walk to the arena with you," Ganesa's father said to her, "and then we have to get ready to leave the city ourselves."

Ganesa said, "Father, there's something I have to say." Worf shot her a glance, wondering if she was about to violate their orders. "I love you," she finished.

They had begun to descend the steps together when Dalal halted. "I almost forgot." He thrust the flat case he was holding at Zamir. "I want you to have this."

Zamir took the case and slowly lifted the cover. "Your mansi collection! Are you sure—"

"Take it." Dalal shrugged. "Don't think of it as a present. Just tell yourself you're hanging on to it until you can give it back to me."

Worf peered over the heads of the boys at the open case. Inside, under a flat piece of glass, were tiny insectlike creatures with brightly colored wings that resembled the petals of flowers.

"Mansi?" Worf said, frowning a little.

"That's what those tiny life-forms are called," Ganesa said. "They're very hard to collect, and almost impossible to find inside the city. Most mansi are found along the riverbanks or out on the plain. You can't capture and kill them—if you do, the colors of their wings will fade almost immediately after death. You have to watch and wait until one flutters to the ground and you see it stretch its wings—that means it's dying. Then you have to store it in an airtight container right away before the wings lose their hue."

"Our son," Ganesa's mother said, "has collected and preserved more subspecies of mansi than almost anyone in Hierapolis."

"Thanks, Dalal," Zamir said softly. "I'll take good care of them." He gently closed the case. It came to Worf then that this world might be like one of those

small creatures, something whose beauty would not
long survive its death.

Geordi La Forge had informed Hakim Ponselle
that he would be arriving at the ancient site in the
Korybantes Desert. "I'll beam down directly to the
chamber where our equipment is," Geordi had told
the archaeologist in his message. "I won't be there
long, so you don't have to meet me."

A component in the monitoring equipment he and
Data had left at the site earlier had failed, then
another, then a third. They had little enough time as
it was, and now this. Impossible as it was, Geordi
had thought he detected a more worried tone in his
friend Data's voice, even a touch of fear, before he
left main engineering to go to the transporter room.

Geordi was hoping that Ponselle would leave him
alone, that he would not have to deal with any
awkward questions. But the older man was waiting
for him inside the chamber, and his wife, Asela
Ibanez, was at his side. On the wall behind the
couple, the images of the small jet black sphere and
the large white pulsating sphere around it were still
visible. Geordi recalled that Asela was an engineer,
but that wasn't going to make this encounter any
easier for him.

"Greetings, Lieutenant Commander La Forge."
Ponselle waved an arm at the monitors and consoles.
"Planning to beam some of this equipment back to
your ship?"

"Actually, I have to replace a couple of components." Geordi moved quickly to one of the consoles
where a module had failed, then took a new module

from the bag he was carrying. "Won't take long." He removed the defective module, then snapped in the new one He hoped nothing else would fail, that they wouldn't have to deal with something simple going wrong down here at the last minute. "Is Professor Rychi still in Nicopolis?" Geordi continued. He knew perfectly well that Rychi was, but was trying to distract Ponselle and his wife; he didn't like the way Asela was staring at the consoles and monitoring equipment.

"He's still there," Ponselle replied, "still deciding which artifacts to beam up to the *Enterprise.*" He ran a hand through his gray hair. "Impossible task." Ponselle let out his breath. "Says he's coming back here afterward, with some of our colleagues and whatever they can bring from the museum. Not that any of it will survive—it'll just get crisped along with us. This place doesn't go far enough underground for us to have a chance, even with that air generator you folks beamed down earlier."

Geordi was silent as he went to another console. The air generators were, of course, part of the cover story, but they would not be needed to replace air that would be lost to the nova as it superheated and then blew away the planet's atmosphere. Still, it would have been implausible to urge people to take shelter without providing the means to replace lost atmosphere and retain it. How effective the generators would be in such a situation would never have to be tested, if all went well.

"But there is something fitting about being here for the end," Ponselle continued, "at least for me, given that it's the last site Samas and I uncovered.

Different people have different ideas about where they want to meet their end. Some folks are staying in their homes, and some are heading for the mountains, I hear. Samas mentioned that. There are even some heading into the desert. Be kind of ironic if a desert storm got them before the nova does."

"I didn't know you had desert storms here." Geordi snapped in the second component, feeling even more uneasy. He suddenly wanted to run another check on all the equipment here, every component and module, but there wasn't enough time.

"Storms don't come often in this desert," Ponselle said, "but when they do, they can be deadly. Samas and I and our team were in the early stages of excavating this place when we spotted a giant dust devil in the east—I mean a funnel the size of a mountain. Covered up most of this site again, and damn near buried part of our team with it." He thrust his hands into his tunic pockets. "You don't want to be out in the open during a desert storm." He chuckled. "Not that we'll have to worry about that much longer." Ponselle paused. "You know, son, messing with that equipment on your part is about as irrational as Samas wanting to come back here with a bunch of old artifacts, but I guess people can do some mighty strange things in the shadow of disaster."

Geordi pulled out the last of the failed modules and installed its replacement. He straightened, then saw that Asela was standing next to him, peering intently at his equipment. "It's kind of odd," she said, "your beaming down here to put in new components when all of this is going to be destroyed anyway."

"We still have to monitor your sun," Geordi said, "and having this monitoring equipment here, in a station linked directly to the device inside your sun, makes that much easier." He wondered if she would believe that.

"You could monitor our sun directly from the *Enterprise,* with your ship's sensors and computer. This equipment seems redundant to me."

"In a situation like this," Geordi said, "I want as much redundancy as possible." He turned toward Asela and perceived the doubt in her round face. She suspects, he thought; she knows I'm up to something. He was grateful for his VISOR, that she could not read anything in his eyes.

He tapped his communicator. "La Forge—ready to beam up."

"It's all right, young man," Asela said. "I know you're plotting something, and that you're probably under orders not to say anything about it. You want us at these old sites, away from our cities, but I don't think it's to protect us from the nova." She folded her arms. "Wonder if I can figure this out." She vanished as the transporter beam caught him, saving him from any more of her probing.

The city of Austra, on the southern coast of the Epictetan continent of Themis, was considered the artistic center of the planet. Worf had heard from Ganesa of how proud Austra's inhabitants were of their aesthetic accomplishments. The city's population of some five hundred thousand people would swell to nearly two million during the popular celebrations of art held there four times a year. Austra's houses and public buildings, long, low pastel structures with wide windows that reflected the city's beauty with their mirrored outer surfaces, stood along a maze of canals leading to the sea. Delicate bridges that looked like webs woven of glass spanned the narrow blue-green waterways.

From the garden outside the Linneaea Gallery, which stood on a hill overlooking Austra, Worf could see most of the city. The people of Austra had always preferred to travel through their city by boat, Ganesa had told him, or to roam its streets and alleyways on foot. Now the canals were clogged with boats carrying people to the brightly painted parking tiers at the edges of the city where they kept their flitters. They were heading north, to a site of ancient monuments on the flat, dry prairie bordering the Korybantes Desert.

Two children clung to Worf's hands. Another child, no more than two years old, sat on the ground holding on to Worf's leg. Ganesa and Ensign Chang were engaged in the delicate task of parting other children from weeping parents. Deanna Troi stood at the gate with Parviz Bodonchar, meeting parents as they arrived with their children. One hundred and four children from this city had won a chance to go aboard the *Enterprise,* and several of them were hardly more than babies.

"I won't leave you!" one woman cried, holding on to her daughter as Yeoman Bodonchar stooped to pick the child up. "I won't leave you!" She clutched at the wailing child as Bodonchar tried to soothe them both.

Children could draw no courage from such people, Worf thought. Austra had already been far more trouble than either Epira or Hierapolis. In those cities the inhabitants had been more disciplined about their preparations, limiting themselves to intermittent outbursts or brief emotional displays. Most of the parents had seemed to realize that weepy farewells would only make the parting harder on their children, as well as delay the away team's progress. A few children from the smaller towns and communities near those cities had been chosen to board the *Enterprise,* and their parents, despite their fears and their grief, had brought them to the designated places in a reasonably orderly fashion.

In Austra, they had beamed down to find a ring of security guards around the grounds of the Linneaea Gallery, ordered there by Minister James Mobutu. The guards had already turned back several parents with children after identity checks showed that their children were not on the list of those to be beamed to the *Enterprise.* There had been many reports of other people in Austra refusing to leave their homes.

Worf recalled that Andrew Kolodny, the council member who had represented this region, had committed suicide. Minister Mobutu, whose home was in Nicopolis, had come here to do the dead minister's work of organizing this evacuation. Minister Kolodny should have realized, Worf thought, that duty required him to stay with his people up to the end, not to desert them. There were a few sound reasons for suicide—to cleanse one's honor or that of one's family, to avoid being an excessive burden to others, to sacrifice oneself for one's comrades in battle—but Kolodny had apparently given in to hopelessness and fear. Others in Austra had followed his example; this city's suicide rate, according to reports, was nearly double that of other Epictetan communities. A fine example Kolodny had set for his people, but perhaps they had elected the kind of leader they deserved.

A group of adults suddenly surged through the gate, pulling their children along with them. Troi, shoved to one side, quickly regained her footing. "Stop!" she cried out. "Please stay calm!"

"My son Ariel's on the list," a broad-shouldered man shouted back, "but his brother isn't. They've never been separated. Can't you take one more?"

"I'm sorry," Troi said, managing to look both sympathetic and determined. "If we make an exception for one, then others—"

"Just one!" the man shouted.

"Why your son and not mine?" another man shouted back. "They're taking my nephew, but not my son." He shook a fist at Troi. "What kind of sense does that make?"

"A few more minutes," a woman with a little girl was saying to Bodonchar. "I just want a little more time with her."

Someone else was shouting at Troi. People outside the gate were demanding to be let in. The cries of infants in the arms of parents rose to a wail.

"Stand back!" Bodonchar said. "Wait your turn!"

Worf let go of the children holding his hands,

scooped up the little boy hanging on to his leg, then strode toward the gate, his two other small charges scurrying after him. "Order!" he called out. "We must have order here!" The people around him shrank back. "The more we're delayed, the less likely any of your children will have time to reach safety. We must get them aboard now!"

The crowd became still. The cries of their children faded into whimpers. "I too have a child," Worf continued, "my son Alexander. He lives with me aboard the *Enterprise,* and I try to set him a good example as a father. Show that you can set one for your own children."

Whether it was his words that moved them, or only the sight of an angry Klingon in their midst, the parents now seemed calmer, or at least intimidated. A few of them backed away while others got back in line, and then one sturdily built young man stepped forward.

"You're setting a fine example, too," the man said. "We're stuck here, whatever happens. You'll be beaming back to your ship before things really get hot, and you're taking these kids with you. Your son will see his father again—you won't have to watch him being taken away, or know he'll die here."

Worf had no answer to that.

"Advising us to leave Austra," the man continued. "What good is that going to do us? Maybe you're just trying to take our minds off of what's going to happen by keeping us busy with this useless evacuation."

"No," Troi said, "you must believe me. We're trying to do everything we can to save you."

"You can't save us. There's nothing you can do. You're just trying to pretend that there is." The man covered his face; another man led him away. Worf turned and walked back to where the first group of children were ready to be transported to the *Enterprise.*

The last of the children had been beamed up from the Bharati Museum. Night was coming; Deanna Troi breathed in air that smelled faintly of flowers. On the other side of the wide canal, in front of the museum, the lights of Nicopolis winked on near houses and along streets, but much of the city was empty. Many of its residents had already left for the archaeological site that overlooked Nicopolis in the foothills of the Aurelian Mountains, or one of the two sites farther north. They might believe that they were going only to their deaths, but they would follow the example of their minister, Mariamna Fabre.

Feeling tired, Troi stood with Minister Fabre, sensing the older woman's deep exhaustion. Almost half the population of this world lived on the western coast of Themis, north and south of Nicopolis, and nearly a thousand children had been beamed aboard the *Enterprise* from the Bharati Museum. It had taken longer than Troi had expected, and her away team still had to evacuate children from Boreas, the only city on the smaller northern continent of Metis. Those children were probably already waiting for them in the Boreas Civic Center.

So few, she thought, but it was necessary to make the effort. If Captain Picard decided that Data's plan was too risky to attempt, and the *Enterprise* left before the inevitable conflagration, those children might be all that remained of this world. She recalled how some of the children had looked just before beaming up—wide-eyed, trying to be brave but clearly frightened, the older ones certain that they would never see their homes and families again, each of them clutching one of the ancient etchings, small sculptures, or archaic artifacts Samas Rychi had given to them.

No, she thought; the children will return, and Epictetus III shall survive. If anyone could make this plan work, Data would, and Geordi La Forge was the best ally he could have in the effort. If there was any chance for their plan to work, Captain Picard could not refuse to give the order that might save this planet, whatever the risk.

"You might as well take this with you," Samas Rychi said as he handed Ensign Chang a small box. "It's an ancient instrument of navigation— something like an astrolabe. It's one of our most valuable pieces, and I suspect it's much more technically sophisticated than it seems."

"I'll take good care of it," Chang said.

Worf, Ensign Mehta, and Yeoman Bodonchar were already on board the *Enterprise;* the children would be settled in their temporary quarters by now. "We have to go," Troi said to the ministers. "You and your aides should leave for the evacuation sites, and we still have the children in Boreas to—"

"Riker to Troi."

Troi touched her communicator. "Troi here."

"Beam up right away," Riker's voice went on. "I

need to talk to you. As soon as you and Chang are aboard, come directly to the bridge. Riker out."

She knew from the commander's voice that something was wrong. There was no reason for her to go to the bridge; she and Chang had expected to beam down with the rest of the away team to Boreas almost immediately. Troi composed herself, not wanting the two ministers to see worry in her face.

"Thank you for what you've done," Fabre said. "Thank you for saving a few of the children and giving us a tiny bit of hope. I know how little that hope is, but it's still better than meeting our end only as helpless victims."

"Two to beam up," Troi said. Chang moved to her side. Rychi was holding up one hand in farewell as the two ministers and their city vanished from her sight.

Chapter Eight

"THEY STILL WON'T LISTEN," Minister Dorcas Dydion
was saying from the bridge's forward viewscreen.
"They refuse to discuss anything with you or any of
your personnel until their demand is met. You must
take the two nereids and their container aboard the
Enterprise. Then they'll release the children."

Riker, sitting in his command station, glanced at
Captain Picard. They should have realized, Riker
thought, that something would happen to compli-
cate matters; getting the children aboard had been
going almost too smoothly. But he had not antici-
pated something as wrongheaded as this. He had
expected hostage-taking as a means a group might
take to save itself. He had expected easily under-

stood selfishness and fear, not this misguided, ignorant selflessness.

Worf was back at his tactical station, looking even grimmer than usual. Ensign Mehta and Yeoman Bodonchar stood at the captain's left. Deanna Troi had just arrived with Ensign Chang; the two hurried toward the captain from the aft turbolift.

"Minister Dydion," Picard said, "the *Enterprise*'s capacity is just about at its limit now. We'll be even more crowded when the last of the children are beamed up. And even if we had the room for those two creatures and their extremely large water tank, we can hardly give in to such threats."

The young minister leaned forward. "Then what do I tell them?"

"Do you think they're actually capable of harming or killing children?" Picard asked.

"I don't know." Minister Dydion shook back her long reddish hair. "I always considered the Tireos group harmless cranks before, but that was under normal circumstances. Our circumstances haven't been normal for a while now. They've got nothing to lose at this point, whatever they do."

"Ask them if they're willing to speak to members of our away team when they return to your planet," Picard said. "Say that we're willing to talk, but tell them no more than that. I'll be in contact again in an hour. If you have a reply from them sooner than that, contact me right away."

"I'll speak to them immediately." Minister Dydion's image vanished.

"What's going on?" Ensign Chang asked.

"Two people from some outfit called the Tireos Oceanographic Institute have sealed off the Boreas Civic Center," Riker replied. "They're holding the children there hostage, along with a few parents who were still saying their good-byes. They refuse to release them until we beam up a pair of sea creatures called nereids, which they claim are intelligent."

Troi shook her head. "There's no evidence for that, according to Samas Rychi."

"And also according to Federation records," Picard added. "I checked. But these people are saying that these nereids have as much right to be saved as the children, that the universe will lose all the members of this allegedly intelligent species if we don't take them aboard."

"Sir," Lieutenant Jacques Bulero said, turning in his seat at operations to face the command area. "Why can't we beam up these fish and then—well, just make sure the tank never rematerializes?"

"It wouldn't work," Riker said. "They might demand visual verification that their demand was met. They might have monitoring devices of some kind on the tank or on the nereids. We can't take the chance."

"Minister Rychi told me after the last council meeting that my former girlfriend is part of this group," Chang said, "the ones who are holding the children." He looked angry at having to admit it. "I can't believe that Teodora would have anything to do with people who would deliberately harm children."

"I'm afraid I know very little about them," Ganesa Mehta said. "About all I've ever heard is that they're a cult of foolish people with grand-sounding academic titles who feel a deep attachment to the sea. They're fairly obscure—I doubt most Epictetans even know anything about them."

"We must decide what to do," Picard said, "and there isn't much time. We can't beam people into the Boreas Civic Center in an attempt to disarm the two hostage-takers—it's just too risky. We might only end up provoking them. But we've got to get the children out of there before Data and La Forge start the last of their tests."

They would, Riker knew, have to leave their orbit around Epictetus III to take up a position at least a million miles from the planet before Data began those tests and moved toward the final steps of his plan—assuming that Picard decided to go ahead with the risky scheme. The *Enterprise* would be out of transporter range, too far away to beam up anyone else from the surface. Again he felt his doubts about this plan gnawing at him.

"It's ironic." Riker looked back; Lieutenant Commander Iris Liang, one of the science officers at the mission operations station, was speaking. "If we do succeed in opening a wormhole," she continued, "and it's large enough for Epic Three to pass through, the Tireos Institute underwater installation should be one of the safer places to be, for them and for their precious nereids. That's what our sensor scan indicates."

"They're determined to save those creatures," Picard said, "and they're assuming that they themselves will probably die. That makes them even more of a threat to those children."

"They have no history of violence," Troi said. "Minister Dydion said so. Perhaps we should meet with them in their underwater station. They might listen."

Riker drew in his breath. "If you go back," he said, "I'm going with you."

Picard said softly, "No, you are not, Number One."

Riker tensed. "The away team is my responsibility. You can't overrule me on that."

"And you can serve them best by staying aboard." Captain Picard gazed at him steadily. "I need you here."

Riker knew his captain too well. He could fill in what the man had left unsaid: I need you here to consider every step of Data's plan with me and confirm that I'm making the right decision; I need you on the bridge if I'm unable to be there; I need you here to take command of the *Enterprise* if I fail, if the responsibility for trying to save a world and its millions of lives is finally too much for me. The immensity of the task, the dilemmas that such an effort presented, might be too much for one man, even a Jean-Luc Picard.

"Yes, sir," Riker said at last. "I'll do my best."

Minister Dydion had an answer for the *Enterprise* officers in less than half an hour. Professor Kwame Landon of the Tireos Oceanographic Institute had agreed to speak to two members of the *Enterprise*'s away team in the institute's underwater facility. The other three were to beam down to the courtyard outside the Boreas Civic Center, where they were to stay within sight of the two men holding the children. They were to remove their phasers and set them down near the stairway leading to the main entrance. They were not to approach the center until they were informed that the children would be released.

It was, Riker thought, progress of a sort. At least the hostage-takers were willing to talk, and might be convinced to let the children go, given enough time. But there was little time, and he did not like the idea of sending two of his people into the institute itself, where they might in turn become hostages.

"I'll be waiting in front of the Civic Center," Minister Dydion said. "It's a good thing Boreas was evacuated just before this happened, and that everybody decided to go. Otherwise, angry parents and citizens probably would have stormed the place by now. I can trust my aides, so let's hope word doesn't leak out. The last thing we need is people coming back here to try to settle this themselves—we could have a riot on our hands."

"I'm grateful for your help," Picard said. "We'll get those children to safety—I promise you that. *Enterprise* out."

"Lieutenant Bulero," Riker said to the operations officer on duty, "see that two portable transceivers are issued to the away team. I have a feeling they're going to need them." He was beginning to fear that there might not be time to get his people safely back to the ship.

Jacques Bulero turned around. "Sir, Lieutenant Commander Data indicates that the progress toward nova seems to be quickening. He wants to begin testing as soon as possible, within the next seven hours at the latest."

Picard said, "Tell him we'll be ready to leave orbit before then." He glanced at Riker.

The commander got up and hurried to the conference lounge off the bridge. The away team would be there, grabbing a quick meal and a little rest while awaiting their instructions.

Parviz Bodonchar and Ganesa Mehta were asleep in chairs. Deanna Troi and Worf sat at the table finishing their food and talking, while Chang Junshing studied a small console screen. Riker woke Bodonchar and Mehta, then quickly told the team what Minister Dydion had said and how little time they had.

"The two of you inside the Tireos Institute will be in the most danger," Riker said. "Even if you talk them into giving orders to their accomplices to release the children, you can't be sure of what they might do afterward."

"I asked the computer for information about the Tireos people," Chang said. "Luckily, a small file about them was transmitted with some of the cultural data from Epic Three—accidentally, I suspect. They not only have a reputation for being harmless, but also pride themselves on being nonviolent. Among other things, they even refuse to eat any seafood."

"That's not surprising," Riker said, "and they wouldn't be the first pacifists to turn violent."

"If they lack skill at arms," Worf said, "and also the inclination to fight, then the two holding the children might be slow to respond to any attack."

"We can't attack," Riker said, "at least not until we have no choice. Once the *Enterprise* is ready to leave orbit, the children must be aboard. They probably won't be safe in the place where they're being held if the captain decides to proceed with opening the wormhole, and by then there may not be time for them to seek shelter somewhere else. That means that as soon as we start running short on time, we have to try to get those children out of there, no matter what's happening with the other away-team members at the institute." That was, he saw now, another reason for him to remain aboard, where he could monitor the progress of Data's plan before giving orders to the away team. Once Data and La Forge neared the last of their tests, he would have to decide what the away team should do.

"Worf," Riker said, "you'll be in charge of away-team operations in Boreas." His heart sank as he realized who would have to be sent to the underwater installation, who would be the best choice to deal with those people. "Counselor Troi, you'll beam down to the Tireos Institute." Her empathic abilities might show her a way to make them see reason.

"Commander Riker," Chang said, "I think I should accompany Lieutenant Commander Troi. My former girlfriend is there. She might listen to me, and that might help us with the others."

"If you broke up with her," Riker said, "seems to me that she might not be that happy to see you. That could work against us."

"She wanted me to choose between her and Starfleet, and I chose Starfleet." A harder look came into Chang's eyes. "If she sees me now, she might convince herself that I regret my decision, and that could work in our favor. I knew Teodora very well, Commander. She's not violent, but she is suggestible and easily swayed. It's probably how she ended up with those cranks." His face softened. "I'm also at least partly responsible for the fact that she's there, I suppose."

Troi had wanted Ensign Chang on the away team in the first place, and was not objecting now. That decides it, Riker thought.

"Troi and Chang," he said, "you'll beam down to the institute. Mehta and Bodonchar, you'll go with Worf. You'll take two portable transceivers with you for use when we're out of communicator range."

"In other words," Chang said, "you may not be able to get us out before leaving orbit."

"Yes," Riker admitted, "but if Data and Geordi's tests don't work out, and the captain orders them to abort their plan, we can try to get close enough to Epic Three to beam you up before we leave this system."

"You mustn't risk having the nova overtake the *Enterprise*," Chang said, "in any attempt to save us."

Riker said, "We won't." He paused. "There's also a chance that we won't have time to get back within transporter range and beam you aboard even if Captain Picard decides to go ahead with Data's plan."

Chang nodded. "In that case, we'll have the same chances to survive that the Epictetans have. That seems fair enough."

"I sense that we're all of one mind." Troi looked

around at the other members of the away team. "Once this last group of children is safely aboard, the *Enterprise* must leave orbit to proceed with the last of the tests and, if the captain orders it, open the wormhole. Nothing should interfere with that, not even getting us aboard."

"I agree," Worf said. "The thought of retreat is most disagreeable, especially when others would have to be abandoned during the retreat. We'll be risking no more than the Epictetans themselves will be if this plan actually works."

"It's my homeworld," Ganesa said. "You know how I feel—you must do everything you can to save it. My life doesn't matter next to that." Yeoman Bodonchar nodded in agreement.

Riker stood up, fervently hoping that Data's plan would save Epictetus III even while knowing that the effort might well not succeed. "I'll give you the rest of your instructions on our way to the transporter room—we're running out of time!"

Dorcas Dydion was waiting for Worf and his two companions in front of the Boreas Civic Center. The building was a long two-story structure made of a gray material that resembled slate. Worf studied the building, noting the tall, narrow windows and the short flight of stairs leading up to the main entrance, as he, Ganesa, and Yeoman Bodonchar walked toward Minister Dydion.

The Civic Center overlooked a gentle slope that ran down to Boreas's harbor. The courtyard was made of tiles that seemed to form a pattern, and soon Worf saw that the images were of whitecaps and waves. The entire courtyard surface resembled the rough, blue-gray ocean in the distance; apparently the people here had their own attachment to the sea. Boreas itself, judging by what he could see from the courtyard, was a city of stark, simple buildings of wood and stone and wide streets lined by tall trees with green needles on their limbs. The treetops came to a point, like spears.

Worf inhaled the cold, clear salt-scented air. Boreas appealed to him more than any of the places he had seen on Epictetus III.

Minister Dydion wore a hooded brown coat and brown trousers. "Greetings," she said as Bodonchar set down the small transceiver he was carrying. "Two of my aides and three members of our security force are in one of the buildings nearby. I sent the others on to our evacuation site. The men inside think everyone's gone, but you have backup if you need it." Worf found himself thinking a little more highly of the woman.

"That's all I can say," Dydion continued. "I have to turn my communicator back on now. The men inside have insisted that a channel be open at all times, so be careful if you have to speak to your captain later." She reached inside her coat and pressed a finger against a pendant hanging around her neck.

"We await your instructions, Minister Dydion," Worf said carefully, knowing that what happened in the next few hours was now up to Troi and Riker. It was going to be hard to wait. He would study the building, try to see how it might be breached without risk to the children.

"You'll have to disarm yourselves. I'll show you where to put your phasers." Dydion turned toward the building and led them toward the stairway.

Troi and Chang were inside a small, simply furnished room. The walls were a pale blue; the three chairs and small couch were upholstered in a deeper blue. The low glass table in front of the couch was adorned with large seashells and carved pieces of driftwood. The door to Troi's left was closed; she guessed that it led to the lock. On one wall, a viewscreen showed an image of brightly colored fish with translucent fins swimming in blue-green waters.

The door to the right slid open; a slender young woman with long black hair entered the room. Troi sensed uncertainty inside her, even fear.

"Welcome to the Tireos Oceanographic Institute," the woman said. "I am Assistant Professor Ashley Harris." A blush rose to her cheeks. "I'm also the pilot of the minisub we use to bring our visitors here, but of course it wasn't necessary to use it for you." She offered them a smile that looked more like a nervous grimace.

Troi gazed at the young woman steadily. "We have very little time," she said, "to resolve this situation."

"Yes. Of course. I'll have to take your weapons." Harris held out her hand; Troi and Chang gave the woman their phasers. "Please follow me."

Harris led them into a corridor, also painted in light blue, to another door at the end. The door slid open to reveal a large room. In the center of the room stood a huge transparent water tank which held two dolphinlike creatures. Light flickered over the dark blue walls of the room, making it seem as if the entire room were under water.

Five people were standing around the tank. The nereids swam to the top of the tank, took in air, then dived under the water as the people watched. "Some of our faculty," Harris murmured.

"The sea creatures?" Chang asked, failing to keep a sarcastic tone out of his voice.

"Of course not," the young woman replied. "I meant the people."

"Do you have any students?" Chang sounded only slightly less sarcastic.

"Well, not at the moment, but naturally we hope—" Harris led them toward the group near the tank. A brown-skinned man with long gray hair pulled into a knot on the back of his neck towered over the others. One of the two women standing with him turned her head, and Troi sensed the sudden tension in Chang.

"Teodora," he said.

"You know Lecturer Tibawi?" Harris asked.

"Jun-shing," Teodora Tibawi said, her black eyes widening as she stared at Chang. "What are you doing here?" She was a small woman with short auburn hair framing a fine-featured face of great beauty; Troi could understand, seeing that face, why Ensign Chang had loved her.

"I'm here," Chang replied, "to try to help you."

"We haven't much time," the tall gray-haired man next to Teodora Tibawi said in a deep, melodious voice. "We must get our brother and sister nereid aboard the *Enterprise.*" He took a step toward Troi.

"I am Professor Kwame Landon, director of the Tireos Oceanographic Institute."

"Lieutenant Commander Deanna Troi," Troi said, "and Ensign Chang Jun-shing." She kept her face composed as Kwame Landon introduced the rest of his colleagues—or accomplices. Teodora Tibawi seemed disoriented, even a bit ashamed, at having to confront her old love in such circumstances. The other people seemed as jumpy as Harris. Troi sensed that all of them were having some regrets about their demand.

Landon ushered her and Chang to cushions in the back of the room; apparently there were no other seats. Chang set down the transceiver; Landon glanced at it, but said nothing. Troi sat down, disturbed by the certainty and determination she was sensing inside the gray-haired man. Some of his disciples might waver, but she wondered if he ever would.

"I must begin with this question," Troi said as Landon and his followers seated themselves. "If you wanted to have the nereids transported to our ship, then why didn't you appeal to your own council? Why didn't you ask them to speak to Captain Picard about possible arrangements?"

Landon's mouth twitched. "Because they wouldn't have listened to us. There isn't one minister among them who has any understanding of our work."

"Then you might have contacted the *Enterprise* yourself and made a request to—"

"There wasn't time. First we didn't think anything could be done, and then your starship was here, and

145

before we knew it, the council had decided you should take some children aboard. They didn't think of the nereids at all."

Troi said, "So now you are threatening children to accomplish your aim."

Landon flinched. He could feel shame after all, Troi noted, maybe even uncertainty, but then she sensed his resolve once more.

"Our way is peaceful," he said. "We seek to emulate the nereid, to live in the sea seeking communion with those who share this world with us, to become worthy of joining them someday."

Troi was facing the tank. The nereids swam to the top again and poked their heads out of the water before submerging themselves once more. Up and down, up and down; they never varied their pattern. Her empathic abilities were not infallible, but Troi could discern no emotions in the nereids, none of the feelings that would require a complex mind to manifest themselves, not even any personality. Perhaps the nereids were too alien for her to sense their feelings. Perhaps they were as utterly stupid as Samas Rychi claimed.

She shifted slightly on her cushion. "Your nereids are likely to die on our ship," Troi said. "We lack the means to care for them properly. You don't know—"

"You wouldn't have to care for them long," Landon said. "All you have to do is take them to a world like ours, with an ocean where they can live."

"But they might not survive there," Troi said. "To transplant a species, to put any species in an alien environment, however similar to their own, is a very difficult— "

"At least they'll have a chance." Landon narrowed his eyes. "Do you really think our human life-forms—the children—are the only beings on this world worthy of being saved? Is it only human lives the Federation values?"

"Of course not," Troi said. "I'm half Betazoid—I know very well that the Federation values all intelligent life-forms."

"You value the human lives here, but not the lives of our nereids. You'd condemn the whole species to extinction. How much confidence do you think that will inspire among the nonhuman members of the Federation? How will your captain explain his actions to the nonhuman members of his crew?"

She wanted to tell him that the intelligent life of this world was what they wanted to preserve, and that the nereids did not qualify as intelligent life, but such a statement would only anger him more. She could not say that the lives of Epictetan children outweighed those of the nereids in this case. She also could not tell him that, if Data's tests were successful, all of the nereids in this world's oceans might have a chance to survive, whether they were intelligent or not.

"Professor Landon," Troi murmured, "I sympathize with you more than you realize. I know what your people are facing, I know you only want to preserve what life you can. But it may be that the only part of your world that will survive are the Epictetan children on board the *Enterprise*." She took a breath. "Do you want them to remember you only as people who threatened other children? Do you want to be responsible for the deaths of children who might have been saved? How are the survivors going to think of you? Isn't holding children hostage and threatening their lives contrary to your own principles?"

Teodora Tibawi lifted her hands to her face, obviously moved. Troi could see that her statement had affected the others as well. Kwame Landon looked away from her for a moment, then lifted his head, and she sensed that she had still not reached him.

"Captain Picard cannot give in to threats," Troi said. "Surely you can understand that. You may only condemn both the children in Boreas and your nereids to death, and then the children who are carried to safety would live to curse your name. That would be your legacy, the only way you'd be remembered."

Other people were entering the room from a door to Troi's left. She felt the mood of the people near her shifting, fluctuating between doubt and fear.

"Kwame," Teodora said, "maybe we should listen to her."

"Really!" Landon said harshly. "They'll say anything to get us to do what they want. Remember, they can leave at will. They don't care about our brother and sister here." He swung one arm violently in the direction of the tank. "They don't care about them at all. We're the only ones who care."

Troi took a breath, hiding her dismay. "Professor

Landon," she said, as gently as she could, "I do know how deeply you care for the nereids, but what you are doing now won't help them. You must believe me—it's possible, if you release the children, that we may be able—"

"Lies," Landon muttered, "all lies. I truly do believe that you want our aquatic brothers and sisters to die. Maybe the council of ministers finally got to you. That's it, isn't it? They won't mind seeing our whole world die if it means concealing the truth about the nereids forever."

The man, Troi realized as if an abyss had opened beneath her, was mad. Perhaps the threat to his world had driven him mad. The others were vacillating now, murmuring among themselves, but she could sense that Landon still intimidated them. She wondered if his followers would be able to overcome their fear of him soon enough to convince him to free the children.

The nereids rose to the top of their tank and dived again, as Troi tried to think of what to do next. She had to wait until Landon's people turned against him, if that was possible. If not, the situation would resolve itself when the *Enterprise* left orbit. At that point, the children would have to stay where they were. Worf might find a way into the building, and rescue them. Perhaps their captors would finally realize that they were all in danger there, and would either let the children go or try to get them to a safer place.

She suddenly knew those thoughts for what they were, wishes designed to ease her conscience. What happened to those children could not be as important as saving a world, and hoping could not ease the hardness of that truth.

And if Data's last tests failed, there might be no safety for anyone on this world.

This mission had grown progressively more disagreeable. Worf chafed at having to follow orders. Inside the slate gray building, twenty-five children of varying ages and five parents were being held by two deluded men, and all he and his comrades could do was wait. The hostages had been herded into a room on the second floor where their captors would have a clear view of the courtyard. Five hours had passed since their arrival in Boreas, and there had been no word from Troi, no order to the men inside from their leader to release the children.

Minister Dydion had surreptitiously shown Worf and his two companions a plan of the Boreas Civic Center, concealing it with her coat as they studied it. Now she was talking to the men inside over her communicator. A useless effort; they weren't listening to anyone.

Worf cursed in Klingon. Ganesa glanced at him, then muttered a curse of her own.

"Enterprise to Worf," Riker's voice said through Worf's communicator.

Worf turned around slowly, keeping his back to the window where the hostage-holders were likely to be watching, then touched his insignia. "Worf here." Dydion was still talking to the hostage-takers over her communicator. Good, Worf thought; she would keep them distracted.

"I've had word from Troi," Riker said. "Kwame Landon is finally close to giving orders to free the hostages. Seems some of his people are balking at holding them any longer. But he's gone off alone to meditate before he gives the order, and we're running out of time. Data's informed the captain that we must leave orbit now, if we're to have enough time to get into the position necessary for his last tests and to open the wormhole safely in front of the planet in its orbit."

Assuming that Captain Picard actually ordered Data to proceed with opening the wormhole, Worf thought; he could hear the doubt about that prospect in Riker's voice. "I understand," Worf replied.

Riker said, "You'll have to—"

"Lieutenant Worf!" Dydion rushed to his side. "Someone's being attacked inside! I heard a scream, and then a man shouting to stay back, and—"

Worf spun around and ran to the stairs, Ganesa and Bodonchar at his heels. He grabbed the phaser he had left on the stairs and aimed it at the door to disable its lock, then ran up the steps and kicked the door open.

There were lifts to the left and right of the main hall and a wide blue-carpeted stairway that led to the second floor. Worf went up the steps two at a time and turned right.

The door to the room where the hostages were being held was open. A baby was crying; he heard a man curse. Ganesa and Bodonchar were right behind him. We should have been ordered to rush the building before now, Worf thought. There were only two opponents, and Worf doubted that their aim with whatever weapons they had was good enough to bring down three members of Starfleet.

Worf went into a crouch, gripping his phaser, and hurried into the room. Two men were on the floor, struggling with each other. Worf aimed and fired, stunning one man; Ganesa's phaser disabled the other.

"Wait!" someone called out. A woman and two boys were in a corner near the window. With them was another man, his face bruised, his arms bound behind his back with strips of cloth, two older children standing guard over him. "Don't hurt us!" the woman went on. "We were the hostages."

A man holding a small child set the boy down, then came toward Worf. "They were getting tired," he said. "We decided it was time to take matters into our own hands." He gestured at one of the men on the floor. "That's one of them. The other one's back there, by the window." He knelt near the other unconscious man. "Hope Carlo will be all right."

Ganesa knelt next to him, took out her tricorder, and did a quick scan. "He will," she said, "when he comes to."

Three men were at the door. Worf guessed that they were the members of the Boreas security force who had been waiting near the courtyard. "We must get the children up to the ship immediately," Worf said, "and then the rest of us must get out of the city." Seconds might count now, even the seconds required to beam him and his comrades to the *Enterprise.* He and his comrades would be gambling their lives on Data's abilities, La Forge's engineering expertise, and Picard's final decision. He glared at the bound man by the window, wishing that he could leave him and his companion behind in Boreas.

Parviz Bodonchar was holding a whimpering baby. He patted the child gently on the back, then handed the infant to an older girl.

"Worf to *Enterprise*," Worf said as he touched his insignia. "The hostages are free—no casualties. We're ready to begin transporting the children."

"O'Brien has informed me that the rest of the children from Boreas are on board," Riker was saying. "Are you sure you're all right there for now?"

"Yes," Troi replied. "Some of the institute personnel are here with us."

Teodora was sitting next to Chang; five other people had remained with them after Landon had gone off to meditate. Troi had sensed the relief inside these people after the matter of the hostages had so abruptly been taken out of their hands. Now they seemed increasingly anxious to assure her and Chang that the children had never truly been in danger.

"We're leaving orbit," Riker said. "The crews on the sublights have finally acknowledged receiving a warning to take shelter. The sooner Data starts doing what he has to do, the better." Troi caught the note of doubt in Riker's voice. "We'll alert you when the decision is made. Riker out."

"Kwame was driven to this," Teodora said to Chang. "He didn't mean any harm. You understand, don't you? He only wanted to save the nereids."

Chang nodded, keeping his eyes averted from the

young woman. Troi sensed weariness in him, and suspected that he was also extremely grateful for having chosen Starfleet over Teodora Tibawi.

The door to her left opened. Kwame Landon came through the doorway and strode toward her; she felt the anger seething inside him. More followers were with him, some clearly hoping to restrain him, others sharing his rage.

"You didn't wait!" Landon shouted. "You didn't even wait for me to tell my colleagues to release their hostages!" He shook his fist at Troi. "You doubted my word!"

"Kwame," Teodora said, "they didn't do anything. Weren't you listening? It was the parents who disarmed—"

"Shut your mouth!" Landon rounded toward Troi. "Do you think I'm going to let you get away with it?"

Troi saw Chang get to his feet; then something struck her from behind. She fell forward and caught a glimpse of Chang struggling with one man before everything went black.

Chapter Nine

"Captain," Data said from his post in main engineering, "we are ready to test the subspace core link."

"Proceed," Picard's voice said from the bridge.

Geordi La Forge was already standing at the central console with Lieutenant Anita Obrion and two other engineering officers. Lieutenant Obrion looked pale. She was one of the most competent of the *Enterprise* engineers, and was clearly aware of everything that could go wrong. Indeed, Data thought, she might be only too aware of both the engineering problems and the immensity of their task. From the tension in her face, he saw that the human implications of the problem—the risks that passage through the wormhole posed to the inhabitants of Epictetus III, the chance that the wormhole might become unstable and doom the planet, the possibility that their plan might bring on the nova too soon—had finally caught up with Obrion.

Those, of course, were some of the possibilities only if they actually managed to open a wormhole. If they failed to do so, they would have an entirely different set of problems.

Data joined the others at the instrument assembly that had been fitted onto the central console, then glanced at Geordi, who gave him a quick nod, and together they began to enter a dual set of commands on the control pads.

"We are taking precautions," Data said, "so that we will not draw a flood of power through the alien suncore device. At first, I considered using a storage device to hold the incoming power before directing it through our warp engines to open the wormhole, but that would risk overload. The best and safest way is to pass power directly from the suncore device through our warp generators to the wormhole target position. That should cause a minimum of buildup within our power-handling systems and avoid a possible massive influx that we could not hold or discharge in time."

"I see," Picard said.

"Additionally, Captain, besides the danger of overload, we have to control the flow for the time needed to open the wormhole, and it may take a large portion of the star's energy output to open and then to keep open a controlled wormhole of the size needed to accommodate a planet. An uncontrolled wormhole would act like a black hole and destabilize this entire solar system."

"But trying to open a wormhole is the only thing we can do," Picard's voice said.

"Yes," Data said. "Do you still wish to proceed?"

"Continue," Picard said.

"I will inform you at every juncture where we will still have a choice to make," Data continued.

"I understand," Picard said.

"First test flow coming in," Anita Obrion said.

"It appears stable and manageable," Data said. "Shall we proceed to the next step, Captain?"

"Yes."

"Insurge overload!" Obrion shouted.

"Correct heavily!" Data ordered.

"Correcting."

"Continue," Data said, and waited.

"Still correcting." Data heard Obrion sigh with relief. "Stable again."

"Set these limits in the program," Data said. "Captain, shall we proceed?"

"We must." Picard's voice sounded strained. "Proceed."

Data watched as the instruments began to register a double flow. "Double flow stable, Captain. Increasing to five times." The flow indicators were silently going up, now showing perfect stability of input to the *Enterprise*'s warp engines, which were now receiving energy not from their usual onboard source, but from the nearby sun. Data reminded himself that the starship's warp engines were down and could not be restarted for several hours. The *Enterprise,* to use an old nautical metaphor, was dead in the water, for all intents and purposes.

"Shall we continue, Captain?" Geordi asked.

Picard did not answer right away. Data supposed that he was waiting for a cue from Riker, who was, given his doubts, functioning as a devil's advocate in this situation. The captain would make his decision regardless of what the commander thought, but an open objection from Riker would not be good for morale on the bridge, especially if he was right on some point.

"Are you certain?" Picard asked. "Are both of you certain?"

"As certain as we're ever going to be," Geordi replied. "We have to act now—the estimated time to the nova is growing rapidly shorter."

"Then we'll proceed," Picard said, and Data knew by the sound in his voice that Riker was not objecting. "It might as well be now as ever. Make it so!"

Data set the program to escalate in stages to whatever level of draw was needed to open the wormhole.

On the bridge, Picard was watching the main viewscreen, which showed an area of space ahead of the planet in its orbit, where the wormhole would open. Invisible subspace energies were tearing at the spot, unraveling the fabric of space-time in order to open and hold a controlled wormhole, into which Epictetus III would enter as it followed its natural orbital path. If the passage went smoothly, continuing the planet's present orbital motion around its star, inertial and gravitational stresses would maintain as smooth a gradient as possible, and the planet would pass without too much tectonic upheaval into a similar orbit around the star fourteen light-years away.

Nothing yet showed in the volume of space ahead of the planet. Picard thought of the fleeing sublight ships. They would have changed course by now in the hope of sheltering themselves from the nova behind one of this system's outer planets. Their crews had acknowledged receiving the warning very late, but they still had a chance.

Picard glanced at William Riker. The commander was still, his eyes on the viewscreen. Picard was sure that his executive officer continued to have grave doubts about this plan, but he was hiding them well. At the forward stations, Miles O'Brien had relieved Jacques Bulero at operations, but Bulero had lingered nearby, as if compelled to keep monitoring the progress of Data's tests, until Picard had finally ordered him from the bridge. Bulero was probably in his quarters now, his eyes glued to a viewscreen when his duty schedule would have had him resting. The same was probably true of every man, woman, and child aboard.

"We have to increase the flow of energy from the star," Picard heard La Forge say with a trace of doubt in his voice.

"I agree," Data's voice said, without either doubt or confidence.

Everyone on the bridge was silent. Picard watched

and waited, thinking that perhaps the entire output of the star might fail to open a hole wide enough and stable enough for the planet to enter. He might as well expect the Cheshire Cat's grin to appear. Pumping the sun would keep shortening the time to the nova. He put that thought out of his mind for now.

"Captain," Data said, "I think we should increase the flow of energy drastically, with the purpose of opening the wormhole before the star begins its fina nova phase. A slower draw of power may delay the opening and leave the planet insufficient time to go through the wormhole, and leave us no time to restart our warp-drive engines and escape this system."

"Is it possible to increase the flow so greatly?" Picard asked. "Sounds a bit circular to me."

"We have no choice now but to keep going," Data said, "or shut down the whole effort. We have to move quickly at this point. The hole must be open and usable before the nova erupts, even if the window will be a narrow one."

Picard looked toward Riker again for a moment, and saw the commander nod.

"Make it so!" Picard ordered without hesitation.

The youngest children, the infants and toddlers, had been the most difficult to get settled at first. Beverly Crusher was housing some of them in sickbay; others were in the personal quarters of crew members who were not on duty and thus were able to look after them. The children aboard the starship had been quick to welcome the young Epictetans and to help get them settled. Nearly all the available living space was now being shared with the young refugees from Epictetus III.

Hastily assembled cribs stood among the biobeds; other infants had been housed in the guest quarters on decks 5 and 6. Raymond Tam, one of the medical officers, was soothing one wailing baby. He rocked the infant gently for a few moments until the cries subsided, then laid the child in a crib.

The youngest children had quieted down, and were not much trouble now. Other children, aged two to six, could be distracted by games or short visits to the holodeck. It was the older ones who worried Beverly most, the children old enough to understand the peril threatening their world, to know that family and friends and all the people and places they had loved and treasured might soon cease to exist. Some of them were refusing to eat, while others shied away from anyone who approached them.

The children had been told, in ways that they could grasp, that there might still be a chance to save their world. It was unnecessary to conceal Data's preparations from them anyway, now that the children were aboard. Almost all of them, Beverly had heard, were now clustered around the available viewscreens in the guest rooms, the personal quarters, even in Ten-Forward. The two girls she had taken into her own quarters had been obsessively monitoring all the communications from main engineering to the bridge before Beverly left for sickbay. They had ignored her gentle urging that they rest, and she had not had the heart to insist that they get some much-needed sleep.

She glanced toward her office. Three children waited there, in need of medical attention for sprained ankles and wrists. She had not been able to tear them away from her office viewscreen.

A nurse at the other end of the room was changing one baby's diapers. More of the babies would wake up soon. Raymond Tam was at a food replicator, taking out bottles of infant formula. Beverly went to help him, welcoming any task that might distract her, however momentarily, from the knowledge that so many lives were now in the hands of a few *Enterprise* officers, and that whatever good she was doing here would be for nothing if they failed.

At the console in main engineering, Geordi tapped in the order for an increased flow of power as if he were playing a musical instrument, and waited for the judgment of his monitors, feeling for a moment that he was a piano player aboard the *Titanic*. He felt sweat break out on his brow and hoped that his crewmates had not noticed.

The instruments were registering a smooth flow of energy, with not even a hint of dangerous spikes. He glanced at the wall display of the warp-propulsion systems. The warp generators were handling the flow.

"Whew," Geordi said, and heard the other engineers sigh loudly in relief.

How quiet it is, Czeslaw Peladon thought as he gazed at the sea from his terrace. The sky was a bluish gray, a little murkier than usual, the air very still, the sun a flat white disk veiled by clouds, but he had experienced days like this before. What was different was a silence so profound that he could easily hear the waves lapping on the shore and the soft musical cries of the furela birds as they skittered across the sand. Epira was nearly empty, its people waiting in their ineffectual refuges.

There was no reason for him to stay in his house. He had sent a message for Krystyna to the *Enterprise* just before Captain Picard's announcement. The sublights, including the one carrying his son, had received their warning and were now in a desperate race toward shelter. He had nothing more to do here, but could not bring himself to leave.

A captain on one of the sublight craft had found the time to send a subspace message to Peladon. He supposed that the *Enterprise*'s communications systems had automatically relayed it to his transceiver.

"What the hell did you think you were doing?" the captain had said. "You were the one who told us we had to go, you were the one who said you and those other two ministers had the council's authority to give us our orders. Save the best of our people, you said, keep the memory of our world alive. I don't think we're going to make it, Peladon, but maybe we deserve to die. At least we know you will, too."

The man knew that the sublight vessel crews had been given a chance to save their own hides as well as those of their passengers. Peladon and his two fellow ministers had even told them to bring their own families aboard in secret, to ensure that they would not have second thoughts. The crews had surely guessed at the truth of what they were doing, even if they had chosen to ignore it at the time, and were now blaming him for their actions in order to escape their own complicity, preparing for when they might have to justify themselves to others—if they survived. The captain's words had stung nonetheless.

Peladon's own message to his granddaughter had been longer. "Krystyna, I think you always knew the truth about me, whether or not you admitted it to yourself. You're too perceptive not to have seen what I was. I lived my life for myself, always. If something required great sacrifice of me, if it was costly, if it involved a matter of principle that offended my practical sense, I could find reasons not to do it. In my work, in my service on the council, in my personal life, whatever I did for others, I always made certain that it benefited me and those closest to me as well.

"And when our world faced its greatest crisis, I put my son Casimir ahead of everyone else, and had you been here, you would have been on that craft with him. I'm astonished by the sudden onset of scruples that kept me from boarding the ship myself.

"You were right to leave, dear child, to choose to live for others instead of only for yourself. I can be grateful now that you were able to love me without following my example."

His message for Krystyna, he thought, had been that of a dying man.

It was time to leave his house, to go to his flitter and get to the site where his aides were waiting, where people would be expecting him to utter useless noble sentiments in an effort to help them to face death bravely. Peladon went to the edge of his terrace, leaned against the vine-draped railing, and gazed up at the veiled sun.

Worf's son Alexander had brought the children to her. Guinan smiled down at them, saying nothing for a few moments, until one little girl tentatively smiled back.

Alexander said, "They're scared." His small face was as fierce as his father's. Guinan was sure that Alexander had done his best to cheer the children, but perhaps the young Klingon's manner was a little too resolute for them. "I told them they wouldn't be so scared with you."

There were six of them, two girls and four boys of about Alexander's age, all of them looking very frightened. There were other children in Ten-Forward, some of them sitting at the bar with a few of the *Enterprise*'s children, others at the tables, still others staring out the huge window ports as if hoping for a view of their planet. Guinan had offered them ice-cream sodas and other treats and had listened as they spoke of the parents they missed and the friends they had left behind. Many of the ice-cream sodas were still untouched, but some of the children were starting to sip theirs.

"My father's on your world now," Alexander said. "He won't be afraid, so you shouldn't be, either. Mr. Data and the engineers are working hard—they wouldn't be doing all of that if they didn't have a pretty good plan. And when my father comes back to the *Enterprise,* you can all go home." Guinan thought she caught a flicker of sympathy in Alexander's dark eyes.

"I'm scared anyway," one boy said.

Guinan knelt and took the boy's hands. "It's all right to be scared," she said. "I'm scared, too. Even Alexander's probably a little bit scared."

Alexander scowled, but did not deny her words.

"All we can do now," Guinan continued, "is try to not show how scared we are."

The boy rubbed at his eyes, then tried to smile.

On the bridge, Picard peered at the wormhole's expected position and saw nothing, not even a slight distortion of the background stars.

He continued to stare at the viewscreen, feeling duty-bound to keep watch for some sign of a wormhole forming, until he sensed that someone was near him.

"Sir," a voice next to him said. Picard looked to his left and saw Ensign Veronica Sorby holding a small tray. "You haven't eaten for hours," the ensign continued. "I've taken the liberty of bringing you some food." He noticed that Riker was standing up now, holding a cup as he watched the viewscreen. Riker had probably sent Sorby over with the food.

Picard stretched, realizing suddenly how much his shoulders ached from tension, then took the tray from her. "Thank you, Ensign."

Sorby had brought him Earl Grey tea and a hard roll filled with vegetables and cheese. Picard bit into the roll, surprised at how hungry he was. He finished the roll quickly and drank his tea while standing and watching the viewscreen, still seeing only black emptiness there. He could not take his eyes from the screen. After all, he told himself, one doesn't see this sort of event often. He did not want to miss the moment. He could not afford to miss it. The burden of the decision he would have to make weighed even more heavily on him.

"Power flow increasing geometrically, Captain," Data's voice said.

"Nova conditions building at the previous rate," La Forge added. "Our efforts don't seem to have made much of an impression yet."

A small mercy, Picard thought as he sat down again, but the nova could not be far off now.

And then he saw starlight ripple as the needle of invisible energy from the *Enterprise* stitched a hole in space-time. Stars near the edges of the growing invisible monster shone as strings of light, then appeared to wink out. Directly ahead, the heavens were being pried open.

Picard felt a moment of disquiet, as if some childhood phobia were visiting him, bringing with it the irrational fear of darkness.

"Nova now quickening," Data said, "but the wormhole is not yet large enough to accept the planet."

An officer behind Picard gasped. There was no going back now, he thought. Epictetus III was on a collision course with the hole, whatever its size; the nova was on, and the *Enterprise*, he reminded himself uneasily, had only impulse engines with which to maneuver.

La Forge said, "The planet is now two hours from the wormhole, Captain. We have no choice but to increase the rate of energy flow precipitously or Epictetus Three won't go through."

No rebirth for this world, Picard thought anxiously, no passage into a safe place, if the hole failed to grow.

"Wormhole opening wider," Data announced suddenly, his voice a bit sharper than usual, "but the overall position appears unstable. It is oscillating from left to right—and it is still not large enough."

"Will it become large enough?" Picard asked.

La Forge said, "We're feeding in more power, but the larger it gets, the more power it requires to get even a few meters wider. Calculating the rate now."

One hour and fifty minutes to go, Picard saw, wondering then if this might be his last mission. "Data, how long to the nova?" he asked.

"Difficult to calculate, Captain."

If only the planet were saved, Picard thought, then the loss of the *Enterprise* would be a small matter. Small, at least, in number of lives lost; not so small a matter to the parents who had given their children over to the *Enterprise*. At every stage of this attempt, he felt the dilemmas multiplying without mercy, and wondered if they would proliferate to a point that would make choices impossible.

"Wormhole oscillations slowing," Geordi said. "Continuing to widen."

Picard waited, feeling that all the decisions had already been made, for better or worse.

* * *

Ponselle watched as Asela monitored the consoles the two *Enterprise* officers had left behind. "The nova's quickening," she murmured. "That's what the measurements here show. What's the *Enterprise* doing, drawing off so much power from our sun? I don't understand it. They'll just bring on the nova even faster."

Hakim Ponselle gazed at the gray wall. The shadows of their sun's interior still danced, as they had since Samas Rychi and he had first entered this chamber. Asela could not have figured anything out by watching those shadows, but she had studied the gauges on the consoles, saw what the readings meant, and had finally deduced that the starship itself was drawing power from their sun.

"There have to be other gauges in this installation somewhere," his wife said, "or devices of some sort. The ancient ones couldn't have had warning of a nova just by looking at the wall—there must be something else here that would have shown them when a nova was imminent."

"Maybe they could see something in those images that we can't," Ponselle said. "Maybe the gauges and such are right in front of us, and we just can't see what they are. Too bad Samas and I aren't going to have time to find them."

"Where is Samas, anyway? He's certainly taking his time."

At that moment, Ponselle heard the sound of voices, then footsteps. He spun around, hurried toward the arch leading into the chamber, and saw Samas Rychi coming down the ramp.

"Samas," Ponselle called out as he went to his friend. "Glad you got here before the end." Rychi gripped him by the elbows, then gave him a quick embrace. In all the years they had known each other, Rychi had never been that demonstrative. His friend had changed.

"Better come and help us," Rychi said. Ponselle hurried up the ramp with him. "We packed up some of the museum exhibits, but we still had to abandon too much."

"Shouldn't have brought them," Ponselle said. "Shouldn't have taken the trouble."

"They'll have as much chance to survive here as anywhere else."

"They won't have any chance of making it through the nova, here or anywhere else," Ponselle said as they came to the next ramp, "and neither will we. Asela's been studying the equipment that those two *Enterprise* officers left behind. Doesn't make any sense, but she says that the starship's drawing off power from our sun, that—"

"I knew it," Rychi said softly. "I thought Captain Picard might have a hidden reason for advising us to leave our cities. I haven't been able to put that thought out of my mind, and then I felt even more strongly that we had to bring whatever we could to this site. I wonder what kind of a plan he's cooked up."

They reached the hall. Two other archaeologists had already dragged a chest through the entrance. Ponselle followed Rychi outside. Fifteen flitters had landed; other archaeologists were unloading crates and boxes from their vehicles. The sky was its usual cloudless blue, and the sun had become the blazing white disk that it usually was at this time of day.

"I almost forgot." Rychi slid open the rear door of his flitter and reached inside for a small case. "I went to your house before I left. I thought you might want some sort of memento."

Ponselle was touched. "You shouldn't have gone at all, Samas."

"Couldn't think of what to bring, so I brought only one item for you—the one on loan from the museum. It's that pendant you found at the site north of Austra ten years ago. I'll never forget it. You were like a child when you saw it."

Ponselle took the case from Rychi and opened it. Inside lay a burnished metal disk attached to a slender chain. The disk was a paler yellow than gold, almost as pale as the sun at noon. The symbol of a star was etched in its center, surrounded by engraved ellipses adorned with jewels of various colors. It had been one depiction of the ancients that had been relatively easy to interpret, although Ponselle still did not know if the pendant had been for a ceremonial purpose or was meant only for adornment.

The star was their sun, the blue gem Epictetus III, and the remaining jewels the other planets of this system, a system that would soon cease to exist. Ponselle touched the pendant lightly, then closed the case and said, "Thank you, Samas."

Almost all of Epictetus III's archaeological sites were on the southern continent of Themis. For Worf and his companions, that particular piece of knowledge had taken on an urgent meaning. The people of Boreas had been evacuated to one of the only two sites that had ever been discovered on their continent of Metis, the site bordering the Dryon Forest that lay nearly three thousand kilometers to the east of Boreas. The only other site was northeast of the city.

Reviving the two men struck by the phasers and getting the children transported to the *Enterprise* had taken a little time. Preventing the five parents from working out their rage on their two former captors had taken even more. By the time the three security-force members with Minister Dydion had taken charge of the two men, and the away team was ready to leave the city, they had run out of time.

The five parents had scattered, running through the streets to their homes for their flitters. Dydion's aides had gone with the security-force people and their two prisoners to a larger flitter. Worf, Ganesa, and Parviz Bodonchar were now in Minister Dydion's flitter, making for the site northeast of Boreas.

Dydion leaned forward in her seat to look at the display panel. "You could have beamed back to your ship," she said, "and now it's out of range. You needn't have stayed."

"There wasn't time," Ganesa said.

"Time?" Dydion shook her head. "Time is the least of our considerations now. There's hardly any chance for us even if we get to this site before the nova begins. Why did you stay? Why didn't the others beam you aboard?"

"We will have the same chances as your people

have now," Worf said. Perhaps the woman would assume that his Klingon pride had caused him to stay behind, that Ganesa was here because she did not want to leave her homeworld, and that Bodonchar had chosen to remain with them. He wanted to tell Minister Dydion that they might have more of a chance than she realized, that they might escape the nova altogether, but said nothing, wondering if Data and La Forge had been successful with their last tests.

Yeoman Bodonchar had brought their portable transceiver. Worf gazed through the flitter's transparent dome at the rugged landscape below. The cliffsides were marked by multicolored striations of minerals, the jagged hills covered with rocks that glittered like jewels; it was a land with its own kind of beauty. But to wait out the planet's passage through the wormhole inside the flitter or in a shelter on this rock-strewn land would be to court death. Even a mild quake could send boulders and rocks hurtling down the cliffsides and hills.

"There it is," Dydion said. "I can see it." In the distance, at the top of a cliff, steely metal surfaces caught the light of the sun. Worf looked west; he could still see the ocean on the horizon. If a wormhole was opened, and the planet's passage through it was extremely violent, a tidal wave might come as far as the cliff. He did not think such a wave would reach the height needed to sweep over the top of the precipice, but could not be sure. There was no way of knowing how much tectonic movement and seismic disruption the passage would cause.

It did not matter. They would have to take their chances here.

"Riker to Worf," a voice said from the transceiver.

Worf leaned closer to the device. "Worf here."

"Wormhole's open," Riker said, "but it's not large enough to swallow Epic Three, at least not yet. Hope you've found shelter."

"We are on our way to the site northeast of Boreas," Worf replied. "We should be there in about five minutes."

"I hope so. The captain still hasn't made his final decision. Riker out."

Worf leaned back. Dorcas Dydion was gazing at him questioningly. He looked away from her.

He could now see the pit at the top of the cliff. Excavating the site had left a crater around the three rectangular monoliths. Etched in the silver metal on the sides of the structures were images of longboats with unfurled sails and spaceships that looked like gossamer parasols.

"Impressive," Worf said.

"That's actually one of the smaller sites," Ganesa said. "The ones near Nicopolis and Austra have about fifty buildings each, much larger than these, and those sites haven't even been completely uncovered yet."

As the flitter dropped toward the pit, the true scale of the buildings showed them to be massive structures, nearly three kilometers tall from the base. Minister Dydion put the flitter controls on manual and landed near a ramp that led to the side of one monolith.

They climbed out quickly. The flitter holding Dydion's aides, the three security-force members, and their prisoners dropped toward the pit. Three other flitters were just behind them, carrying the five adults who had been with the children.

As the other flitters landed near them, Worf and his comrades followed Dydion up the ramp. "How do we get in?" Bodonchar asked.

Dydion stopped and extended an arm to the smooth metal surface, brushing it lightly with her fingers. A doorway opened before them, yawning ever wider until it was twenty meters high and nearly twenty meters wide. They stepped through the door into a vast hallway illuminated only by the string of small light globes the archaeologists in charge of the site must have left behind.

Along both sides of the hallway stood rows of monumental metal sculptures of beings that seemed remarkably humanoid and yet also extremely alien. Worf looked up at one sculpted face. The look of pride and disdain in the slightly lidded eyes and curving mouth revealed an arrogance beyond even that of the proudest of intelligent beings; it was a look that, had he not been a Klingon, might have made him feel small and weak, a creature who would forever be at the mercy of much greater forces. And above, on tiers reaching up into the darkness, were still more of the sculptures, a ladder of images reaching to the heavens.

Nothing could touch them. That was what the images seemed to say. They spoke of beings who could bend all the forces of nature to their will. Worf stared at the reflections of the images in the mirror-like surface of the floor, hoping that this race's ancient monuments would be able to withstand the forces that would now be hurled against them.

Data said, "The wormhole is still not big enough to accommodate the planet."

Miles O'Brien was hunched over his operations console; Veronica Sorby sat bolt upright at control. There was no sound on the bridge except the intermittent beeps of instruments and panels. In little more than an hour, Picard realized, wormhole and planet would collide. There was nothing to be done now except to restart the *Enterprise*'s warp drive and leave when Epictetus III entered the wormhole—if the nova gave them that much time.

"The wormhole still seems to be widening," La Forge said, "but slowly. It may be enough, Captain. We could increase the rate of power flow, but that would risk losing the stability we now have."

"We await your order," Data said. "What shall we do?"

Picard glanced back at Iris Liang. The science officer's green eyes held a look of controlled terror. Riker sat stiffly at his station, betraying his doubts only with a slight shake of his head.

"Increase the rate of power flow," Picard said. "Do everything you can to make it large enough for the planet to pass through." His decision had been made. "I'm going to make an announcement now, to be sent on emergency channels to every transceiver and communications device on Epictetus Three capable of receiving subspace messages." There might still be time for any people who had remained in the cities to get to safety.

On the viewscreen, the nearly invisible wormhole waited for the planet. As Picard watched, Epictetus III swam into view from his left, a living jewel being offered up to a cosmic monster.

"Message coming in from the *Enterprise,*" Bodonchar said. Worf strode to the yeoman's side, refusing to allow himself to hope.

He knelt near the transceiver. "Captain Picard of the *U.S.S. Enterprise* to Epictetus Three." By then, the others had gathered around Worf and Bodonchar. Worf knew by the sound of the captain's voice that his decision had been made.

"We have succeeded in opening a wormhole along your world's orbital path," Picard continued. "Your planet will pass through this wormhole an hour from now, to emerge in a planetary system fourteen light-years away, in an orbit that should be at a safe distance from that system's sun. In this way, we hope to save not only your lives, but also your entire planet. I must warn you that the passage is likely to be violent, that quakes, tidal waves, and other seismic disturbances will result. Most of you will survive, however, especially if you stay alert. Bear in mind that this passage is survivable. A nova would have given you no chance at all. Those of you who are not at evacuation sites should proceed there immediately. If you are too far away from a site to get there within an hour, then at least get away from the coastline."

"Then we don't have to go down the ramps to the

lower levels," Dorcas Dydion murmured, and Worf saw that she was still trying to absorb this startling news. "We don't have to huddle underground waiting for the nova. We're going to escape it altogether."

"That is what we are hoping for," Worf said, aware of the dangers that still lay ahead.

Dydion clutched at Ganesa's arm. "You knew about this. You must have known all along."

"We knew," Ganesa said. "We had orders not to say anything."

"We weren't sure," Worf said, "if we would be able to accomplish such a feat."

"I see." Dydion let go of Ganesa and sat down next to Worf. "I do know something about politics. My guess is that Starfleet Command and the Federation Council told your captain not to promise anything he couldn't deliver—for the good of the Federation, of course."

"He still may not be able to deliver it," an aide muttered.

"But we have a real chance now," Ganesa said. "Our whole world has a chance."

"I repeat," Picard said, "that anyone near the coast should immediately head inland." Worf did not want to think about how close to the coast they were. "If you cannot get to an evacuation site, go to a stretch of open land, wait there, and remain inside your vehicle. Do not head for mountain slopes where there are likely to be landslides."

Worf stood up. "This message will be repeated now," Picard said. Dydion pressed her hands together and leaned closer to the transceiver. "Captain Picard of the *U.S.S. Enterprise* to Epictetus Three. We have succeeded in opening a wormhole along your planet's orbital path. . . ."

"I repeat that anyone near the coast should immediately head inland." That was Captain Picard's voice. Troi inhaled slowly; her head hurt. "If you cannot get to an evacuation site, go to a stretch of open land, wait there, and remain inside your vehicle. Do not head for mountain slopes where there are likely to be landslides."

What was going on? Troi tried to ignore the throbbing in her head. "This message will be repeated now," the captain continued. "Captain Picard of the *U.S.S. Enterprise* to Epictetus Three. We have succeeded in opening a wormhole along your planet's orbital path. . . ."

Others were talking now, drowning out Picard's words. One of the voices sounded like Chang's. He was giving an order, telling somebody to restrain someone else.

"Just sit down," Chang said, "and stay calm. Do you understand? We'll be safe here, probably much safer than we'd be almost anywhere else. All we can do now is wait."

Troi heard the soft, high-pitched whine of a tricorder. She was being scanned. She opened her eyes and saw Ensign Chang leaning over her, Teodora Tibawi at his side.

"You're all right," Chang said as he put his tricorder away.

"I have a hard head," Troi said as she slowly sat up. The back of her head still throbbed. "How long was I out?"

"I'm not sure. I wasn't paying much attention to the time."

Troi gingerly felt her head and winced. She longed to lie down and rest; the strain of the past days was catching up with her. She looked around the room and saw Kwame Landon sitting cross-legged on the floor near the water tank, his head bowed. Another man sat next to him in the same posture; two men were standing behind them, as if keeping guard.

"What happened?" Troi asked.

"Professor Landon violated our principles," a young man near her said, "and Associate Professor Dixon-Martins should not have struck you as he did." He waved in Landon's direction. "With the help of your associate, we managed to restrain them. They are meditating now on the outrageousness of their deeds. It was wrong to hold those children hostage—we know that now. When we heard Captain Picard's message, we realized that he meant to save us all from the start, that he hadn't neglected the nereids. Professor Landon should never have given that order. It was wrong to hurt you."

"That is not our way," Ashley Harris added. "We don't practice violence."

Troi was picking up a few sensations from them. They seemed genuinely sorry, but she also sensed that they were worrying now about what might happen to them later if their world managed to pass through the wormhole safely. Being accomplices of

180

adults who had threatened the lives of children was a grave offense on most worlds; their fellow Epictetans were likely to judge them harshly. She felt their fear, and saw their apprehension whenever they glanced at Chang. The ensign had subdued their leader; adrift now, they would turn to Chang to guide them, at least temporarily.

"This message will be repeated now. Captain Picard of the . . ." Chang leaned toward the transceiver and muted the sound.

Teodora sat back on her heels. "They will be all right, won't they?" She gestured toward the water tank. "The nereids, I mean."

"Of course," Chang said, sounding faintly exasperated.

"Most of the nereids in your oceans will survive," Troi said, "if this plan works." The nereids in the tank were still rising to the top and diving again, not varying their repetitive motions at all.

"Do you feel all right now?" Harris asked.

"I think so," Troi said.

"We really are grateful you're here, for what you've done," Harris said. "It's almost a miracle. I was so sure that we—" Troi sensed the wild, conflicting emotions inside Harris; the unexpected reprieve had apparently unbalanced her even more. "Perhaps I could show you and Ensign Chang more of the Tireos Institute."

Troi thought of refusing, then decided against it. These people, even with their worst fears gone, were still too insecure and unstable to provoke. "Very well."

Harris led them through one doorway to a small adjacent room where the sea could be viewed through an oval viewport, then to a meeting room and lounge. Kwame Landon and a few of his early supporters, Harris told them, had bought the facility from the University of Nicopolis when it was abandoned by its oceanographers for a more advanced one nearer the city. Professor Landon's revelation about the true nature of the nereids had apparently come to him in this very meeting room. Troi restrained herself from asking Harris if his revelation had been backed by even an iota of evidence.

More people had come into the large room when they returned. Troi guessed that almost all of the institute's forty people were now here. More men and women approached her, gave their names and academic titles, and offered more apologies for the actions of Professor Landon and Associate Professor Dixon-Martins.

"Please forgive us," a blond young man with the title of assistant professor said.

"We were only trying to save our brothers and sisters of the sea," murmured an older woman who called herself a professor.

"Violence is not our way," said a muscular man who had introduced himself as Lecturer Paulo Wiegand.

"Our two erring colleagues will reflect on their transgressions," Associate Professor Gena Huong said softly, "and tell you themselves how remorseful they are."

Troi endured the muttered expressions of regret,

offered in almost identical language, as patiently as she could. These people were irrational, deluded, and frightened, but were managing to control themselves; she would not do anything to anger them.

Three people left the room and returned with trays laden with food and drink, which they set on the floor in front of Troi and Chang. "This food is from the sea," a young woman told her. "We eat no fish and no animal flesh at all, and certainly nothing even distantly related to the nereids, but these vegetables and fruits do come from our oceans." Troi stared at the leafy green vegetables and brightly colored fruits on her tray, but did not feel like eating.

Chang was not eating, either. "When this is all over," Teodora was saying to him, "perhaps you can visit for a while. Your captain won't mind that, will he? Maybe you'll even want to settle here permanently someday."

The young woman, Troi thought, was oblivious to their situation, to the possible future consequences of her group's ill-considered actions, even, apparently, to Chang's increasingly obvious irritation.

"I should have been more understanding, Junshing," Teodora continued. "I didn't have to let Starfleet come between us. You do care, don't you? Otherwise, you wouldn't be here now." Chang glanced at Troi, raised a brow, and rolled his eyes slightly. Troi tried not to grimace.

"Riker to Troi." The voice was coming from the portable transceiver next to Chang. "Entrance into wormhole is imminent."

"Still here," Troi said, leaning toward the transceiver. "Still safe." There was no point mentioning her minor injury now, or Chang's brief struggle with Landon and his associate.

"We'll beam you back as soon as it's over and we can get within transporter range. Riker out."

Teodora raised a hand to her cheek, looking terrified. The reality of the risks they still faced had finally penetrated to her. Chang reached for Troi and gripped her hand.

Chapter Ten

ON THE VIEWSCREEN, the green-and-blue planet was a stately ship of life nearing the port of the wormhole. Picard strained forward in his seat, holding his breath, as if he might somehow miss the entry between heartbeats.

"We're holding it steady and stable," La Forge said, "and the wormhole's finally large enough!" His voice quavered, as if he did not quite believe that it was all happening as planned.

Picard felt a surge of hope as he stared at the screen, even though he knew that small accelerations and decelerations of the planet were already shifting tectonic plates, opening and closing fault lines, rocking bodies of water into motions that might swell into monstrous waves. Volumes of atmosphere were moving against their usual patterns of heat flow, and polar ice fields were cracking. The planet was not a rigid ball, but a fragile, elastic layering of crust and mantle, liquid and solid cores, spinning at sixteen hundred kilometers per hour and moving toward the hole at more than one hundred thousand kilometers per hour. The smallest changes in these motions would cost lives—and it could not be otherwise. A planet was not the *Enterprise,* which could control gravity and the unwanted effects of inertia and acceleration.

"It's going to work," Riker said, rising to his feet. "It's really going to work."

"Epic Three in the side pocket," La Forge said. That sounded more like Geordi. Picard almost laughed in relief. Miles O'Brien reached over and slapped Veronica Sorby on her back; she let out a raucous laugh. The renewed wave of hope that Picard felt sweep across the personnel on the bridge was almost tangible, filling them all with renewed energy and determination.

Then, as he watched, something seemed to cut across a portion of the planet's northern hemisphere, just above the northern continent and just below the polar icecap, as if the planet were an apple being thrown through a piano wire at two hundred kilometers an hour.

For a moment, Picard did not realize what he was seeing. Then he knew that it was the narrow edge of the wormhole, so thin that it could not be seen, fine enough to cut blood vessels in half. If anyone was standing in its path, the boundary would slice, cleanly in two, every cell it encountered, right down

to the smallest platelet. The action was swift, reminding him of the old trick of pulling a tablecloth
out from under plates, glasses, and silverware.

"No!" Riker shouted as the small section of Epictetus III separated from the rest of the planet and
began to pass above the wormhole, continuing in the
planet's orbit.

"The hole," La Forge was saying with dismay, "it
twitched downward suddenly. Nothing we could
do . . ."

Maybe it wouldn't cause too much harm, Picard
told himself, clutching at any reason for hope. On
Epictetus III, air and water would already be rushing
in to seal the wound, then exploding into mountain
ranges of live, volcanic steam. But the severed piece
had been far from the planet's centers of population
and away from the sites where people had gone to
wait out the passage. Most of the Epictetans still had
a chance to survive any additional seismic and
atmospheric disturbances caused by this unforeseen
wounding.

While he was still watching the viewscreen, the
small inverted plate of ocean and ocean floor, suddenly deprived of the planet's gravity, was stripped
of everything that was not firmly attached. Irregu-
larly shaped masses of ice and water, of stones and
soil, bits and pieces almost too small to be seen,
lifted slowly and gracefully from the plate, leaving
only the bare crust. The pieces were forming un-
countable billions of tiny globes, with their surfaces
flashing to vapor. The vapors crystallized, becoming
trillions of glittering points of light, a gigantic snowstorm in space.

"Captain!" Iris Liang cried out at her mission operations station. Picard jumped to his feet, hearing the desperation in her voice, and turned to face the science officer. "Sensors show an installation on that fragment," she went on. He turned back to the screen, but could not see anything through the blizzard. "Location verified," Liang murmured, but by then Picard had guessed at the horrible truth. "It's the Tireos Oceanographic Institute."

"Distress call coming in," another officer called out.

Riker sat down at his station and leaned forward. "It's Troi," he said, "calling for help. She and Chang are on that fragment."

Picard's stomach twisted inside him. "Troi!" he shouted as the wormhole swallowed Epictetus III. "Troi! Chang!" But there was no answer.

Chang had let go of Troi's hand. Teodora was whispering something to him. Suddenly Troi felt herself being hurled forward, as if being yanked by a gigantic rubber band.

She flew past the tank, dimly aware that others were flying helplessly toward the walls, and caught a glimpse of water shooting in a wide stream from the tank. The two nereids hit the wall with a sickening snap. Someone screamed, but the scream was cut short. Troi threw up her arms as she struck the wall and heard thuds as others hit the surface near her.

For a moment, she was afraid to move. Then, gradually, she became aware that she was still lying against the wall, that she had not fallen to the floor, and that there was water around her. She glanced to her left and saw a heap of bodies lying on the wall, as if it were a floor.

Someone was weeping; she heard moans, and struggled to understand what was happening, then saw the portable transceiver lying at an arm's length from her. She wriggled toward the transceiver and reached for it, hoping it still worked, and touched the Send control.

"Troi to *Enterprise,* Troi to *Enterprise*—we need help. Don't know what's going on. Can you hear me? We need help. Troi out."

The transceiver was silent. She hooked its strap over a metal wall brace, wondering why it and she were still on the wall instead of having fallen to the floor. Far above her, she saw the opposite wall, insisting to her that it was now the room's ceiling. She sat up and saw people strewn across the wall on which she was sitting; several bodies lay in a heap. The water tank was on its side; the nereids, covered in blood, were obviously dead. Cushions were scattered everywhere.

A few people sat up. The Tireos Institute, Troi realized, had suffered a gravitational or inertial change of some kind. She could feel a weak gravitational force now. As she got to her feet, she saw Teodora crawling toward Chang.

"Jun-shing, Jun-shing," Teodora moaned; she looked up at Troi. "Help him."

Troi knelt next to Chang and reached for her tricorder, but she could sense nothing from him— no feelings, no emotions, no sensations at all. She set the tricorder for a mediscan and passed it over him, knowing even as she did so that it was a useless gesture.

"Teodora," she said at last, "he's gone."

Teodora shrieked. Troi seized her by the shoulders and held her. Teodora screamed again. Troi scanned her quickly, then put her tricorder away. "Listen to me!" She clutched Teodora's arm. "All you have are some bruises. You have to help me with the others. Do you understand?"

Teodora nodded, her whole body trembling.

"Come with me." Troi got up and pulled the other woman to her feet. They crept slowly along the wall to a group of four people, obviously dazed, their emotions in turmoil; one of the men looked up at Troi with wild, crazed eyes.

"You said we'd be all right," Gena Huong muttered, shaking her head. "You said we would be all right."

Troi checked the four quickly with her tricorder; one man had bruises, another had a concussion, a woman had fractured two ribs. "That woman's ribs must be bound," Troi said to the uninjured man. "She broke two. Do you know how to handle it?"

"Yes," the man replied.

"Use your shirt for a bandage." Troi led Teodora toward the next group. They lay in a heap, and she could not sense anything from them. Again she took out her tricorder to verify the deaths. Ashley Harris was one of them, her neck broken. Paulo Wiegand's body was next to Harris's. Kwame Landon was gone, his corpse lying not far from the bodies of his beloved nereids.

Troi continued her grim task, scanning every

person in the room, alive or dead. Teodora followed her, helping to make slings for injured arms and propping pillows under broken legs. Of the forty-two people in the room, ten were dead, three unconscious, and the rest had injuries ranging from slight contusions to fractured limbs.

It could have been much worse, Troi told herself; they were lucky that the room's only furniture had been cushions, and that no one had been crushed by the water tank. Then she remembered that Ensign Chang Jun-shing was dead.

"What's happened?" one woman called out.

"A quake," a bearded man said. "Was it a quake? What's going to happen to us?"

"It wasn't a quake," Troi replied, certain of that much. "Somehow, we've lost most of our gravity."

"I do feel much lighter," a young woman said. "How can that be?"

"This gravity can't be more than that of a large asteroid," an older man said, "but that's impossible—how could the whole planet—"

"I don't know," Troi said.

"Something's happened," the bearded man said. "The plan didn't work, did it? Your captain's plan didn't work, and now—"

"Please stay calm," Troi insisted. "You're all safe for now." She doubted that was true. "I'm going to try to take a look at what's outside. Just wait here and don't move around. I sent out a distress call to the *Enterprise,* so Captain Picard will already know we're here. I promise you that he'll help us." But she knew that immediate help from the starship was not likely.

She found that she was able to creep along the wall of the circular room if she moved slowly in the lighter gravity. It was as though the institute had been turned on its side. She came to the doorway that led into the small room with the wide window; the door was closed. Troi feared that the door's mechanism might not work, but then, as she touched it with her foot, the door slowly slid open.

She stretched out on the wall and peered through the doorway. She could see the oval viewport from here; it revealed a snow-swept desert landscape instead of an ocean floor. A hazy sun was trying to burn through the blizzard, and it seemed to be growing brighter. Had the nova come already, stripping away the oceans? What could have reduced the gravity of Epictetus III to that of an asteroid? It made no sense at all.

Then a possible answer came to her. She was no longer on the planet, but on a fragment torn from it in some way. The snowstorm was the head of a comet, and the institute was now at the new comet's center.

Troi felt weak as she crawled back from the passageway. She took a deep breath and felt her lungs straining, then moved toward the display panel next to the door. The gauges told her what she already suspected, that the station was losing air.

She went back to where the survivors were waiting and took Teodora aside. "Don't say anything," Troi murmured, "and don't react when I tell you this. Air is leaking out of this place. I assume you have emergency tanks. Do you?"

Teodora nodded. "We've got some oxygen tanks with our diving equipment, for when we used to—"

"Can you get to those tanks?" Troi interrupted.

"I think so. They're kept in a storage room." Teodora clutched at Troi's sleeve. "The emergency air system should be coming on."

"Unless it's damaged." Troi glanced toward the others. "You know these people better than I do, Teodora. Find three or four who aren't badly hurt and who won't panic, and take them with you to get those tanks. I'm going to contact the *Enterprise* again."

"Do you think—"

"Just get the tanks!"

Teodora left her. Troi went to the transceiver, wondering if her earlier message had reached the ship, if this one would get through, if the *Enterprise* was trying to raise her and had been unable to contact her.

She pressed her fingers against the Send plate. "Troi to *Enterprise,* Troi to *Enterprise.* We need help." She looked at Chang, lying nearby, and felt a sudden tightness in her throat. "Troi to *Enterprise.*" Tears sprang to her eyes, but she was still too stunned, too shaken, to weep.

"The planet's gone in," Riker said, gazing at the viewscreen. Epictetus III had vanished into the faint glow of the wormhole. "I hope they make it to their new sun." He leaned over his controls. "Riker to Troi, Riker to Troi."

Picard gritted his teeth. The planet could be suffering any number of disasters by now, and his ship was still in danger. They could lose both the planet and the *Enterprise,* Data had said. Picard knew that the worst-case scenario was still possible.

"Troi to *Enterprise."* Her voice, weak as it was, seemed to fill the bridge.

"Deanna!" Riker shouted. "Can you hear me?"

"Affirmative . . . think the transceiver was partially damaged. We're here, in what was the Tireos Institute's undersea base. There's almost no gravity. What happened?"

"A small piece of Epictetus Three was sliced off by the edge of the wormhole," Picard replied. "You're on that piece. Is the base still airtight?"

"No . . . losing air slowly. Using emergency tanks from diving equipment, but they won't last longer than two or three hours for all of us. Thirty-two survivors, three of them seriously hurt and unconscious, twelve more with broken bones. Captain Picard . . . Wil . . ." Troi's voice faded out for a moment. "Ensign Chang is among the dead."

The news had the force of a blow. Riker's face contorted; Picard's hands grasped the sides of his chair. In all the years that he had been a starship captain, the pain of losing someone under his command had never lessened.

"I'm sorry," Riker said, and Picard knew that Riker would be thinking of how he had chosen Chang for the away team, how he had sent him to the undersea installation with Troi, that he should have gone there himself as commander of the away team and was alive now because he had not gone, because Picard had ordered him to stay aboard.

"Data," Picard said, "you heard all of that. What can we do?"

"I am not sure, Captain," Data replied. "The nova will go in less than two hours. We no longer have enough time to restart our warp engines and escape. Therefore, we have no choice but to follow Epictetus Three through the wormhole, and we can accomplish that only if we start our impulse engines immediately."

Picard frowned. "Can we approach the fragment, close enough to beam the survivors aboard, and still make the hole?"

"We can approach," Data said, "to a distance of less than forty thousand kilometers and get a fix on Counselor Troi and those with her, then set an entry trajectory for the hole. But having only two hours in which to accomplish this is, as you might put it, cutting it close."

"Do we have impulse power?" Picard asked.

"You have it now," La Forge replied.

"Ensign Sorby," Picard said to the officer at the command station, "you're supposed to be a good pilot."

"One of the best pilots who ever came out of Starfleet Academy." The young woman hunched forward over her console. "If I do say so myself."

"You have a chance to prove that now," Picard said. "Follow that fragment and get us within transporter range and away in the best possible time."

"Yes, sir. Plotting and entering fastest course maneuver now."

Picard looked toward Riker. "Number One, get to

the transporter room on deck six and prepare to beam survivors aboard."

Riker was already out of his seat and heading aft. "O'Brien, come with me," Riker called out. "Liang, take over at ops." O'Brien bolted from his chair and followed Riker to the turbolift as Liang hurried forward to his station.

"Hang on, Troi," Picard said, "and be ready to beam up. We're coming to get you!"

"It'll be all right," Troi said to the people trapped with her, trying to keep her voice steady. "They're coming to take us out. Your world has passed into the wormhole, except for this fragment. They'll beam us aboard and then we'll follow in the *Enterprise.*" Before the nova flares, she added silently to herself, and suddenly imagined the planet in the wormhole, with the air and ocean surging into the area that had been cut away, then rising in massive clouds of steam.

Teodora and the three people who had gone with her had found only enough tanks for ten people. Slightly injured people were sharing air with their more severely injured companions. Teodora was kneeling next to the three unconscious people, holding the mask over each of their faces in turn, then scanning them again with Chang's tricorder. Troi inhaled, gasping slightly; it was becoming increasingly difficult to breathe. A man passed a breathing mask to her; she drew in some of the oxygen. Decompression would soon affect them, bringing on light-headedness; their blood would begin to fizz like carbonated water.

"You," Troi said, gesturing at two of the men. "Move the people with broken legs over there." She pointed to the people Teodora was tending. "Captain," she continued, leaning closer to the transceiver, "we have to beam up the most severely injured people first. They're about seven meters away from me. Ensign Chang—" She swallowed hard. "Ensign Chang's body is near them. You can get a fix on them using his communicator."

"Transporter room," Riker's voice replied. "Riker here, and I've got O'Brien with me. Can you hold on until we're closer?"

"Yes," Troi said, willing it to be so.

"Steady," Picard said as the *Enterprise* neared the fragment. It had taken nearly an hour to build up enough impulse velocity to overtake the piece of Epictetus III on the far side of the wormhole. The tiny portion cut from the planet had been receding from the ship at more than ninety-five thousand kilometers an hour, with an initial distance from the *Enterprise* of nearly nine hundred thousand kilometers.

"Data," Picard continued, "I assume the hole will still be open when we come back to enter."

"I think it will last that long," Data replied from main engineering, "but we are no longer keeping it open and stable with our suncore power feed. There is no way to tell how long it will be before it begins to drift into chaos."

More and bigger risks, Picard thought, on top of the ones we're already running. To abandon Troi was unthinkable, but might become necessary; she would tell him herself to leave her there rather than put his ship at too great a risk.

"Warp drive is still offline," he said.

"For a minimum of ten hours," La Forge agreed, "too late to outrun the nova."

"Ensign Sorby," Picard said, "how soon?"

"Closing."

As the comet's core, shrouded by mist and haze, grew larger on the viewscreen, Picard thought of sailing ships overtaking whales, and wondered how Epictetus III was faring during its passage through the wormhole. Possibly it was already through to the other side, but perhaps not; time was hard to measure inside a wormhole. He was, he realized, trying to stretch out time himself, since a nova's bloom could not be predicted exactly; even a mistake of fifteen minutes would prove fatal to his ship.

That was frightening enough, but an even worse fear was that Epictetus III had not emerged into a suitable orbit around the target star, but instead was somewhere in interstellar space, already starting to lose heat. People might be gazing up at a black sky empty of a sun, knowing that eventually, in a matter of weeks, the air would grow colder, then flow as liquid. Or the planet might have come out too close to the target sun, even collided with it; or Epictetus III's axial tilt might have become chaotic. The possible wrong turns were simultaneously nightmarish and dramatic, but there had been no choice except to risk them. He wondered if that lack of choice could possibly comfort him if the number of lives lost turned out to be very large.

"Captain," Data said then, "I have accomplished all that I can here. I am leaving everything in Geordi's capable hands and requesting permission to come to the bridge."

"Permission granted." Picard forced himself to dismiss the realm of pure possibility from his mind, concentrating on what was likely, what they had planned for—that Epictetus III and its people would at least survive the nova, even if that meant having to evacuate the planet later on, when more starships could be sent to do so.

He watched the screen as the *Enterprise* pivoted and overtook the fragment tail-first, impulse engines decelerating to bring the ship into a near pause over the fragment, ready to beam the survivors aboard and poised to accelerate toward the presumed safety of the wormhole. The coming nova was to his right now, its steadily increasing glare beginning to brighten the edge of the viewscreen.

The fragment appeared at the bottom of the screen. Small patches of surface were visible through the snow. As Picard watched, more snow erupted in giant streamers from vents in the fragment of seafloor.

Data emerged from the aft turbolift and hurried to his bridge operations station, relieving Iris Liang.

"We're at thirty-five thousand kilometers," Data said.

Picard touched his communicator. "Picard to Riker. Fix on Troi and beam survivors aboard!" Then he leaned forward and peered at the snowy piece of crust that was all that remained of Epictetus

III in this solar system. The ice geysers were still spewing, in what seemed to him an oddly festive way.

Lieutenant Jake Dane was on duty in the transporter room on deck 6, along with Lieutenant Jane Webber, when Riker arrived. Miles O'Brien went to the console to supervise the operation. Riker let out a sigh, relieved to have all three of the officers there with him, just in case anything went wrong.

But nothing could go wrong with the transporter. He refused to believe that something would.

"We're locked on," Webber said, her Australian accent more pronounced than usual, as Beverly Crusher and the emergency medical team Riker had summoned entered the room.

"Deanna!" Riker said, touching his insignia.

"Yes," her voice replied, sounding even weaker than it had earlier. "Got to—air pressure dropping to critical. Get the people with Chang aboard first."

"Gotcha," Dane muttered, his lanky body slouching over the console. "Beaming up Counselor Troi—we'll have her aboard in a moment."

"Survivors aboard, Captain," Jane Webber's voice announced, "and on their way to sickbay."

"Lieutenant Commander Troi isn't with them," Jake Dane added, "but we'll get her up as soon as possible."

Picard was not surprised. Troi had probably stood aside at the last moment, choosing to be transported with the last group. The *Enterprise* was still closing with the fragment, and would do so until its closest planned approach, less than fifteen thousand kilometers; that would make possible the use of the shorter-range emergency transporters if the main ones malfunctioned. Everyone would be brought safely aboard. Already, he knew, six people were coming aboard every two minutes.

Then Picard thought of the away-team member they had lost. "Number One," he said, "see that Ensign Chang's body is brought aboard when all the survivors are safe. He was a fine young officer, and I want a proper funeral for him."

"Yes, sir," Riker's voice said softly. Perhaps Chang's body should lie on Epictetus III, the world his starship had saved—if the planet had survived. Picard hoped that Worf, Mehta, and Bodonchar would not be sharing his grave.

He waited, staring at the image of the fragment on the viewscreen, until Lieutenant Webber's voice said, "Webber to bridge—all survivors aboard, Captain, including Lieutenant Commander Troi!"

"We've brought Ensign Chang aboard, too," O'Brien said softly.

Picard sat back and watched as the screen's starboard side caught a brief glimpse of the threatening nova. Then he looked back along the now empty orbit of Epictetus III, where the wormhole waited.

"Full ahead!" he ordered.

Chapter Eleven

THE FLOOR LURCHED under Worf, then rushed up to meet him, slamming against his arms as he fell.

He lay against the mirrored surface, feeling the ground shudder. A major quake, he thought, and it was hitting close enough to Boreas to knock down a good share of the city's buildings.

The trembling subsided. Ganesa was lying near him; he got to his feet and helped her up. Dorcas Dydion sat near Bodonchar, the hood of her coat thrown back, arms wrapped tightly around her legs, obviously frightened but unhurt. The other people with them were looking up at the monumental alien sculptures as if preparing to pray to them.

"That was a bad one," one of Dydion's aides said at last. "I've never felt a quake that strong."

The planet must be in the wormhole by now, Worf realized as he went to the base of the nearest giant statue and studied it, then scanned it with his tricorder. The structure seemed unaffected by the quake; his quick scan had not revealed even the smallest of cracks. Even so, he wondered how much more punishment the building could take.

"Worf," Ganesa called out, and then the ground heaved and threw him forward again, and continued to buck under him. This quake, he realized, would be even worse than the first.

As the *Enterprise* came up on what had to be called the "back" of the wormhole, meaning the part that could not be entered, Picard thought of the stationary breach as a hole in the endless wall of space-time, and wondered what would happen if something ran into the anomaly from this side. Would there be anything there?

He waited as the ship's course took it above the wormhole's position and farther back along the missing planet's orbit.

Then, still according to the plotted maneuver, the impulse engines stopped, and the starship pivoted one hundred and eighty degrees to face the mouth of the wormhole. The threatening sun, growing brighter by the minute, raced across the center of the viewscreen and disappeared, leaving an electric glare at the screen's left.

"Captain!" La Forge shouted from main engineering. "The wormhole is oscillating up and down."

Picard tensed in his chair. "Can we enter?" he asked, his eyes on the screen.

At operations, Data peered at his console, then looked up at the bridge viewscreen. "I am not sure," Data replied. At the wormhole's edges, stars were flickering and being stretched into strings, as if someone were trying to redo the cosmic scenery.

Commander Riker came back to the bridge and hurried to his station. "There may be a window," La Forge's voice continued, "where the wormhole's motion will not touch us, as long as the motion isn't too wide."

"Scanning now," Data said.

"Scanning here, too," La Forge called out. "Yes— if the oscillation doesn't increase—we can enter, at least."

"I agree," Data said.

"Is the wormhole still completely open all the way through?" Picard asked. "I'd hate to have you tell me that we have to power it up again."

There was a short silence before La Forge said, "To be safe, I'd say maybe we *should* power it up again, just to make sure the wormhole stays open— not only for us, but possibly for the planet. What do you say, Data?"

"I am fairly certain," Data murmured, "that the planet has already emerged."

"That's my guess, too," La Forge responded. "The wormhole seems stable enough now, by what we can measure from here, but I have no idea for how long. No one's ever done this before."

Picard stood up, paced in the direction of the viewscreen, then looked around the bridge. "Well, do we go through? Do any of you object?"

"Not me," Veronica Sorby said as she looked up at him.

"I say we go," Iris Liang said, and the other science officers nodded in agreement.

"Of course we have to go." Riker was scowling. "Do we really have any choice?" he continued. "It's the wormhole or the nova, but what's the use if the hole has gone bad?"

Data turned around, glancing from Riker to Picard, then said, "To tap the suncore power feed again at this late stage in the nova's progress might be futile if the wormhole has in fact remained stable all the way through. But if it has not, we might not have enough time to benefit from shoring it up— because doing that would quicken the nova still more. We could be caught in it before we can shut down the tap and go through. However, it is likely that if we enter the wormhole now, we will emerge on the other side."

"But in what condition?" Picard asked.

"That is difficult to assess, Captain," Data replied. "At this point, as with Epictetus Three, the most important consideration is that we survive in whatever way possible."

"I have to agree with that much," Riker said. "Some chance is obviously better than zero."

Picard studied both officers carefully, but it was clear that they had no more to say. He knew what Data was saying: that the *Enterprise* might come through heavily damaged, meaning they might have to abandon the ship, use emergency evacuation procedures to transport everyone to Epictetus III—

assuming that the planet was there and in reasonable shape, that their shuttlecraft weren't badly damaged, and that their transporters still worked—and then call for help from there. A crippled, perhaps irreparably damaged starship, evacuation to a possibly unstable planetary environment—he didn't like it at all, but Data was right: survival in any condition had to be paramount.

Picard heard the aft turbolift whisk open. He looked back as Deanna Troi came out on the bridge and took her seat at his left in the command area. There was a bruise on her forehead, her uniform was stained and had rips at the shoulders and knees, and her face was drawn. She had not rested, or even taken the time to change her uniform, but had come to the bridge in case she might be needed. He felt a sudden pride in her, and in all of his crew.

"I thought you'd be in sickbay, Counselor," Picard said, "or else resting in your quarters."

"Dr. Crusher says I'm fit for duty," Troi said softly, "and I wanted to be here."

"Welcome back." Picard looked away from Troi, knowing that she had to be at her station, to see their venture through to either disaster or success. He was, he supposed, no longer in a position to deny his crew anything.

"Geordi," Picard said, "how much longer before we regain warp capacity?"

"Seven or eight hours," La Forge replied.

"Can we hurry it up?"

"By only an hour or two at best."

"Maybe we should wait," Riker said, "and go into the wormhole only when we absolutely have to. The

206

nova may be late . . ." He did not sound convincing to Picard.

"That is possible, Captain," Data said, "but then we might face the even greater risk of a deteriorating wormhole, one from which we may never emerge."

"But the wormhole might already be impassable," Picard replied, knowing that Riker was about to say it.

"We have to risk it anyway," Lieutenant Commander Liang said. "Nova's close now."

"Nova's gathering real steam," La Forge said from main engineering. "I think it's going to blow."

"Mr. Data," Picard said, "an unambiguous recommendation, please."

Data's yellowish eyes gazed at him steadily. "I believe we have just enough time to power up the wormhole, whether it needs it or not, and enter before the nova strikes."

Picard nodded. "Then if we take that insurance policy, I think we're ready." Riker glanced at him, but Picard could not read his expression.

"I agree," Troi said, and Riker looked a little more at ease.

On the viewscreen, the wormhole was still playing its elusive game, blotting out a portion of the starfields, smearing stars into lines near its edges. I might have already sent a planet to its destruction, Picard told himself. He might not be blamed for it, but he was responsible; there had been no alternative except to let millions of people die without trying to do anything for them. Small consolation, he thought, if both the planet and the *Enterprise* were lost.

"Geordi," he said, "open the suncore feed and repeat the procedure for opening the wormhole."

"Yes, Captain. Automatic repeat now."

As Picard waited, invisible fingers of force reached into the wormhole, energies stolen from the coming fury of the nova, playing with the stage set of the cosmos, tearing open the scenery to meet the demands of imperiled intelligent life.

"Geordi," Picard said, leaning forward, "cut away when we can't wait any longer."

"That's just about now, Captain."

Data said, "The wave front of the nova is on its way, and will reach us in—"

"Impulse power—full ahead!" Picard ordered, looking into the blackness of the wormhole, seeing the flare of gas and debris entering the hole.

"We're going in," La Forge announced as the wormhole grew to cover the viewscreen. Data and Sorby strained forward at their consoles. As the wormhole blotted out the forward view, Picard felt as though the ship was suddenly motionless in an infinite blackness, trapped in a solid black substance.

Then he felt a sharp jolt and grabbed the sides of his chair.

Two of the engineers were thrown to the floor. La Forge turned toward them, noticed that they were getting up and did not seem seriously hurt, then turned back to the display console in front of him.

"The wormhole twitched, Captain," La Forge said. "Just our luck to go through during a really big twitch." He looked up from the display console to the master situation monitor on the wall. Lights were flashing on the stern of the cutaway display of the *Enterprise,* telling him the bad news even as the voice reports were beginning to come in. "We didn't quite make the window."

"Damage report!" Captain Picard said.

"It's clipped our tail some," La Forge replied. "We've lost three of the Bussard ramscoop warp-field coils and our aft torpedo launcher."

"No life-support affected," Anita Obrion said.

"Just luck," La Forge said. "Means we can ignore the damage for now." He did not have to add that the loss might cost them dearly if they needed to rely on their warp drive later, when and if they emerged from the wormhole.

The sun had set, and now the stars were gone as well. The heavens had faded, to be replaced by a black vault banking insistent flames. The lights of Epira winked on, small jewels surrounded by darkness.

Czeslaw Peladon's terrace rumbled under his feet; he heard the ground moan. The furela birds were usually out on the beach at night, scurrying among the shell-shaped lights looking for any crumbs left behind by daytime visitors, but the birds had flown away as soon as the sky turned black. Even the ocean had retreated, fleeing east and leaving beached fish behind.

The silence of the deserted city was upon him once more. It was time for him to leave his house, to go to the site west of Epira, the site that might not become a mass grave after all. There was a chance for all of them now; his world might escape the nova. Krystyna might need him later if her parents did not make it to safety. His aides, after Captain Picard's completely unexpected announcement, would be trying to maintain order and wondering where he was.

And then a terrible thought seized him: the sublight ships, if they survived, would become a heroic monument to his memory, but only if his world perished; and deep within himself, surrounded by an army of shame, he heard a voice without conscience wishing it, even if it meant his death. He would live out his life in disgrace only if his world survived. Captain Picard and his crew might have taken his last chance at greatness from him.

Peladon forced himself to rise. He went into the house, and the darkness seemed to follow him, making the lights inside glow more faintly. He descended the stairs to the garden, where his flitter awaited him. The ground shook again; that quake had been closer.

A sound came to him from the east, the singing sound of a distant, inhuman voice holding the same note. He got into the flitter. As he touched the control panel, the ground lurched again; his flitter was quickly aloft. He began to fly west, then turned back for another look at the city, wondering, as he came in very low, if he would ever see Epira again.

The singing sound was closer, growing into a roar. Streaks of light shot across the black sky, illuminating the ocean below. Peladon saw the wall then, a black wall of water that towered above Epira's tallest buildings, a wall so high that he could not see the top. That was where the ocean had gone—to rise up into this wall.

The tidal wave rushed upon Epira with a deafening howl. Peladon slapped his control panel, knowing even as his flitter shot up higher that he would not have time to rise above the watery cliff. The wave stood in the air, still far from breaking, a glistening black mirror of frozen time—

—and he passed into it.

"View aft," Picard ordered.

The viewscreen switched in time to show something that reminded him of a black shutter closing behind the ship, cutting short the light from the nova's seething electric glare as the *Enterprise* slipped behind the cosmic scenery.

"We seem to be going through smoothly," Data said after a few moments. "I register no bumps or asymmetries in the field around us. There appears to be plenty of room." Data's last words sounded as if they had been imperfectly recorded and were being played back at a slower speed.

Good, Picard thought, at least something's going right, but his thoughts seemed sluggish and prolonged. Time distortion, he told himself. But Hawking had said it wouldn't be this way; the twentieth-century physicist had missed something in his equations. Then Picard's mind locked and his thoughts came to a stop. . . .

* * *

The sky was dark, yet flickered as if a fire were raging behind a black curtain. Dalal Mehta sat inside the flitter with his parents, watching the sky and feeling the ground intermittently shudder.

They had been among the last to leave their city, to follow the swarm of flitters to the ancient site in the north of the vast, flat plain of tarendra grass. Dalal's mother had refused to leave Hierapolis until she had convinced three neighboring families to come with them.

"If they wanted to stay in their homes," Dalal's father said when they were finally in their flitter, "would it have mattered? Going to the sites isn't likely to save anyone."

"Starfleet's up to something," Dalal's mother replied. "I think the *Enterprise* officers have other reasons for wanting this evacuation. I know my own daughter—Ganesa was hiding something from us. There was something she wanted to tell us but couldn't—I'm sure of that." She sniffed. "I have an instinct for such things."

The Mehtas had landed their flitter only to find themselves at the end of a long line of evacuees, packs on their backs, moving slowly toward the huge pit of the excavated site. Several aides to Minister Nowles moved up and down the line, directing people and soothing those who seemed most frightened. Occasionally, people halted, refusing to walk down the massive ramps into the crater of metallic monoliths. Other aides guided them to one side, to calm them and to keep them from holding up the line.

"No need to rush," an aide said to the Mehtas.

"There's plenty of time for everyone to get safely inside." Dalal knew it was important to prevent panic. His parents had often complained that Rohin Nowles was a windbag and a cynic, but the minister and his aides were keeping good order here.

And then waves of people were suddenly turning away from the pit and moving back to the field of flitters, pushing back those behind them. Dalal struggled to keep his footing as people pressed in around him. Someone shouted, and then a council aide with a sound amplifier was moving toward the crowd of people near the Mehtas. "Message!" the aide shouted, holding his amplifier disk over his head, "message from the *Enterprise*," and then Dalal and the hundreds around him heard of their miraculous chance at deliverance.

The Mehtas, unable to push their way through the crowds that were soon surging away from the site, had gone back to their flitter to wait. We have a chance now, Dalal thought, clinging to that thought, remembering the evening when his parents had struggled to tell him that a nova would soon destroy their world, that they and everyone they knew were doomed. They had sat up with him, answering his questions, soothing him, holding him as he wept in terror. Their calm courage had made it a little easier to ignore the hollow, sick feeling inside himself and to conquer the intermittent surges of panic that threatened to overwhelm him. Now, there was hope.

The ground shuddered, as it had been doing for some time, then shook under them. Dalal grabbed at his father's arm. The plain rippled again, as if it had suddenly been transformed into a liquid surface.

Dalal gripped his armrests, feeling nauseated, wishing that the rolling, wavelike motion would stop.

He cried "Father—" and the word caught in his throat, then left him in a long low growl. The ground was heaving more slowly now, rising and then falling again, and suddenly Dalal was unable to move.

The air was heavy. He felt it pour slowly into his lungs—and then, from the grassland near their vehicle, thousands of mansi flew up from the tall tarendra blades as time regained its flow. All around, as far as he could see in the soft yellow light cast by the flitters, millions of the tiny creatures hovered, colorful flowers dancing on air, and then they abruptly fluttered to the ground.

Dalal opened the door near him, leaned out, and quickly reached for the mansi that had fallen near him, but their wings were already extended in death, their bright blues and yellows and reds fading even as he watched.

Rychi had heard Captain Picard's announcement on his communicator, just as he was about to leave his plasteen-domed office. After that, the archaeologists, except for Ponselle, joined Asela Ibanez in the gray-walled chamber to watch the severing of the sunlink as their world entered the wormhole. The flickering light and shadows on the walls suddenly vanished. The only light in the chamber now was the glow of a few globes near the arch.

The device that had kept the nova at bay had been destroyed by the nova it had held back for so long.

Asela and the others were still murmuring among themselves about the ancient technology. Rychi left the chamber and went up the ramps to the hallway, where Hakim Ponselle was sitting by the open doorway. There was nothing to be seen outside now except a blackness that had swallowed everything, but Ponselle seemed driven to keep watch there anyway.

"The nova might already have started," Rychi said as he sat down next to the older man. "The shadows on the walls below are gone now. Asela was saying earlier that if two Starfleet officers could come up with a plan to move this whole planet out of harm's way, then an ancient race with a technology far beyond ours should have been able to think of doing the same thing. So if they knew a nova was coming, why did they abandon this planet? Why didn't they take it with them?"

"We don't know that they abandoned it voluntarily," Ponselle said. "All we can say for sure is that the old ones suddenly up and disappeared."

Rychi contemplated all the etchings he had viewed, all the images and artifacts he had pored over in museums and at sites. The ships were a constant in the alien artwork, and yet some of the depictions seemed to be more than ships. Etchings that he had dated to the ancient civilization's most recent era had shown vessels so laden with people and provisions, even with animals and trees, that they seemed to be seagoing arks; a few had looked more like islands than ships. Islands sailing the high seas, he thought, and indeed some of the ancient maps had shown islands in places where none could be found now. Those maps had not agreed with one another, either; none of them showed the islands in the same locations. An ocean that was over ninety percent of Epictetus III's surface, only two relatively small continents, islands that seemed to wander . .

"To travel on the ocean here," Rychi heard himself say aloud, "to sail any distance from land, must have been incredibly frightening for them at first."

"You're not telling me anything we don't know," Ponselle muttered.

"Sailing a long way out to sea, far from land, and being able to get back would have been a real accomplishment," Rychi continued. "There would have been no place to land, not unless they either turned back the way they had come or kept going until they'd sailed practically around the world. They would have had to take a lot with them. Maybe ships, even large ones, weren't enough. Maybe their ships became more like islands."

"Samas, what are you—"

"Listen." The insight suddenly flared in Rychi's mind, blazing with the force of a nova. "Their ships, their oceangoing vessels—they were more like arks, or like seagoing habitats. They had to be— experience would have taught them that a lot of ships were never seen again, and their expeditions would have eventually shown them that there was nowhere beyond Themis and Metis to land. After a while, they would have been prepared for long voyages, for staying out on the ocean for years— maybe for good."

"I still don't—"

"Hakim, I think they might have finally abandoned their continents for the oceans. Maybe just a few did at first, and then others followed, and then all of them left, and that's why we look at their sites here and think that they suddenly vanished from this world."

Ponselle rubbed at his gray beard. "Don't tell me you've swallowed all that Tireos Institute nonsense."

"I'm not talking about the nereids," Rychi said. "The ancient people of this world might have lived on the sea, in island habitats, and then abandoned this planet just as they had abandoned the land earlier. They could have built mobile habitats to sail the ocean of space—they might be a culture of mobiles now, free of planets. Their earlier experience here, on the sea, would have prepared them for that kind of existence."

"You might have something there." Ponselle leaned forward, clearly excited. "You might—but then what's this place doing here?"

"They must have built it before they abandoned the land for the sea," Rychi replied, "when they needed a sunlink to warn them of when the nova was coming. But you always thought it might be more than just an alarm system of some sort. Maybe it was. They didn't need their planet anymore, so they left it for some future race. And maybe they left this installation in the hope that whoever settled here would be able to understand what the suncore link was and then discover how to use the suncore device to control the star, maybe even to get enough power to move this planet."

"Could be," Ponselle said, "but you're giving them a lot of credit for benevolence."

"And if this world's old ones left the land for the

sea," Rychi continued, "then it's from their homes on the sea that they would have left for space. That's where we might find more ruins, more recent sites—in the sea."

"If we get through this wormhole alive," Ponselle said.

Light blazed across the sky, died, and then filled the sky again. Rychi narrowed his eyes, then saw four curving bands of light heading in his direction.

Flitters, he realized, and got to his feet. Perhaps the people in them had gone into the desert to await death, and had then heard the communication from the *Enterprise.* They would be seeking shelter now, knowing they might live, and this site was the only shelter here.

Ponselle quickly stood up. "Hakim," Rychi said, "keep standing in this entrance—we have to keep it open so they can see it."

"But you don't know how many more flitters are behind that bunch."

"We'll shelter as many people as we can," Rychi said.

The flitters came closer, then landed several hundred paces away. The sky was still flashing. As the strangers got out of their flitters, they seemed to be moving in unconnected and discontinuous motions.

"Come on," Rychi shouted, "you've got to get inside," and then he saw other flitters behind them—ten, twelve, possibly more. A few had lights on under their domes, and he could see that they were crowded with passengers. Maybe there wouldn't be enough room for them all.

"Come on!" he shouted again. "Move!" The wind

was rising on the desert. Usually the most violent winds, the ones that raised the sand into giant funnels, blew from the east or the west. This wind was coming from the north, but he knew a big storm was coming.

"Hurry!" Rychi shouted, knowing that a flitter would be no protection against such a storm; a sand funnel could lift it and sweep it away. Two adults and two children ran past him on their way inside, followed by another family. "Hurry!"

Veils of sand were lifted by the wind, obscuring the more distant flitters. The people inside them might not be able to see the dimly lighted entrance where Ponselle was standing. Rychi left the entrance and ran for the nearest flitter, pressed the door open, and turned on both the light inside its cabin and the light band that circled the outside of the craft, then hurried to the next flitter. The wind gusted, almost lifting him from the ground. By the time he had turned on the inside and outside lights of five flitters, the sky was completely dark and the sand was lashing his face. Then he felt rain, a hot black stinging rain.

He staggered back to the entrance, guided by the lights. Ponselle caught him and hung on. The wind shrieked. The two men waited as more people made their way through the swirling sand to the space near the entrance illuminated by the flitters.

"Samas!" Ponselle shouted above the wind. "Got to close up!" Rychi waited, refusing to leave the entrance, until he was certain that there were no more people outside.

At last Ponselle pulled him inside; the door

whisked shut behind them. The shriek of the wind was gone, replaced by the whimpers of children and the gasps and whispers of adults. People sat along the ramp and in the hallway that led to Rychi's makeshift plasteen office.

"I notice some of you carried packs in here," Ponselle said. "I trust it's food and water. Think we better take inventory—we might have to last here awhile. Then—"

An invisible hand slammed Rychi to the floor. People shouted and screamed as the ground shook. Rychi heard a deep loud ringing, as if the alien station were a bell being rung by a giant. He reminded himself that the structure would hold, that it had been here for eons, that every scan ever done had confirmed that it could withstand even the most massive quakes. It would have to hold. He covered his head with his arms and waited for the shaking to stop.

Worf did not know how long the third quake had lasted. It had been even worse than the first two, jolting the ground, persisting until he thought it might never stop. The alien monument sheltering him and his companions might finally collapse around them and become their grave.

Then the ground was suddenly still. Worf managed to sit up only to find himself unable to move, unable to turn his head, unable even to breathe.

He sat there, facing Ganesa, who had awkwardly propped herself up with one arm, as if she had been frozen in the act of trying to get up. Worf realized that this might be exactly what had happened, that the wormhole through which they were traveling was slowing their perceptions of time. Yeoman Bodonchar was near Ganesa, caught in a crouch. The other people that he was able to see were not moving, either.

His thoughts seemed to be coming to him at normal intervals. Perhaps human beings were affected differently, or maybe the temporal distortion did not affect the firing of synapses and the activity of the brain and nervous system. Perhaps having his thought processes affected would have been preferable to this, to feeling that his body had become a prison. A mental eternity might pass while he sat here, his thoughts racing forward frantically inside a body trapped in one endlessly prolonged moment of time.

They had thought only of getting this planet through the wormhole and of making sure that the *Enterprise* was not caught by the nova. Worf found himself imagining an Epictetus III that might emerge to orbit its new sun, but with people driven mad by the temporal distortions they had endured.

Worf struggled to control his thoughts. He would not allow himself to go mad, not even if he had to sit here for a subjective eternity.

Then he saw Ganesa move, ever so slowly, as she raised herself into a sitting position. She opened her mouth and a deep rumbling came from her. "Woorrrrrrfff—"

There was a sudden rushing in his ears, and he found himself moving normally, able to stand up. "Worf," Ganesa said again. "Are you all right?"

221

"Yes." Worf shook himself, then helped her to her feet.

Bodonchar was standing up now, holding out his arm to one of Minister Dydion's aides. The aide stood up, then pushed his arm away, shouting, "I've got to get out of here!" The muscular yeoman grabbed the woman; she twisted in his grasp. "How do we know this building won't collapse and bury us? I have to get out of here!"

"You're safer here," Minister Dydion said as she quickly approached the woman. "If this structure were unsound, that last quake would surely have brought it down."

"I can't stay here!"

"You don't know what's out there," Dydion shouted back.

"I don't care!" the woman screamed. "I can't take it anymore!"

"You must, you foolish woman," Worf said in his deepest, most commanding voice. "We may still be traveling through the wormhole."

The woman clung to Dydion, looking terrified of Worf. Good, he thought; fear often worked to maintain order when reason failed. "The quakes may have made the outside even more hazardous," he continued. "Step outside, and another quake may shake a rock loose that would crush you. A tidal wave may be on the way, or have already struck— this structure could even be under water by now."

"Until we're sure of what it's like out there," Ganesa said, "we're better off waiting here."

"How are we going to know?" one of the two prisoners from the Tireos Institute asked. A security-force member gestured angrily at the man. "Sooner or later, we'll have to take our chances outside."

"Maybe we'll shove you out first," one of the five parents with them replied, "you and your accomplice. If you two don't die, then we'll know—"

"Enough!" Dydion shouted. "This isn't going to get us anywhere!" As if to emphasize her words, the floor trembled slightly under them.

"We will know it's safe," Worf said, "when the *Enterprise* contacts us." He gestured at the portable transceiver Bodonchar had carried inside earlier.

The Epictetans seemed convinced for the moment. Bodonchar let go of the woman he had been trying to calm, then went to Worf. "Maybe we should try to raise the *Enterprise* now," the yeoman said in a low voice. "Might as well find out how long we may have to last in here."

"I'll try to contact our ship," Worf replied. "You and Ensign Mehta watch the others. If any people try to leave, stun them with your phasers. If we must forcibly restrain them to save their lives, we shall."

Bodonchar nodded. Worf stomped toward the transceiver, cursing the Epictetans silently for the fools and cowards they were. Not all of them, of course. Minister Dydion was bearing up well, and his comrade Ganesa had not let him down.

He knelt by the transceiver and touched Send. "Worf to *Enterprise*, Worf to *Enterprise*, respond." There was nothing except a strange whistling sound. "Worf to *Enterprise*. Ensign Mehta, Yeoman Bodonchar, and I are safe with Minister Dydion and a few of her people. We are inside the archaeological site to the north of Boreas." The whistle rose to a high-pitched whine. "Worf to *Enterprise.*"

The ship might have been lost. Epictetus III might still be inside the wormhole, or might have emerged in an orbit too far from or too close to its new sun. If the *Enterprise* was lost, there might be no rescue for anyone who had survived on this planet, no time for other starships to reach them, no time for evacuation.

He would prepare himself for the worst. With the provisions Minister Dydion and her aides had brought inside from their flitters, they could all last for a little while. After that, it would be necessary to go outside, whatever awaited them there, to bring in the food and water the five parents had so carelessly left in their three flitters—assuming those flitters could be found. If the *Enterprise* was not heard from by then . . . he would not think further ahead than that right now.

He leaned over the transceiver. He would raise the other members of the away team. He should be able to contact them, given that they would still be on the planet. "Worf to Troi, Worf to Troi," he said, and wondered why she had not tried to communicate with him by now. Perhaps Troi and Chang had been harmed, or worse, by the people at the Tireos Institute; he swallowed the rage evoked by that thought. "Worf to Troi," he repeated, but there was no answer.

Chapter Twelve

TIME SWEPT HIM UP in its current, and sent him forward once more. Picard, his thoughts clear again, looked around the bridge.

Troi took a deep breath, then leaned back in her chair, shaking her head. Riker got to his feet and turned to face the science officers.

"We're all right," Iris Liang said.

"Frightening," Veronica Sorby murmured, glancing back at Picard. "Being stuck like that—it was even worse than being dead, more like having your own body turn into a coffin." She shuddered.

"Captain!" La Forge's voice called out from main engineering. "The wormhole is collapsing behind us."

"Full impulse," Picard ordered.

"We have full impulse power now," Data said from his forward position. "Obviously our second attempt to control the wormhole was incomplete. It is clear that we do not know what amounts of power are needed to open and control a wormhole in a predictable way."

"Did the planet go through?" Picard asked.

"That is difficult to say, Captain," Data replied. "It does not seem to be ahead of us."

"Will the collapse catch us?"

"Calculating the speed of collapse now," Data said.

If it caught up with his starship, Picard knew that there would be a moment of implosion and the *Enterprise* would simply cease to exist as the collapse swept on. If Epictetus III was still in the wormhole, the planet would share the same fate. He did not want to think of that possibility, that it had all been for nothing, and that he would know it in an instant before the end.

Some of the children had started screaming when the temporal distortion was past. They were quieting down now, some being calmed by friends or *Enterprise* crew members, others perhaps by their own pride or their fear of embarrassing themselves in front of strangers.

Guinan circled Ten-Forward, moving from one group to another, smiling, assuring the young ones that everything would be all right even as she worried about what might be happening on their world. Many of the children were clearly exhausted, but still refused to go to their assigned quarters to sleep.

She sympathized with them even more than they knew, having lost her own homeworld so long ago.

"It's because time isn't the same inside a wormhole," one dark-haired girl was explaining to a group of children. "That's why you felt that way, like everything had stopped." She was about eleven or twelve, Guinan guessed, older than the others. "Don't worry—we'll be all right once we get through to the other side."

"You seem to know something about wormholes," Guinan said.

"Not a whole lot." The girl looked up at her, and the contemplative look in the child's brown eyes made her seem older. "It's just that trying to understand what's going on keeps it from being as scary."

"I know exactly what you mean," Guinan said.

"What's going to happen to us?" a boy asked. "I mean, if we—if our world doesn't—"

"Don't even think about it," the girl said.

"That's good advice," Guinan murmured. "Don't even think about it." At least not until you have to, she added silently. She glanced toward the window ports, then sat down with the children.

"The collapse is slow," Data said, "so we are keeping ahead of it, but I cannot predict how long that will last."

Picard relaxed a little. "Time to exit?" he asked.

"Our sense of time is still being affected, Captain, so I cannot say."

"The collapse is gaining on us," La Forge's voice said.

"Captain," Data said, "our speed is now increasing."

Troi, who had been sitting on the edge of her chair, sank back against her seat. Picard let out a sigh of relief. "Good going, Geordi!"

"Thanks for the compliment, but it's not our doing," the chief engineer replied.

"Data?" Picard asked.

Data leaned over his console. "I believe I see. . . . The collapsing field of the wormhole behind us is pushing us forward, which means that the collapse may never reach us."

As Data was speaking, Picard saw flashes of light on the viewscreen. Then, suddenly, a bright yellow-white sun appeared, flooding the bridge with light. Picard narrowed his eyes against the brightness and glimpsed Epictetus III ahead, catching its new sun's light.

A jolt shook the *Enterprise.* "The wormhole has closed behind us," Data said.

"The planet's orbit," Picard said, hearing the anxiety in his own voice, "how is that?"

"Scanning now," Iris Liang said from behind him. "Appears nearly as predicted, but the planet's axial tilt is off by a degree."

Only a degree, Picard thought. Data had calculated it just about perfectly. He and Geordi had earned just about every citation and honor Starfleet could bestow, not that either of them would be thinking of that; saving a world and its inhabitants would be reward enough.

Everyone on the bridge was silent for a long time, seemingly content to gaze at the viewscreen as the marbled blue globe of Epictetus III grew larger. The upper half of the northern hemisphere was shrouded in a spreading pool of dark clouds, but otherwise the planet looked much the same. At last Veronica Sorby called out, "Whoo—ee!"

Troi laughed.

"Data," Riker said, "I'll never doubt you or Geordi again."

Data turned in his chair. "I do not think you will keep that promise, Commander," he said solemnly. "It is in the nature of human beings to doubt, and as our executive officer, being dubious of proposals and demanding that they be justified is one of your obligations."

Riker grinned. "You know, if we threw a party in your honor, to thank you for what you've done, you'd probably deliver a literal-minded stem-winder about exactly how you arrived at your plan that would put us all to sleep."

Data wrinkled his brow. "I believe a speech is often called for in such circumstances, but I would hope mine would not produce somnolence among the guests."

Riker chuckled. Epictetus III swelled on the screen; the officers on the bridge erupted into cheers.

"Entering orbit," Data said.

The sky was growing lighter in the east. In the west, a thick bank of clouds obscured part of the sky. Dalal Mehta pressed his hands against the dome of the flitter and looked out at the plain. The tall blades of tarendra grass bowed in the wind, then straightened as the wind gradually died.

"Dawn is coming," his father said softly. "I didn't expect to see another dawn."

Dalal had been watching the stars for a while. They were all unfamiliar constellations. He searched the sky in the east and saw new morning stars, a cluster of eight, and another group of stars that were like the ornaments of a cosmic fan. A brightness above the horizon became the fire of a rising sun.

Dalal opened the door and slipped outside. Other people were standing next to their flitters, gazing east at the new sun. He breathed deeply of the morning air, and it was as if someone had turned the universe on again.

"They're through," Parviz Bodonchar shouted, "the *Enterprise* got through," but Worf had already heard Commander Riker's voice on the transceiver. He strode quickly to Bodonchar's side and knelt next to him.

"*Enterprise* to Worf," Riker said.

Worf leaned toward the transceiver. "Worf here." Ganesa hurried to him. "Ensign Mehta, Yeoman Bodonchar, and I are unharmed," Worf continued. "We are at the archaeological site to the north of Boreas. Minister Dydion and some of her people are here with us—they're uninjured as well."

"We'll be close enough soon to beam you aboard," Riker said, "but it's safe for you to go outside now. Epic Three's in an optimum orbit—axial tilt off by only a degree. We're just starting to get damage reports—seems most of the cities suffered heavy damage from quakes and tidal waves. Epira and Austra are almost completely under water."

230

Ganesa let out a gasp of dismay.

"Most of Boreas seems to have been hit by a tidal wave," Riker added, "and much of that city has been destroyed, but that wave's receded. Same with Nicopolis—a tidal wave reduced most of its structures to rubble, but a few still stand. Hierapolis, except for some minor quake damage, is almost untouched." Ganesa lifted a hand to her mouth. "It won't have a riverfront now, though—the river's changed course. It's now flowing almost ten kilometers away from what used to be the waterfront. The archaeological sites all seem to have held up well. Looks like there's been an increase in volcanic activity, mostly along the faults on the ocean floor, and a few aftershocks in various places, but we'll know more after we've done a complete scan. The biggest change is that the entire northern polar icecap is, at least temporarily, a sea of steaming water."

"We have been trying to reach Counselor Troi and Ensign Chang," Worf said, "but have had no response. Are they safe?"

"Troi's aboard the *Enterprise*. A small piece of Epic Three got sliced off by the wormhole—where the Tireos Institute was located. We had to get close enough to beam the survivors aboard, and that required some quick maneuvering—I'll tell you all about it when you're back." Riker was silent for a moment. "We lost Ensign Chang—he died on that fragment."

"Oh, no," Ganesa murmured. Bodonchar bowed his head.

"He died with honor," Worf said.

"His body's aboard." Riker paused. "We'll try to get you back as soon as we can."

"Understood," Worf said. "There is enough food to last us for several days."

"Do what you can in the meantime to assist Minister Dydion."

"Yes, sir. Worf out."

"Enterprise out."

Minister Dydion was standing near him. Worf got to his feet. "May I use your transceiver?" she asked. "I should contact my people now, find out how they are."

"Of course. Yeoman Bodonchar will stay here with you, in case you need his assistance. I will go outside and see if our vehicles have survived the passage." Worf looked in the direction of the others and saw that Dydion's security people had their two prisoners under control, then walked to the entrance. The doorway yawned open; he went outside, followed by Ganesa.

The new sun had risen, but a bank of black clouds loomed in the north; he smelled salt in the air. The areas between the monuments were strewn with large rocks. The archaeologists had excavated the site like an open-pit mine, and there were cracks in the sides of the pit. One of the flitters had been crushed under a boulder, but the other vehicles seemed untouched.

Ganesa went to a flitter. "Get in," she said. "We might as well see if at least one of these flitters is still working." She slipped into the craft; Worf got in next to her.

Ganesa's hands moved over the control panel. The flitter shot into the air and out of the pit; she brought it down and landed near the edge of the cliff. Below, Worf saw sand, pools of water, dead fish, and green ropes of sea flora scattered over the rocks; a tidal wave had come inland as far as the bottom of this precipice.

"As long as my people have their lives and their world," Ganesa said, "the rest can be rebuilt." She touched the controls again; the flitter lifted, then dropped slowly toward the other vehicles.

Minister Dydion came outside as the two got out of the flitter. She looked tired, and her long hair hung limply over her shoulders. "I got through to the Dryon Forest site," she said. "A few people, about three hundred or so, panicked and fled into the forest, but everyone else stayed inside the monuments or else near them. There don't seem to be any deaths, except for some of those who went into the woods—a few of their bodies have already been found. Casualties are minor—broken limbs, bruises, and the like. We were very lucky, even if we did lose almost all of Boreas."

Worf lifted his brows.

"I overheard that part of your Commander Riker's report," Dydion continued. "We'll just have to rebuild—maybe a bit farther inland." Her mouth twisted. "I wish Edmond—I wish my husband were here to see it. How I wish he hadn't given up. I wish that more than anything."

Her husband might have taken his life, but the woman had not taken his way out, had stayed to see things through. Worf could respect her for that. But he could also see how her sorrow was tainting her joy in knowing that her world would now live.

A brief report from Minister James Mobutu, who was with the refugees from Austra, had mentioned ten thousand deaths in the south so far. Now Picard was listening to a report from Minister Rohin Nowles, who informed him that at least a thousand people from Hierapolis were dead. Nowles expected that figure to increase, since several thousand people had ignored instructions and had apparently gone to meet their expected deaths near the Kuretes Mountains or in the Korybantes Desert. The desert and mountains had, apparently, claimed lives spared by the nova. One witness said he had seen one encampment of people in the mountain foothills buried under a rockslide.

"There were also some severe desert storms," Minister Nowles continued, "worse than any we've had in the past, according to reports." His face sagged with fatigue; he ran a hand through his graying hair. "I'm just grateful most of our people went where they were supposed to go, futile as it seemed at the time. Rychi's faith in the old sites was justified, I suppose, although not quite in the way that he expected. There isn't much more to say, Captain Picard."

"We'll get any emergency aid you need to you as soon as possible," Picard said. "Starfleet Command and the Federation Council have been informed of your situation, and help is on the way."

"We're grateful to you," Nowles said softly, "more

grateful than I or anyone can say, or will ever be able to say." His image vanished.

Picard felt a moment of satisfaction, but knew at once that it could never grow into a feeling of triumph. Too many were dead.

Another message was coming in: the face of Mariamna Fabre appeared on the screen. "Captain Picard," she said quickly, "we've come through pretty well, but with many losses. We're still getting reports, but along the western coast, we've lost at least five thousand people so far, and thousands more are unaccounted for. Some were people who, it seems, either refused to leave their homes or left them when it was too late. Our fatalities in the west may go as high as fifty thousand, and I'm not counting the severely injured. Medical teams are already on the way to several locations."

"Some of our people will be beaming down to help," Picard said, "as soon as we know what kind of aid is most urgent."

"Right now, it's probably food, water, and medical supplies," Fabre said. "All our people here in the west have been told to stay where they are for the time being."

Picard was relieved to see that the woman's sturdy, stalwart manner had not deserted her, and was profoundly grateful that she had survived. "We'll start beaming down a flow of replicated supplies to all the evacuation sites immediately," he said.

"Thank you." Fabre smiled. "It could have been so much worse. Whatever difficulties we have to face now, we'll all remember that."

Picard looked down for a moment, not knowing

what to say, wondering why he was being thanked, with so many dead. He knew what answer he should give himself, but he wondered if it would ever help. When he raised his head again, Minister Fabre's image was gone.

"Minister Nowles gave me a quick report on your city," Rychi called out to the people crowded into the installation's hallways. "You'll have to remain here for a few days, but luckily most of Hierapolis is still standing."

A few people cheered; most were silent, perhaps thinking of how easily they might have died instead of surviving to see their world's rebirth.

"We have enough food and water to last that long," Rychi continued, "and by then you should be going back to your homes. If not, we can call on the *Enterprise* to beam some more supplies down to us." He had decided not to ask Captain Picard for help unless it was absolutely necessary; he had heard enough reports already to know that people in other locations were in much greater need. "If you go outside, please take care not to wander too far from this site. The weather may be unsettled for a while—you don't want to get caught in another sudden storm."

When he was finished, some people got up and wandered toward the plasteen dome to line up at the latrines. Others, clearly exhausted, made pillows of packs and stretched out on the floor to sleep; still others went to the ramps that would take them down to the suncore-link chamber. Hakim Ponselle had told everyone to leave their provisions there, so that they could be parceled out fairly; no one had objected.

About one hundred and forty people were now sheltered in this station, a tiny fraction of the people who had been lost. Rychi, after listening to brief reports from other ministers, expected the fatalities to number at least one hundred thousand, and he was probably being too optimistic.

The entrance opened; Ponselle came inside. "How is it out there?" Rychi asked his friend.

"Think you might want to come and see for yourself," the older man replied.

Rychi followed him to the entrance and went outside. The sky was its familiar noontime blue, the new sun as bright as the one they had fled. To the south, flitters were scattered across the orange sand, most of them obviously greatly damaged. They were, he thought, going to have to request transportation when it was time to leave.

As he turned to go back inside, he glanced east and froze. Not more than twenty paces from the installation, a rift had opened in the ground.

"That's what I wanted you to see," Ponselle said. "If that fissure had opened up just a little farther west, it would have swallowed us."

Rychi shuddered, then walked toward the edge of the rift. It was about one hundred meters wide and ran north and south; he could not see where it ended. He peered into the crevice, estimating that it was nearly a kilometer deep.

"Guess we got lucky," Ponselle said as he came to Rychi's side.

Rychi inhaled the warm, dry air. His world still

lived, and now there would be time to learn more of the secrets of its former inhabitants. He might even find the key to their writing.

A thought came to him. If the old ones had indeed left this world to become interstellar mobile-dwellers and nomads, they might have returned to gaze upon their old home once more out of nostalgia. They might have left a record of their travels, of contacts with other intelligent species, perhaps even a record of those contacts that might turn out to be the Rosetta Stone that would allow him to understand their written symbols. And, if they had left the land for the sea before venturing into space, the sea might be where such an artifact would be found.

He would learn what he could, and others would have the chance to build on his work. The sites would still be there, the monuments that had saved so many lives.

"Got a lot of work ahead of us," Ponselle said, and Rychi knew that the other man was thinking similar thoughts.

Two members of the *Enterprise*'s security team were on duty in the hallway. The door opened; Troi entered Ganesa Mehta's quarters. The uninjured women from the Tireos Institute had been housed here, in Ensign Mehta's quarters, and the men in Worf's rooms, after the traditional Klingon weapons Worf kept had been removed from the walls.

The women were sitting on the floor, most of them looking tired and unhappy. Troi felt as exhausted as they looked, and the news she had brought would not cheer them. She had asked Commander Riker to be allowed to visit them, worn out as she was. This would be her last task before she went to her own quarters to sleep.

"I have sad news for you," she said. "Your friend Ford Veniam has died in sickbay." Three women sighed, and she sensed their sorrow for their dead colleague. "His body will be returned to your world for burial according to your customs as soon as possible. Your other friends are recovering."

Teodora Tibawi looked up, her beauty still unmarred by her recent ordeals. "Are we still prisoners?" she asked.

"You're not prisoners," Troi replied, although in a way they were. Commander Riker had ordered them confined, knowing that the Epictetan authorities would expect to have them returned for whatever judgment would be rendered there. There was also the chance that a few of them might try something desperate or risky, or attempt to escape somehow.

"What's going to happen to us?" Teodora said.

"I can't answer that. Your fellow Epictetans will have to make that decision. You'll stay here until it's time to send you back. We want to get the children home first, so you may be here for another few days, but it won't be longer than that. By then, your other injured friends should be well enough to join you."

Commander Riker did not feel that these people deserved much consideration. Troi had sensed that even before he confirmed it. "Don't be too gentle with them," he had told her. They had aided and abetted two men who had held children hostage, and that the children were alive and unharmed was largely a matter of luck. But Troi could sense the remorse in these women; and they had demonstrated some courage when they were trapped with her. She doubted that they would ever threaten anyone again.

"It won't go easy for us," a blond woman said.

"Maybe your people will be so thankful for what's happened that they'll be merciful and forgiving." Troi paused. "All I can do on your behalf is to send a report to the council of ministers telling them that you truly regret your actions, and that your biggest crime was being too easily swayed by others. It might help if I mentioned that none of you tried to harm me."

"Are there any more reports of casualties?" Teodora asked.

"The estimates now are about one hundred and forty thousand fatalities, and there will probably be more." Troi pressed her hands together. "But it could have been much worse." It could have been twenty million, she reminded herself. "I have to leave you now—I told Commander Riker that I would speak to the men also."

She was turning to leave when Teodora got up and motioned to her. "Lieutenant Commander Troi," she said, "I have only one favor to ask of you."

"And what is that?"

"I want to be at Jun-shing's funeral, to pay my last respects. It's probably my fault anyway, what happened to him. Maybe he wouldn't have been at the institute if—"

Troi took Teodora's hands, feeling the tension of guilt inside the other woman. "Ensign Chang knew his duty, Teodora. He might well have volunteered to go there anyway." Tears trickled from the young woman's eyes. "I'll do what I can to see that you get to attend the funeral," Troi continued. "Captain Picard wouldn't object to that, I'm sure. He's already asked a couple of ministers if Ensign Chang can be buried on Epictetus Three, and they said that they would be honored—"

"Don't bury him there." Teodora pulled her hands away from Troi's and wiped at her eyes. "He wouldn't want it, I know he wouldn't want it. I have to speak for him now. He loved Starfleet, not that planet. He'd want to be in space. Don't put him in the ground."

"I'll tell the captain what you said," Troi murmured, thinking of Chang. She had not known the young officer very well, but instinctively felt that Teodora was right. "I think he'll agree—I know he will."

A message was coming in from Worf, on the heels of a report from one of Minister Peladon's aides. No rest for the weary, Picard thought as he listened to the Klingon. Worf, Ensign Mehta, and Yeoman Bodonchar were going to travel with Minister Dydion to the evacuation site near the Dryon Forest. Her aides had reported that temporary shelters and sanitary facilities were being set up, and that most of the people were unharmed. The three away-team members could be beamed aboard later from there.

Picard rubbed at his eyes. He had not felt tired while receiving and responding to the almost constant reports from Epictetus III, making his log entries, and giving Vida Ntumbe, Pietro Barbieri, and the Federation Council a preliminary report. But the reports from the planet were tapering off, and his exhaustion was beginning to catch up with him. Other officers had come on the bridge to replace Ensign Sorby and Science Officer Liang, and he now had a fairly complete picture of conditions on the planet.

The passage had cost that world nearly a hundred and fifty thousand lives, and at least that number of people were seriously injured, but emergency hospitals and shelters were already going up. Within ten more of their days—the Epictetan day would now be a few minutes longer—the first cargo-carrier starships sent by Starfleet with emergency aid and personnel would be in orbit around the planet. Within a few months, they would be well on the way to rebuilding their damaged and destroyed cities.

But so many people had been lost. He hoped that those mourning them, and those who were grieving for the suicides who had given up all hope, would not judge him and his officers too harshly.

"Captain."

Picard started; Data was standing at his side. "Captain, Commander Riker has retired to his quarters, Geordi has gone off duty, the others on the bridge have been relieved, and I have verified that almost all of the children we brought aboard are finally sleeping. I would most strongly recommend that you get some rest yourself."

"I shall. You'll have to watch over things here." Data would see to the *Enterprise*'s repairs, and handle any important messages, because Data never tired. "There's just one thing I have to do first." He had promised Beverly Crusher that he would let her know as soon as he had news of the sublight ships, and the report of their survival had come in only a few moments ago.

He was about to touch the panel in front of him, then paused. "Mr. Data," he said, "I'd like your opinion. What would you have done about the Epictetan sublight craft?"

"Exactly as you did, Captain. I have considered the matter, and conclude that, given the moral dilemmas involved, those people should be picked up by the two Epictetan cargo-carrier starships that are still on their way home. Therefore, as you did, I would have sent a subspace message to the captains of the *Olympia* and the *Carpathia* directing them to pick up all survivors."

"Yes," Picard said. "Those who fled should be judged by their own people." He still felt uncharitable toward the people aboard the fleeing vessels. Perhaps he was being unfair. Had Epictetus III been lost, and the *Enterprise* also lost in the effort to save that planet, the people aboard the sublight ships and the cargo carriers would have been all that was left of their world. Surely it would have been better to have a few survive than for all of them to have vanished. Better that there be someone to remember their world than no one at all; that must have been what at least some of the people fleeing in the sublight vessels had thought. Perhaps they were not all cowards in love with their own skins.

It was yet another of the knotty moral dilemmas

with which Epictetus III had bound his heart and mind.

Beverly decided to send the subspace message to Krystyna Peladon from her office, and then go back to her quarters to sleep. It occurred to her that she might be more eloquent after she got some rest. She yawned, then gulped down more coffee. She would send the message first. Krystyna should know as soon as possible.

She smoothed down her hair, then leaned toward the small screen, ready to send her message. "Krystyna," she said, "I'm sending this directly to you, and not through Wesley. Your parents are safe. All of the sublights managed to shield themselves from the nova by getting behind several planetary bodies in your outer solar system—your former solar system. The two Epictetan cargo-carrier starships will reach them within sixty hours and beam everyone aboard, then continue on to Epictetus Three."

She paused. There wasn't much more to say about Krystyna's parents. Their reception on their home-world would not be a warm one; there would be recriminations, perhaps worse, maybe even trials. But perhaps not. It was difficult to predict, after all that had occurred.

"This is going to be harder to say," Beverly continued. "Captain Picard also told me that your grandfather hasn't been seen ever since your world entered the wormhole. He never showed up at the evacuation site where he was expected, and the last message any of his aides received from him was sent from his house in Epira. They're now assuming that he never left the city. Krystyna—" Beverly's hand tightened around her cup.

"Krystyna Peladon at Starfleet Academy for Dr. Beverly Crusher," the computer said, and Krystyna's face appeared on the screen.

"Dr. Crusher," the young woman said, "I heard all that, I—" She drew back a little and Beverly saw that Wesley was with her. "I know what it's going to be like for my parents. They should have stayed, they—" Krystyna shook her blond head. "I had a message from Grandfather. I think he must have decided to stay in his home, no matter what happened. After I heard his message, I had the feeling I'd never see him again."

"I'm sorry," Beverly said softly.

"He said that I was right to leave." Her eyes glistened. "He admitted that he was wrong about a lot of things. My father always did what Grandfather wanted him to do, and now he'll pay for that. At best, people will ostracize him and Mother—they won't forget." She looked away from the screen. "I'll have to be the best kind of Starfleet officer. It's the only way I can restore my family's honor."

Beverly wondered if Krystyna would ever return to Epictetus III. It would be easier to stay away, not to have to deal with her parents' shame and the judgment of others about what her grandfather had done. Then Krystyna lifted her head and Beverly saw the determination in her eyes, the strength in her face. She would go back to her homeworld, and Beverly thought it likely that she would make that world proud of her.

"I'll come to see you the next time I visit Wesley,"

Beverly said. She watched her son as he slipped his arm around Krystyna's shoulders. Perhaps their friendship would eventually deepen into something more. Wesley, she thought, would be fortunate to have someone like Krystyna Peladon, if the relationship survived the changes in her.

Chapter Thirteen

IN HIS DREAM, Picard was looking back at the solar system of Epictetus III through the *Enterprise*'s telescopes. But the system was fourteen light-years away, so he saw the sun and its planets intact, just as they had been fourteen years ago. The light he saw was coming to him from a past in which the people of Epictetus III were living their lives as though their world would always be solid and enduring and their sun an eternal shining presence in their sky.

He awoke just as he was getting ready to shout a useless warning across time and space, and knew again the terrible cost of what he and his crew had done.

* * *

The cost of saving Epictetus III was again on Picard's mind as he stood in the main shuttlebay next to Ensign Chang's casket. He had seen something of himself in the young man—Chang would have been a distinguished officer someday. Now his family would have to mourn a man whose brilliant promise had been cut short.

Commander Riker stood next to Picard. Troi was there with Teodora Tibawi, Ensign Chang's former love. Worf, Ganesa Mehta, and Parviz Bodonchar, who had beamed aboard only a couple of hours earlier, had also come to pay their last respects, and behind them stood the many friends the young officer had made during his brief tour of duty on the *Enterprise.* All of the mourners, except for Teodora Tibawi, were in full-dress formal Starfleet uniforms.

Picard had made his speech, mentioning Chang's fine record and the posthumous decorations that would be his. Riker had told of how often Chang had beaten him at poker, while Troi had spoken of the courage and dedication she had sensed in him. They had all spoken eloquently, but Picard somehow felt that more should have been said about a man who might one day have been a starship captain.

He was about to turn toward the operations control booth to signal to the flight-deck officer when the words seized him. "Ensign Chang Jun-shing reminds us," he said, "that we must be willing to risk much in the performance of our duties, even be willing to give up our lives. As we mourn his loss, we have to remember that this brave young man willingly took that risk."

But his words suddenly sounded hollow. Chang

had chosen to risk his life in the performance of his duties, but his death had been by chance; some would even call it a useless death.

There had been no choice for the people who had died on Epictetus III. He had enlisted them in the cause of saving their world, knowing that some of them were likely to die in that effort. That all of them would have been lost had he and his crew not acted did not seem entirely to justify his course of action. He had gambled their lives, and those of his crew, because he had believed that he had only two choices—to attempt to save the planet with a desperate and risky plan or to let almost all of the Epictetans perish with their world. But what if those had not been the only two choices? What if there were a third choice, or any number of possible alternatives that he and his officers had simply been unable to glimpse? Perhaps if he had refused to go along with Data and La Forge's proposal, another way might have been found to save Epictetus III without such a great loss of life.

To gaze at Ensign Chang's black metal casket was also to remind himself yet again of how reckless his gamble had been, of how easily everything might have been lost. A twitch in the wormhole had severed a bit of the planet, hardly more than a sliver, and Chang Jun-shing was dead as a result. The wormhole might have cut Epictetus III in two, or sliced off the entire continent of Themis and all of the people there. He might have watched the death of a world knowing that his actions had brought it to its end.

Picard felt the tension in his shoulders, the tightness in his stomach. This was all a delayed reaction, he told himself, the kind of feeling people often had when a grave danger was past, and the realization of how close they had been to death was fully upon them. It was normal to feel the turmoil of emotions that had been suppressed during the crisis, now that the crisis was over.

At last, unable to think of anything more to say about Ensign Chang, he turned toward the control booth and lifted his hand. The casket began to glide toward the shuttlebay's exterior space doors. Slowly, the doors opened, revealing the blackness of space, and then the casket shot forward, to take up its wide cometary orbit around Epictetus III's new sun.

Worf stood in the arched hallway inside Hierapolis's Riverside Arena, near the open main entrance to the building. The brown-haired infant he was holding wriggled in his arms, then tried to grab at the metallic chain sash he wore over his Starfleet uniform. He scowled at the child; she stretched her hand toward his beard. Outside, on the wide stone stairways that led down the steep hillside to the arena, families had already gathered to welcome their children home.

He had beamed down with Ganesa Mehta, Ensign Hughes Holman, and four other crew members of the *Enterprise.* All of them carried infants or small children in their arms. Worf heard a faint, high-pitched sound behind him and turned to see a glittering column of light. Small forms quickly took shape inside the column; eight more children had beamed down.

The *Enterprise* personnel were supposed to wait until all the children had been transported there before leaving the arena, but the first group of arrivals had run outside before anyone could stop them. People rushed down the nearest stone stairway and surged around the children, calling out names. A young couple hurried to Ganesa; she peered at the name bracelet on the wrist of the infant she held, then handed the child to the pair.

"Order," Worf called out as he went outside, "we must have order here," but no one was paying any attention to him. A redheaded girl pushed her way through the crowd and threw her arms around a younger red-haired boy. An older boy holding an infant peered at the child's name bracelet, then surrendered the baby to a couple before hurrying off to his own parents. Soon Worf was in the middle of a joyous crowd of people laughing and shouting and crying out names.

The child he was holding began to squirm, then to wail. Someone plucked at his sleeve. "Kathryn Henries," a voice said near his elbow. Worf looked down to see a small blond girl tugging at the cuff of his uniform. "Kathryn Henries," she said again, "I'm looking for her, and you've got her. I'm Kristin Henries—she's my sister."

A tall blond man and a short brown-haired woman were standing behind Kristin Henries; the woman's brown eyes glistened with tears. Worf checked the child's name bracelet as the baby let out a piercing shriek, then handed her to her mother. "Thank you," the woman said as the infant's cries subsided. "Thank you for taking such good care of her."

Worf was about to reply that others had looked after her, that he had done no more than beam down with the child, but the family was already hurrying toward the flitters that stood near the arena.

"Ganesa!" Dalal Mehta was pushing his way through the crowd toward his sister. "You got leave!"

"No," Ganesa replied as she hugged the boy, "I didn't get leave, I'm still on duty." She smiled. "But I'll have a little time to visit with you and Mother and Father before I have to go back. And I'll probably be beaming back again to help with some of the relief efforts, so I should get to see you again."

"We were lucky," Dalal said. "Most of the city's still here."

"I know."

"Our house doesn't have any damage at all," Dalal continued. "A lot of people from Hierapolis are volunteering to help out in other places, since there isn't as much to do here." He craned his neck. "Where's Zamir? I came here to meet him."

"He should be along at any moment," Ganesa said. Worf turned toward the arena, searching for the stocky form of Dalal's friend. Riverside Arena now overlooked a vast expanse of reed-covered mud flats instead of the Arion River.

Another group of children came out of the arena, Zamir Yesed among them. Worf, who towered over most of the people around him, raised an arm and motioned to Zamir.

A dark-haired couple suddenly rushed past him. "Zamir!" the woman shouted. "Zamir!" The two had to be the boy's parents. Worf strode after them, Ganesa and Dalal right behind him.

"Zamir," Dalal called out when they were near, but the Yeseds had already claimed their son. Zamir's father threw his arms around the boy, and then his weeping mother embraced her husband and son both.

"All right!" Zamir said. "You'd think I'd been gone for ten years." His father let go of him, but his mother was still hanging on, hugging him tightly as Zamir fidgeted. "You're going to crush me if you don't let go." He managed to free himself from his mother's arms as Dalal reached his side.

"Welcome back, Zamir," Dalal said. He clasped Zamir's hand once, then let go. Worf supposed that Dalal did not want to embarrass his friend further with any excessively emotional displays.

"I'm glad to be back," Zamir replied. "I was worried about you, Dalal. It must have been a lot scarier down here."

Dalal shrugged. "It wasn't so bad."

Zamir greeted Ganesa, then Worf, and introduced the Klingon to his parents. They gaped at him in silence much as their son had when first meeting him. At last Mr. Yesed found his voice. "We'd better go home now," he said to Ganesa. "Zamir's grandparents will be getting impatient—they're waiting to welcome him and hear all about the *Enterprise*."

"I didn't get to see that much of it," Zamir said, "just the holodeck and some of the crew quarters and this place called Ten-Forward where they gave us treats. Most of the time we were watching viewscreens and monitoring reports."

"Part of our roof collapsed," his mother said, "and it was the part right over your room, but we should have it fixed in a few days." Tears were still streaming down her face. "I'm so glad you're back, dear. You have no idea how hard it was, having to wait down here without knowing what would happen." She wiped at her eyes. "I thought I would go out of my mind."

"It's all right," Zamir said. "I'm here now—it's all over." He glanced toward Dalal and Worf and rolled his eyes, but was obviously happy to see his parents. "Wait, I almost forgot." He took off his pack, opened one flap, and pulled out Dalal's small, square case. "Your mansi collection, Dalal. I took good care of it. They put me and two other boys in Lieutenant Jensen's quarters—he's a biologist, so he really liked seeing your collection. He wants to come here if there's time and look for some mansi himself."

"Come over to our house later, Dalal," Zamir's father said as he led his wife and son toward the stone steps. "I know you boys will want to talk."

"I'll be there," Dalal said.

Other people were ascending the stone stairways that led down to the arena, their children in tow; a few families were going home in flitters. Three small children, two dark-haired boys and a girl with a long brown braid down her back, were still waiting with Ensign Holman. Worf frowned. Many of the parents and children were leaving now, and several families were still waiting by the arena's main entrance, but those three children had remained unclaimed.

"Mother knew," Dalal said to his sister. "She said so, when we were leaving Hierapolis. She said that she knew you were hiding something from us, that your commanding officers had to be planning something."

Ganesa smiled. "I guess I can't fool her."

"We could have all died," Dalal whispered, and for a moment Worf expected to see tears in his eyes, but the boy composed himself.

A flitter was landing in the courtyard next to the arena. A man with graying hair got out of the vehicle; Worf recognized Minister Rohin Nowles. "Ensign Mehta," Nowles called out as he approached them, "I'd like a word with you."

"Of course," Ganesa said.

"I hope you can help." Nowles glanced at Worf from the sides of his eyes, looking distinctly nervous; Worf gazed at him steadily until the man turned back to Ganesa. "Being an Epictetan yourself as well as a Starfleet officer—well, I think you might be most helpful with this particular problem."

The minister drew Ganesa aside; Worf and Dalal kept near them. "I've checked the list of children that the *Enterprise* took aboard," Nowles continued in a low voice. "The parents of three of the children you beamed up from Hierapolis died during the passage—that's been confirmed by witnesses. I thought you should know as soon as possible."

Nowles glanced at the trio of children who were still waiting for their parents to claim them. The three showed unease as the minister looked toward them; Worf saw that they knew something was wrong. The older boy looked up at Ensign Holman with wide, dark, apprehensive eyes; the girl slipped her arm around the younger boy. "My guess is that those three are the ones who lost their parents."

"We'd better verify that," Ganesa murmured. Worf waited with Dalal as Ganesa and Nowles went to Holman and engaged in a whispered conference.

"Poor kids," Dalal said.

"It is a hard thing to lose one's father and mother," Worf said, thinking of the Klingon parents he had lost in a Romulan attack and of the human parents who had reared him to adulthood.

Ganesa and Nowles left Holman and came back to the courtyard. "We'll have to find places for them to stay," Nowles said, "at least until we can find new homes for them. They don't have any relatives in Hierapolis, according to the records, and with things as unsettled as they are, it'll take time to contact any relatives elsewhere." He paused. "And someone's also going to have to tell them that their parents died in a rockslide near the Kuretes Mountains." It was clear that Minister Nowles did not want to give the three children the unhappy news himself.

"I'll tell them," Ganesa said.

"Thank you, Ensign Mehta."

"And I'm sure my parents would be more than willing to make a home for those children for as long as it's necessary."

"Ganesa's right," Dalal said. "They'd be happy to take them in."

"Well." Nowles heaved a sigh of relief. "Thank you again. I'll be in touch with your parents as soon as I find out about any relatives. Right now I'm expected at Riverview Center."

He got into his flitter; Worf watched as the vehicle lifted from the ground. Minister Nowles, he suspected, was not one of the more admirable examples of his friend Ganesa's people.

"This isn't going to be easy," Ganesa said, "telling those children about their parents."

"I know," her brother replied.

Worf said, "It is better that they hear it from you than from Minister Nowles."

"It's because of what we did," Ganesa said, "what Captain Picard decided we had to do, that those children are orphans. I suppose I feel just a little bit responsible for what's happened to their parents."

"Look at it this way," Dalal said. "If the *Enterprise* hadn't done anything, those kids and their parents would all be dead. It's better to have it this way than nothing at all."

Ganesa smiled slightly. "I'll try to keep that in mind." She put her arm around his shoulders. "I'd better go tell them now. I might need your help, Dalal."

Dalal gripped his mansi collection more tightly. Worf stepped back. His presence might only alarm the bereaved children more when they first heard of their parents' fate. But he would stay near, in case he might be needed. It might help them later to speak to one who had also been orphaned as a child.

The ensign led her brother away. Worf gazed after

Ganesa and her brother as they walked toward Hughes Holman and the three orphaned children.

Beverly Crusher had beamed down to the out-skirts of what remained of Nicopolis with Commander Riker and Counselor Troi. Riker and Troi, after conferring with Mariamna Fabre, had been taken to the archaeological site in the Aurelian Mountain foothills overlooking the city, where they were to assist Samas Rychi, who had recently arrived at that site to oversee the construction of temporary shelters.

Beverly had gone with Minister Fabre to the Tarvala Medical Institute, one of the few structures in Nicopolis still standing. Patients were now being housed in classrooms and laboratories as well as in the wards, and the Epictetan relief efforts were still stretched thin. Beverly and members of her medical team had come to offer some much-needed assistance until a medical team from Hierapolis arrived.

She was sitting with Raymond Tam in one of the lounge areas, taking a short break until it was time to examine and treat more patients. The Tarvala Medical Institute was on a high hill in the south of the city, and the wide window in this lounge offered a view of most of Nicopolis. It would have been a beautiful view once, Beverly thought, a view of a graceful crescent-shaped city overlooking a blue-green ocean. Now the ocean was murky and brown, its waters filled with silt, and the beach was littered with dead fish. Nicopolis was a maze of channeled scablands strewn with parts of buildings, broken beams, dislodged boulders, flattened furniture, and slender trees torn from their roots.

"I wish," spoke a voice near her, "that you could have seen Nicopolis before." Beverly looked up as Mariamna Fabre took the seat next to her.

"I looked at some images before I came," Beverly said. "I know what you lost."

Minister Fabre looked tired. She had welcomed Beverly and her team to her world, had directed them to the wards where they were most needed, and then had gone about her own work. In addition to frequent consultations with her fellow ministers about relief efforts and plans for rebuilding, she was also helping to care for the patients here. Mariamna Fabre, Beverly had discovered, had trained as a nurse before deciding to pursue musical theory and composition; now her medical skills would be used.

"I spoke with Captain Picard a few moments ago," Fabre said. "I was sure he'd want to know what the council of ministers decided to do about all the people who fled in the commandeered sublight vessels."

"I'm a little curious about that myself," Beverly said.

"So am I," Raymond Tam said. "What did you decide?"

"We're not going to put them on trial. I'm not quite sure what we could charge them with anyway. Dereliction of duty? Desertion? Treason? Stealing government property?" Minister Fabre shook her head. "We'd probably have to concoct some new charge after the fact, and most of us don't care for that idea—it sets a bad precedent. Some of those people have children—it's hard not to feel a little sympathy for people who grabbed at the chance to save theirs from what seemed to be certain death. Some of them could probably argue that they didn't really understand what they were doing, that they believed that the council had authorized their flight and chosen them fairly. And before condemning them, a lot of us would have to look deep inside ourselves and ask if, given the chance, we might not have done the same thing." She leaned back in her chair. "So we decided not to do anything. We have enough to do already without engaging in useless recrimination. At any rate, two of the ministers who commandeered the sublight craft are dead, and the third has resigned from the council."

Beverly sipped her cup of tea. The people from the Tireos Institute had not been so lucky. The two men who had gone to Boreas to take the children there hostage would be tried, while the other Tireos people were likely to be put on a kind of probation at best. Maybe that had made it easier for the ministers to do nothing about the much larger number of people who had fled in the commandeered ships; the Tireos Institute folk would serve more easily as scapegoats, being a small group widely regarded as both marginal and deluded. The decision of the ministers was a practical solution, even if Beverly had doubts about its justice.

"Life here will be hard for those people anyway," Fabre went on. "Many will ostracize them. Everyone will know that they ran away."

Beverly thought of Krystyna Peladon, who had

said much the same thing. There would be others besides her trying to live down their parents' dishonor. "Perhaps that's enough justice," Beverly said.

"By the way," Fabre continued, "I was wondering about Captain Picard. Of course I don't know him as well as you probably do, but—he seems a bit abstracted."

"Abstracted?" Beverly asked.

"Worried. Disturbed. I don't quite know how to put it. Given all we've been through, it's not surprising, and I'm sure it's nothing serious. His advice has been most helpful in resolving a few problems, and he is, if I may say so, an extremely charming man. But once in a while, I would notice a distant look in his eyes."

Beverly had noticed the same thing herself; Mariamna Fabre was observant. Beverly supposed that Captain Picard was still wrestling with the choices he had made, but she knew that he would eventually resolve whatever was troubling him. If she had any serious concerns about his state of mind, she—the only officer aboard the *Enterprise* with the power to do so—would have relieved him of duty. Commander Riker, who knew Jean-Luc Picard better than anyone, would not have left his side to beam down to Epictetus III if he had any doubts about the captain's ability to handle his duties. She would have thought less of Picard had he been the kind of man who would remain untroubled by the dilemmas Epictetus III had presented.

"I've known Captain Picard for some time," Beverly said. "My late husband served under him. Once I blamed Captain Picard for my husband's death, but I learned better a long time ago. I think you were very fortunate that the *Enterprise* was the closest starship to your world when it was threatened."

"So do I." Fabre smiled. "This wasn't a rescue I would ever have imagined."

Chapter Fourteen

"You're here early, Captain," Guinan said.

Picard took a seat at the bar. "I thought I'd stop by before going on duty."

"What's your pleasure?"

"A cup of coffee will be fine," he replied.

"Espresso? Cappuccino? Rilorean coffee laced with whipped cream?"

"Just plain black coffee—hot."

Guinan moved down the bar to get it. Ten-Forward was nearly empty; almost every crew member not needed on board in engineering, maintenance, life-support, or child care was on Epictetus III, helping out. The starships promised by Starfleet would be in this system and in orbit around the planet within a few days; Geordi and his engineering team would have the *Enterprise* fully repaired by then.

Guinan set a mug of coffee in front of him. "If there's enough time," she said, "I wouldn't mind visiting one of Epic Three's archaeological sites before we leave this system. That is, if I wouldn't be in the way." Her smile broadened. "Those structures intrigue me. I'd like to see them close up."

"Do you think your race might have had contact with the planet's original inhabitants sometime in the past?" Picard asked.

Guinan peered at him from under lowered eyelids, looking even more mysterious than usual, and he knew that she would not answer that question.

"Guinan," he went on, "I keep asking myself if we did everything that was possible."

"You did everything you could."

"But I wonder if there was something else we might have done, something we just couldn't see. I suppose what I wanted was a perfect solution that would have harmed no one."

"Perfection," Guinan said, "isn't something any intelligent being should ask of itself. Ask for perfection, and you may poison what's possible."

Picard nodded. "You're right, of course." He sipped some coffee. "We're not omnipotent, we can't ever expect to be. And yet, with so many lives at stake, perhaps the universe could have given us just one moment of perfection."

Guinan rested her arms on the counter. "About perfection—it's not always obvious what it should be." He had been thinking that same thought, responding to himself, before she said the words. Her hand gripped his gently for a moment, then released it.

Picard was in his ready room, about to begin an entry in his captain's log, when his comm panel showed an incoming message from Riker.

He touched the console. "Picard here." An image appeared on the small screen in front of him. Commander Riker was sitting next to Samas Rychi on a cot inside what looked like a plasteen shelter.

"Captain," Riker said, "almost everyone near Nicopolis is now housed in some kind of temporary shelter, with water and food available. Those who aren't in domes or tents are living inside the monuments for now—we've put in cots and latrines. Professor Rychi spoke to Minister Dydion a little while ago. She told him that some of her people are going to set up shelters near Boreas—what's left of Boreas—but that most of them are remaining at their evacuation site for now."

"The climate's more temperate near the Dryon Forest," Rychi added, "so they're better off staying there near the monuments until more shelters can be built."

"I'll be back aboard in less than an hour," Riker said, "but I'd like to return with a few of our engineers to see what we might do for the people in the north."

"Very well, Number One," Picard said. "Take any of our engineers Geordi can spare. He's nearly finished with repairs anyway."

Riker nodded. "I'll come to the bridge when I'm

aboard, give you a fuller report before beaming back here. Things are going a little more smoothly than we expected."

"Captain Picard," Rychi said, "I hope that you'll have time to visit at least one of our archaeological sites yourself before you leave this system."

"I'll make the time," Picard replied. "Surely."

"And when we're back to normal here, you must come back and spend more time with us. I think we can promise your crew a diverting shore leave then, especially if they come during one of our arts festivals. Minister Mobutu tells me that the people of Austra are determined to rebuild their city just as it was before—maybe with a few improvements."

"We'll definitely return," Picard said. Perhaps then, when he saw this world flourishing once more, he would finally be at peace with his decision. "And naturally I'll want to see even more of your sites then."

"I'll give you a guided tour," Rychi said. "Those ancient sites saved many lives. We would have lost millions more without them."

Rychi had changed. No longer was he the self-absorbed, somewhat fainthearted man Picard remembered from his first discussion with the council of ministers. Rychi might easily have remained that sort of man if he had not been tested by his world's ordeal. Perhaps, Picard thought, that was something else to consider whenever he wondered if he had done the right thing.

"I'd better go," Rychi continued. "I've got to meet with the city planners and then our emergency services director, and once things settle down, Rohin

Nowles thinks the council should consider a planetary name change." Rychi smiled. "He doesn't think it's appropriate for us to keep the name of Epictetus Three, given that our old planetary system no longer exists and we're the second planetary body out from the sun in this system. Others will no doubt argue that we should keep our old name as a bond with the past. I'll be thankful when everything's settled enough to make that kind of trivial debate a burning political issue."

Picard laughed, and the laughter came more easily to him than it had for some time.

Rychi said farewell; Riker repeated that he would be aboard in an hour, then signed off. Picard sat at his table for a while, feeling his darker thoughts crowding into his mind again.

He was about to resume work on his log when the door insisted that someone wished to enter the ready room.

"Come in," Picard said softly.

Data entered; the door slid shut behind him. "It was good to see you on the bridge today, Captain. You appear to be more rested than you have been in some time."

Picard did not answer.

"I came to tell you that the *Carpathia* and the *Olympia,* the Epictetan cargo carriers, will be in this system within four days. Their captains have just sent a subspace message saying that all of the people who fled from Epictetus Three are now safely aboard."

Picard nodded, but remained silent.

"I have been thinking about what might have

happened to the alien Epictetans," Data continued, "if you would care to hear."

"Yes, of course, Data. Continue."

"The key element in my theory comes from the very use we made of their sun—to draw power. I conclude that this is possibly what they did also—and then, when their star became unstable, they stabilized it long enough to free themselves of their planetary life. To be more exact, they used and then discarded their sun. Perhaps they did not expect that their sun would move beyond a mild variable state. They thought, perhaps, that they could control it. And perhaps they might have, if they had not, as I suspect, developed an interest in mobile habitats. But once they left, the suncore stabilizer began to deteriorate—all of which may explain the signs of instability in this star."

"Very astute, Data," Picard said, trying to show more interest.

"On balance, Captain," Data continued, "I think the operation went very well."

"Yes, I suppose so." Picard replied more sharply than he had intended. "After all, most of the patient lived. Yet there are so many dead, Data, too many—each life a world destroyed, a mind that will never come again."

Data lifted his brows slightly. "May I point out," he said, "that we did all that was possible in so short a time. It was not within our power to do more. We could not entirely prevent what gravity and inertia would do to a planetary geology when we let Epictetus Three through the wormhole. We were given an opportunity—"

"Data, you're an embodiment of rationality," Picard said impatiently. "It's your basic nature, you were designed for it. You can't know the disquiet I feel over the dead. Oh, we were clever and humane, without a doubt, but far, far from perfect."

Data gazed at him steadily. "But I do understand, Captain. I know that human beings form bonds of sympathy for one another, as part of your biology, and that this is the basis of your ethical systems. And even greater is the bond of friendship, which is a more rational bond, especially when based on knowledge and respect. May I speak to you now as such a friend?"

"Of course," Picard said. "But you don't have an unconscious, as we humans do. You have a database, and all of it accessible. We have a stew of memories and impulses, out of which things float up and then have to be dealt with."

"That is essential," Data said, "to the open-ended creativity of your species."

"Maybe it's overrated. Your orderly mental background serves you well, and also shields you from pain. I wish I could be more like you."

"I am not a stranger to a sense of danger," Data said, "or to dissatisfaction with myself and others."

"Yes, of course. I don't mean to sound as if I'm disagreeing with you."

"But following from the crux of the problem, I would agree that even though this operation was not perfect—"

"Two hundred and fifty thousand dead is far from perfect," Picard cut in. That was the most recent figure, given to him earlier when he came on the bridge; maybe it was even higher by now, and would climb higher still.

"But it *was* a solution, Captain, and even in human terms, a far from ignoble one. In fact, it was an unprecedented rescue."

Picard sighed. "Quite right, Data. It was a solution. Maybe perfection is a demand that grows out of an appalled imagination. Thank you for reminding me that we have not, even with the losses, failed. It might help if you kept reminding me of that occasionally."

Data nodded. "I will do so now. It occurs to me that you are dwelling overly much on the dead. However great those losses, think often of all those who will live that would have died. Nearly twenty million, to be exact."

Picard leaned forward. "Did Counselor Troi suggest that you talk to me?"

"I must confess that she did, almost immediately after she beamed up."

"Thank you, Data," Picard said, feeling a strong mixture of gladness and sorrow. "I think I see. She knows very well that your rationality can be a tonic to me, and even more so now."

"I believe she had that in mind, Captain."

Picard restrained his feelings as he stood up. Together, he and Data went out onto the bridge. Troi, looking rested, sat at her station, ready to advise him about the human storms that were running their course on the planet below. Riker emerged from the aft turbolift and lifted an arm in greeting as he hurried to his station.

Picard went to the command area and sat down at his station. On the viewscreen, Epictetus III swam in its new orbit—and his mind flashed forward some fourteen years into the future, to the moment when the planet's people would see a nova brighten their sky, and be reminded of their deliverance.

About the Authors

Pamela Sargent and George Zebrowski have been watching *Star Trek* ever since the 1960s, when they were students at the State University of New York at Binghamton.

Pamela Sargent sold her first published story during her senior year in college, and has been a writer ever since. She has won a Nebula Award, a Locus Award, and been a finalist for the Hugo Award; her work has been translated into eleven languages. Her novels include *The Sudden Star, Watchstar, The Golden Space,* and *The Alien Upstairs.* Her novel *Venus of Dreams* was listed as one of the one hundred best science-fiction novels by *Library Journal. Earthseed,* her first novel for young adults, was chosen as a 1983 Best Book by the American Library Association, and has recently been optioned for motion pictures. Her other acclaimed science-fiction novels include *The Shore of Women* and *Venus of Shadows; The Washington Post Book World* has called her "one of the genre's best writers."

Sargent's most recent novel is *Ruler of the Sky*, a historical novel about Genghis Khan. Gary Jennings, bestselling author of the historical novel *Aztec*, said about *Ruler of the Sky:* "This formidably researched and exquisitely written novel is surely destined to be known hereafter as *the* definitive history of the life and times and conquests of Genghis, mightiest of Khans." Elizabeth Marshall Thomas, author of *Reindeer Moon* and *The Hidden Life of Dogs*, commented: "The book is fascinating from cover to cover and does admirable justice to a man who might very well be called history's single most important and compelling character." Sargent is also the editor of *Women of Wonder, The Classic Years* and *Women of Wonder, The Contemporary Years*, two anthologies of science fiction by women.

George Zebrowski's twenty-six books include novels, short-fiction collections, anthologies, and a forthcoming book of essays. His short stories have been nominated for the Nebula Award and the Theodore Sturgeon Memorial Award. Noted science-fiction writer Greg Bear calls him "one of those rare speculators who bases his dreams on science as well as inspiration," and the late Terry Carr, one of the most influential science-fiction editors of recent years, described him as "an authority in the SF field."

Zebrowski has published more than seventy-five works of short fiction and nearly a hundred articles and essays, including reviews for *The Washington Post Book World* and articles on science for *Omni* magazine. One of his best-known novels is *Macrolife*, selected by *Library Journal* as one of the one hundred best novels of science fiction; Arthur C. Clarke described *Macrolife* as "a worthy successor to Olaf Stapledon's *Star Maker*. It's been years since I was so impressed. One of the few books I intend to read again." He is also the author of *The Omega Point Trilogy*, and his novel *Stranger Suns* was a *New York Times* Notable Book of the Year for 1991.

Zebrowski's most recent novel, written in collaboration with scientist/author Charles Pellegrino, is *The Killing Star,* which the *New York Times Book Review* called "a novel of such conceptual ferocity and scientific plausibility that it amounts to a reinvention of that old Wellsian staple: Invading Monsters From Outer Space." *Booklist* commented: "Pellegrino and Zebrowski are working territory not too far removed from Arthur C. Clarke's, and anywhere Clarke is popular, this book should be, too." Their *Star Trek* novel *Dyson Sphere* will be published in 1997.

Pamela Sargent and George Zebrowski live in upstate New York.

STAR TREK
FIRST CONTACT

Captain Jean-Luc Picard and his crew take the new Enterprise NCC-1701-E to the limits of adventure in this stunning new motion picture event. Be there at the birth of the dream, and witness the ultimate battle with the most dangerous enemy the Federation has ever encountered. There is no thrill like First Contact.

A VIACOM COMPANY

1264

STAR TREK®
CHRONOLOGY

THE HISTORY
OF THE FUTURE

A completely revised edition of the bestselling
official illustrated time line of the incredible
and ever-expanding Star Trek universe—
presented for the first time in full color.

From the founding of the Federation, to Zefram Cochrane's
invention of warp drive, to James T. Kirk's early days in
Starfleet Academy®, to the voyages of the *Starship
Enterprise*™ under Captain Jean-Luc Picard, to the newest
adventures of the *U.S.S. Voyager*™, this book provides a
comprehensive look at *Star Trek*'s incredible history. The
STAR TREK CHRONOLOGY documents every impor-
tant event from every *Star Trek* episode and film, and
includes both stardates and Earth calendar dates.

by **MICHAEL OKUDA** and **DENISE OKUDA**

POCKET
BOOKS

**Available in trade paperback
from Pocket Books**

718-01

Coming in mid-December...

STAR TREK
THE NEXT GENERATION®
#44: THE DEATH OF PRINCES
By John Peel

On the planet Buran, newly linked to the Federation, a mysterious disease devastates the population—and turns them against the visitors from the *U.S.S. Enterprise*™. Meanwhile, on nearby Iomides, a renegade Federation observer has disappeared, intent on violating the Prime Directive by preventing a tragic political assassination.

Also coming in mid-December...

#81: MUDD IN YOUR EYE
By Jerry Oltion

After millennia of warfare, the planets Prastor and Distrel may have finally achieved a lasting peace. Investigating on behalf of the Federation, Captain Kirk is shocked to find out that the architect of the peace is none other than that notorious con artist, Harcourt Fenton Mudd!

Printed in the United States
By Bookmasters